RETURN
to the
IRISH
BOARDING
HOUSE

BOOKS BY SANDY TAYLOR

SANDY TAYLOR

RETURN
to the
IRISH
BOARDING
HOUSE

bookouture

Published by Bookouture in 2024

An imprint of Storyfire Ltd.
Carmelite House
50 Victoria Embankment
London EC4Y 0DZ

www.bookouture.com

ISBN: 978-1-83525-583-4
eBook ISBN: 978-1-83525-582-7

To my best forever friend. Chalk and cheese, but only on the outside. Through the laughter and the tears, we wrote songs and poems and painted pebbles on the beach. Darling Wenny, the wind beneath my wings, and we said we wouldn't look back.

PROLOGUE

She sat on the bench, looking across Merrion Square at the house. It was three storeys high and made of red brick. Stone steps bordered by rusty railings led up to the wide front door, with paint so dirty and scratched it was hard to tell what colour it might have been. Many of the windows were cracked and broken, bits of coloured curtain fluttered in the breeze, as if trying to escape. This tall, elegant house must have been beautiful once, but now it looked neglected and unloved.

She became obsessed with it; it seemed to call to her, bringing her back time and time again, to sit on the bench and imagine how it could be if it was hers. It touched her heart in a way she barely understood.

At night, as she lay on another filthy, bug-ridden mattress, the house came into her dreams, and in her dreams, she walked through large airy rooms and up a wide sweeping staircase. She looked out over the square and saw a lone figure sitting on the bench, someone who looked a bit like her. It didn't matter that the dreams made very little sense, she always woke feeling happy.

A FOR SALE sign was stuck to one of the filthy downstairs

windows. One day the sign would be gone, and she would never come back, for on that day the dream would be over.

She stood up and started to walk away. At the edge of the square she turned and looked back at the house: if it was hers she would paint the front door bright red.

CHAPTER 1

DUBLIN, 1956

Mary Kate

It was the most beautiful soft day. The sky above the old stone church was a clear blue, stretching above the graveyard like a canopy. Bright yellow daffodils moved gently among the graves. This was a time of new beginnings, a time of new life and of hope, it was not a time to die.

Mary Kate touched the warm grey stone. 'Sean Barry, beloved husband, brother and friend'.

Only two years had passed since they had stood together in the little church beside the waters of Glendalough, promising to love each other in sickness and in health. Two wonderful years of a love that had filled her heart and touched her soul in a way that no one else ever could, nor ever would.

There had been no illness, no pain, no warning of what was to come, just a deep sleep that he had never awakened from, leaving her with a world that she didn't want to live in. A future filled with sadness and disbelief; how could she go on without him? How could she live without the love of her life, her soulmate, and her best friend? What was the point of living at all?

What sort of God would give her such a precious love, only to take it away?

After Sean had died, she hated leaving the cottage; she had been afraid of all the space beyond its walls, all the space that she couldn't fill. Someone once said that when a heart breaks, you must find a way to cover the cracks but what are you supposed to cover them with? No wise words could ever replace the emptiness that had once filled her with such happiness.

She couldn't eat, she couldn't sleep, and she was angry, she was so angry that she could barely contain it. She had stood in the garden and wailed like a banshee into the dark night. There was no space left in her heart, for anything or anyone, not even her friends. No one else's suffering touched her, no one else's pain could match hers. She only wanted Sean and if she couldn't have him, then she didn't want anyone.

She ventured out only to visit his grave, but it gave her no comfort.

They had gloried in the changing of the seasons, each one bringing its own special magic. Spring, when the flowers they had so lovingly planted, burst from the soil. Walks in the autumn woods as the leaves tumbled about their shoulders and squelched beneath their feet.

In winter they would lay in bed listening to the rain lashing against the windows and the wind buffeting the walls of the little cottage, safe and warm in each other's arms.

Now she hated it, for every season reminded her of him. She neglected the garden they had both loved and been so proud of, and as autumn gave way to winter, she tormented herself with thoughts of him, cold and alone in that cold lonely place, and it broke her heart. She had dreams of clawing at the soil to be beside him and to keep him warm. What little sanity she had left told her that she was sliding into madness and that she needed help.

· · ·

Mary Kate had been brought up by her beloved grandparents and when they had died, she had been thrown out of the only home she had ever known and forced to find lodgings in Dublin. These had been lonely years, years of dead-end jobs and run-down boarding houses, each one worse than the next, no friends and no one who cared whether she lived or died. She'd decided to jump into the Liffey and end it all but God in His wisdom had other plans for her. Her mother, who had abandoned her as a child, had gifted her more money than she could ever have dreamed of, and her life had changed. Years of poverty and loneliness were behind her. Eight years ago, she had opened her very own boarding house in Dublin that had brought strangers into her life, strangers who had become the family she had always wanted.

She took the bus back home and stared unseeing out of the window, with only Sean's face filling her mind and her body with everything that was now lost.

Mary Kate got off the bus and started to walk up the lane towards her cottage, the home that she and Sean had fallen in love with, the beautiful little cottage in the shelter of the Wicklow Hills. Her steps slowed as she got closer, for there would be no Sean pottering in the garden or walking towards her with that lovely smile on his face.

Her heart fell as she saw someone sitting on the bench. She had hidden away for the last few months, not wanting to see anyone, or having to listen to any more words of wisdom about how lucky she had been to have known such love. She wouldn't even open the door to the local priest, who took to giving impromptu sermons through the letter box. The thing was, the letter box was on a spring that suddenly clamped down with such force that it nearly took the poor man's nose off. He didn't come back.

The figure on the bench stood up and she could see that it was her dear friend Moira. Mary Kate stared at her.

'Well, aren't you going to ask me in for a cup of tea?' said Moira. 'Because if you're not, I'm going to sit here all night and I shall sing very loudly.'

Mary Kate reluctantly opened the door and Moira followed her inside.

Moira looked at her dear friend, who had barely any flesh on her and her heart broke. 'I have a proposition,' she said.

'I've lost my husband, Moira,' said Mary Kate. 'I am in no mind to be listening to propositions.'

'Hear me out,' said Moira. 'Just hear me out.'

Mary Kate sighed. 'I'm listening,' she said.

'I've had enough of teaching, my heart isn't in it anymore.'

'What's that got to do with me?'

'I'm hoping that it will have a lot to do with you.'

'In what way? I want nothing but to be left alone, I'm sorry, Moira, you're my friend but please go.'

'I'm going nowhere, Mary Kate Barry, and I will have my say, whether you want to hear it or not.'

'You always were stubborn, Moira Kent. So, tell me if you have to, then please go on your way.'

Moira took a deep breath. 'I want to reopen the boarding house, and I want you with me.'

Mary Kate's eyes filled with tears. She walked across to the window and looked out at the pretty garden, where her and Sean had spent so many happy hours, filling it with wildflowers that attracted the bees and the small creatures who needed a safe place to go about their busy little lives.

Could she open the boarding house again? Did she even want to? She remembered the day that the dilapidated building had been brought back to life and in a way brought her back to life as well. She smiled when she thought of all the people who had passed through the red door. Colleen, who had run from her parents and her home, to save the life of her unborn child. Darling Jessie and Abby, who she'd taken from the orphanage and who had become the children she never thought she would have. Orla and Polly, who filled the rooms with their youth and their laughter, and dearest Moira, who finally confessed that it was the house where she had grown up. When Mary Kate married Sean Barry, she had given the boarding house to Moira, who opened a little school. So many lives had been touched and so many lives had touched hers in return.

Maybe there was a future for her, maybe she could be happy again. She could almost hear Sean whispering in her ear, 'Go for it, my darling girl, and I will be beside you every step of the way.'

Mary Kate turned back into the room and walked into Moira's arms. They would bring the Irish boarding house back to life and they would do it together.

CHAPTER 2

Moira

The boarding house needed redecorating from top to bottom; Moira wanted Mary Kate to feel at home as soon as she walked through the red door. Sticky fingers now graced the walls, along with the remains of the artwork that she had taken down. The beautiful carpets needed replacing, as muddy shoes and boots had almost obliterated the pretty pattern. James Renson's wife Erin and her sister Gerry took curtains away to be cleaned and Moira worked with them on the choice of colours for each room. They had decorated the house when Mary Kate had first bought it and Moira knew that they would do a great job.

This was the house where she had grown up, but she had come here as a guest. It had taken some time before Moira admitted to Mary Kate that the boarding house had once been her childhood home. She never fully understood why she had chosen to come back, for once her mother and little sister had died there were no more happy memories and she had felt nothing the day she left.

Mary Kate had become her dearest friend and it broke her

heart to see her so unhappy. Persuading her to reopen the boarding house had been the right thing to do, the only thing to do, and she had no regrets. Yet, there had been a part of her that was sad. She had said that she hadn't the heart for teaching anymore but that wasn't the truth. Running her little school in the beautiful old building at 24 Merrion Square had been a joy and she had loved every minute of it. She had been given a second chance to become a better teacher, the kind of teacher she should have been, but hadn't known how. Life had broken her and she had vowed to never again let anyone touch her the way her little sister had. Not only had she suffered because of this but so too had anyone who tried to get close to her.

She had done a disservice to the girls she had taught at Clifton College, her previous teaching position, and she felt ashamed. She hadn't even tried to get to know them, she had been a cold and distant woman and she knew by their faces that they hated coming into her classroom. It had been Mary Kate who had shown her that the love you give away comes back to you in so many ways. 'My grandad used to say that you reap what you sow,' she'd said.

And so she had put her heart and soul into caring for these children who had come into her life, celebrating each success, however small, and letting them know how special they were. She wanted the children to feel proud of their achievements when they left her school and not be made to feel like failures. Every morning, herself and Abby waited for the children to burst through the red door, their shiny faces grinning up at them, happy to be there and ready for the day ahead. At home time, Moira would stand on the steps, shaking each little hand, and smiling as she watched them running towards their parents, proudly holding out their latest pieces of artwork.

There were no lessons on the final day, instead, they played games and picnicked in the garden. Their beloved dog Guinness had a wonderful time being spoiled by the children, who shared their food with him. They had arrived that morning wearing their best clothes, clutching presents and flowers and cards. How different from the day she had walked away from Clifton College – there were no flowers or gifts that day. She knew that no one would miss her, in fact they were probably glad to see the back of her and she could understand why. She had educated them but given nothing of herself. When the last child left the little school, it had been a different experience entirely, she closed the red door and burst into tears.

Eliza and Abby were sitting at the bottom of the stairs.

'You look very sad,' said Eliza.

Moira wiped her eyes and smiled at her. 'I'm sad and happy at the same time. Now isn't that silly?'

'Not at all,' said Eliza. 'I had a desperate toothache once and it made me sad but then yer man yanked it out and I was happy again. It was a bugger of a tooth.'

'You swore,' said Abby. 'Did you get that from your mammy?'

'I did,' said Eliza. 'Isn't it a grand word?'

Abby made a face. 'I'm not so sure about that.'

'I'm sad because the children have left,' said Moira. 'But I'm happy, because I think they liked me.'

'And why wouldn't they?' said Eliza. 'Yer a grand woman altogether.'

'Thank you, dear, thank you for saying that.'

'Yer as welcome as the flowers in May.'

'It's going to be awful quiet around here, isn't it? With just the four of us rattling about the place,' said Abby.

Moira smiled at her. 'It won't be quiet for long, darling. This house will soon be filled with new guests and best of all, Mary Kate will be coming home, now isn't that marvellous?'

'It's spectacular,' said Abby. 'I mean, I'm awful sad that Sean died, because he was very kind and Mary Kate loved him, but I'm awful happy that Mary Kate is coming back.'

'That's a big word,' said Eliza.

'What's a big word?' said Abby.

'That "spec" word you just said. It's even bigger than bugger.'

'Oh, Eliza,' said Moira, 'what are we going to do with you?'

'You can take me down to the kitchen for a grand slab of Mammy's cake.'

'Great idea,' said Moira. 'A piece of your mammy's cake is exactly what's needed right now.'

'Will it make you happy again?' said Eliza. 'Mammy's cake always makes me happy.'

'And *you* always make me happy, darling girl.'

'Good job I was born then, wasn't it?' said Eliza, grinning.

Abby raised her eyes to the ceiling and followed Moira and Eliza down to the kitchen.

CHAPTER 3

Mary Kate

Last night she had hardly slept, she didn't know how she was going to leave the little cottage where she had been so happy. It wasn't just four walls that she was leaving, for every brick held precious memories and every room still echoed with the sound of their laughter. Why did she think she could leave it all behind? She would tell Moira that it was too soon, she couldn't do it.

But she had woken up with her grandfather's words in her head: 'No good ever came of living in the past, Mary Kate, best to cut all ties and move on.'

She got out of bed and walked over to the window. The garden that had given them both such joy was overgrown with weeds and brambles, the flowers choked in darkness. She looked around the room, it felt cold and empty. She'd thought that this was her safe place, but she'd been wrong, for she'd made it her prison. Sean wasn't here, this cottage was not the keeper of his memory: she was.

She closed her eyes. 'Will I be alright, Grandad? Will I be

happy again?' and there was his voice as clear as if he was standing beside her.

'The flowers will find their way towards the light, Mary Kate, for their roots are strong and so are yours. They will bloom again, and so will you. Leave as fast as you can and never look back.'

'I will, Grandad,' she said out loud. 'I will.'

And now she was standing on the pavement looking up at the boarding house. Another beginning, another new start.

She placed her hand on the red door, and it opened. She almost stepped back out, as a huge cheer went up and she was looking at all her friends who were filling the hallway.

'Welcome home,' said Moira. And Mary Kate burst into tears.

'I knew this would happen,' said Mrs Lamb. 'The girl is overwhelmed, what on earth were we thinking? Come and sit down, Mrs Barry, you've had a shock.'

Mary Kate smiled at her. 'They're not sad tears, Mrs Lamb, they're happy ones.' She looked around at all her friends. 'How could I be sad when I'm so lucky?'

'Moira has that trouble,' said Eliza. 'She gets happy and sad at the same time. Now I had this desperate toothache...'

'If you say another word about that tooth,' said Abby, glaring at her. 'I swear by all that's holy, I'll hang you off the banister by your two ears.'

'I'd best be quiet then?' said Eliza.

'Yes,' said Abby, 'you best had.'

Oh, it was good to be back, thought Mary Kate, as she followed Mrs Lamb into the sitting room.

'I'm sorry we gave you such a fright,' said Moira.

Mary Kate shook her head. 'It was a shock alright, but a lovely one. Thank you.'

She looked around the room at her friends who had gathered to welcome her home and to celebrate the re-opening of the boarding house. She knew how blessed she was, for every one of them had, in their own way, brought happiness and meaning into her lonely life.

When Mary Kate had first set eyes on 24 Merrion Square, it had touched something inside her. What she saw was a house without hope, a house that no one cared about, a house that had given up, just like she had. When she had walked away that day, she couldn't get it out of her head. It was as if the house was calling to her. When she received her fortune, she knew exactly what she was going to do. She could have bought any house she desired; she could have bought a mansion if she'd had a mind to but she knew exactly which one she wanted. There were some who thought she was mad, a single woman taking on the ugliest house on the square, and some who said that it would be better off demolished and something fancy put in its place. Mary Kate knew that there were some who were sitting back, just waiting for her to fail. As it turned out, they had a desperate long wait and God love them, they were only green with envy. Her beloved grandfather used to say, 'Jealously fires an arrow and only wounds itself.' He had a wise saying for every occasion and told her that however bad life might become, there would always be red-letter days, if you looked hard enough for them.

Sean Barry had his own building firm and was recommended by her solicitor, James Renson.

The day that her and Sean had stood side by side looking at the house, she knew that James had done her a huge favour, because when Sean saw the house, he didn't see an ugly duckling, what he saw was a swan. The renovation became a labour of love to him and as the house began to grow, so their love for each other had grown with it.

Every part of the house had Sean's mark on it, from the high ceilings to the magnificent marble fireplace and the beautiful windows. The last thing to be finished was the door and she'd asked Sean to paint it red.

'Why red, Mary Kate?'

'In memory of my grandfather's red-letter days,' she'd said.

'Then red it shall be,' he'd said, smiling.

Maybe that was the moment she had started falling in love.

The Clancy brothers were belting away rebel songs on the radiogram as if their lives depended on it and they had her brain mashed.

She walked across to the window and looked out over the square.

Abby followed her and held her hand. 'Are you sad?' she said softly.

Mary Kate looked down at darling Abby and her eyes filled with tears. She was about to make a fool of herself.

'Is it because Sean died?'

'Now, Abby,' said Moira, 'you're going to make Mary Kate unhappy and you don't want to do that, do you?'

'I think she's already unhappy, Mammy. You are, aren't you, Mary Kate?'

She stroked Abby's beautiful fair hair. 'I am, my love, but I'll be alright soon.'

James, who was her solicitor and dearest friend, tapped his glass and started to speak: 'I think we should all stop pretending that we're having a great time and acknowledge that someone very dear to us is struggling to put a brave face on it. Now, will someone please turn off that bloody music.'

'I'll do it,' said Eliza. 'I can do it, can't I, Mammy?'

Mrs Lamb touched her daughter's cheek. 'You can, my love.'

Eliza, in her twenties, was a child in the body of a woman; she had the biggest heart and enchanted everyone who met her. Her mother, Mrs Lamb, had come to the boarding house looking for the position of cook and Mary Kate had liked them both. They brought with them kindness and loyalty and good food.

James smiled at Mary Kate. 'We may not be able to quell the storm, my dear friend, but we can walk beside you through the rain.'

'Or under an umbrella,' said Eliza. 'We have a good big umbrella, don't we, Mammy?'

'I'm sure we have, Eliza. I'm sure we have.'

Eliza looked very pleased with herself. 'It will keep Mary Kate from getting wet.'

'It will indeed, pet. How clever of you to think of it.'

James raised his glass. 'Let us raise our glasses to this wonderful woman, who I feel privileged to call my friend. She has touched all our lives and asked for nothing in return. To Mary Kate.'

'To Mary Kate.'

'Oh, James,' said Mary Kate, wiping her eyes, 'you'll have me bawling, sure I've done nothing that any good Catholic woman wouldn't have done.'

'You're wrong there,' said Colleen. 'You took me in when I was a scared young girl, carrying a child. You never judged me, you never asked me for money, you just quietly accepted me and gave me shelter and a home for my baby, I shall never forget what you did for me.'

Abby tugged at her skirt, like she used to do before she could talk and wanted your attention. 'And you took me and Jessie from the convent, when you'd only wanted the one orphan.'

Jessie grinned. 'That's because you were glued to my side, Abby – Mary Kate didn't have much choice.'

They all laughed, and everything felt better. She was surrounded by people who cared for her and she knew that it was these dear friends who would take her towards the light.

'Put the Clancy brothers back on, Eliza,' she said, 'and let's have a bit of a jig.'

Just then the doorbell rang. 'I'll go,' said Eliza, jumping up.

'This could be our first lodger,' said Moira.

'I very much doubt it, Moira, we only advertised it yesterday.'

They could hear some talking in the hallway and then Eliza came back into the room.

'Who was there?' said Mary Kate.

'A poor soul called Banana.'

'Banana?' said Mary Kate.

'Are you sure you got that right, Eliza?' said Mrs Lamb.

'Oh yes. She said her name was Banana and she was looking for somewhere to rest her weary head.'

'Did she really say that?'

'No, I made that bit up, but she's definitely called Banana.'

'Who in God's name would call a child Banana?' said Moira.

'Well, perhaps it was because she looked like a banana. Maybe her mammy looked in the cradle and thought, I'll call you Banana.'

'Don't be ridiculous, Eliza,' said her mammy.

'I'm not being... that word you said.'

'Ridiculous,' said Colleen.

'Thank you, Colleen.'

'You're very welcome, Eliza.'

'Now I've forgotten what I was saying. Oh yes, I'm not being um.'

'RIDICULOUS,' they all chorused and started laughing.

Mary Kate dabbed at her eyes. 'And where is this poor weary head now, Eliza?'

'I told her to sit on the stairs while I fetched you. Did I do right?'

'Don't you always do right, my love?' said Mary Kate, walking towards the door.

'I do,' said Eliza, grinning.

Mary Kate was smiling as she walked into the hallway. The woman sitting on the stairs was wearing a bright yellow coat. No wonder Eliza called her banana. The woman stood up. 'My name is Alana Kennedy,' she said, smiling.

Mary Kate smiled and held out her hand. 'Mrs Barry,' she said. 'Are you looking for lodgings?'

Alana nodded. 'Do you have vacancies?'

'You can have the pick of the house,' said Mary Kate. 'We are reopening after a bit of a break. You will be our first guest.'

'Then I would like to stay.'

'We have a bit of a party going on in the front room, so I will get Eliza to show you around and you can decide on which bedroom you would like.'

'You have a lovely home,' said Alana.

A lovely home, thought Mary Kate. That was what she had always wanted her boarding house to be, a home to whoever found their way through the red door and today was the new beginning. *I'm going to be alright, Grandad*, she said to herself.

CHAPTER 4

Bridie

Bridie Toomey had been sitting on a bench in the bus station for more than an hour.

She was so cold, she could hardly think. The last time she'd worn these clothes it had been summer but now it was autumn, and a bitter autumn at that.

He wasn't coming, was he? She'd been a fool to think that he would, but she had believed him when he'd said he loved her, she had believed in a future that she could only have dreamed possible. A little cottage in the country, a fire in the hearth and a door to shut out the rest of the world.

Too late now for children but Stephen had held her and said, 'We will have each other, Bridie, and that will be enough.'

She smoothed back what little hair she had left and looked around her. The place was teeming with people who all seemed to have a purpose, racing around, dragging cases and yelling at their children. Bridie had only one purpose and that was to be safely in Stephen's arms. Everything would be alright then, it would all have been worth it.

As the middle one of four sisters, she had had a happy child-hood and a privileged one at that. They had all attended the Loreto convent, the private school on the outskirts of Dublin, with its distinctive brown and yellow uniform, complete with a felt boater, held in place with a bit of elastic under the chin. She had been the clever one, coming home with glowing reports that she hoped would make her mother proud.

It was only as she grew older that she realised it wasn't enough to be clever. Her sisters were popular – they always had a friend hanging off their arms, giggling away in corners. Whispers and secrets that they never felt the need to share with her. They were invited to birthday parties at posh houses and followed everywhere by a bunch of spotty boys. On St Valentine's Day a raft of cards would come flying through the letter box, followed by shrieks of delight from her sisters as they ran down the stairs. Every year Bridie would have one card, always the same handwriting, which she knew for a fact had been written by their father. She thought that it was very sweet of him but somehow it made the whole thing worse.

Bridie had no idea why she was so different; she once asked her mother what was wrong with her. 'There is nothing wrong with you, child,' her mother had answered, closing her book. 'What a curious question.'

Her mother had obviously thought that was the end of it and returned to her novel. She didn't like curious questions and pushed her glasses up her nose in a very precise way, but Bridie had persevered.

'I really do think that something is wrong with me, Mother. I'm beginning to notice that I am very different to my sisters.'

Her mother had a habit of saying that she didn't like to be put in a position. No one knew what position she was talking about, we only knew that she didn't like to be put in one. And best avoided at all costs.

'Have you nothing better to do, Bridie, than to stand there

bombarding me with this bizarre dialogue? You have put me in a position and probably a very imminent bilious attack.'

So, she had committed the ultimate sin of putting her mother in one of her positions and even worse, one of her bilious attacks.

Bridie had always found her mother to be a very complex person, in fact she had never met anyone quite as complex. She would say, 'I am having one of my heads, or I can feel one of my colds coming on or I'm having one of my turns.' It was as if she claimed sole ownership of her various ailments. The weirdest one was when she was having the vapours, which occurred when she and my father had 'words' – they never had arguments just 'words'. Her sisters found it hilarious and would pretend to swoon, clutch their heads, and throw themselves on the bed.

Bridie eventually found out why she was so different when she overheard a conversation between her mother and a neighbour. It happened the night before her older sister Caroline's wedding. The pair of them were sitting in the good room, drinking sherry.

'Well, at least you will always have Bridie, Mrs Toomey, for there will be no wedding bells ringing for the poor girl. It must be a great comfort to know that she will take care of you in your old age. I always think that it's a blessing to have one plain daughter in the family.'

Bridie didn't listen to any more of their conversation but went upstairs to her bedroom. Her heart was broken. When she eventually pulled herself together, she dried her eyes and walked across to the mirror and stared at her reflection. It was the same face that she had been looking at all her life and she had never thought that there was anything wrong with it. She wasn't cross-eyed, like poor Imelda Cronin down the road. Her ears didn't stick out like Danny Coyne, who her sisters said looked like a car with its doors open. Maybe when you were beautiful, you could get away with being unkind. Well, if that was the case then maybe it was better to be plain, and being plain wasn't the worst thing in the world. She could see and she could hear and she wasn't crippled, she could still have a good life and had no intention of looking after her mother in her old age – she could jolly well look after herself.

Both ends of the bus station were open to the elements, causing a tunnel of Arctic air blasting through the place that would take the nose off you.

She watched as the woman sitting next to her stood up and hurried towards one of the buses. Bridie noticed that she had left her coat behind and was just about to call out when something stopped her. She waited until the bus pulled away, then picked up the coat and put it on. It was bright yellow, a bit racy for her but it was lovely and warm. She would own up to her sin the next time she went to confession. Anyway, it wasn't really stealing, was it? It was just a bit of a borrow, caused by necessity; she was sure that God would understand.

She put her cold hands into the deep pockets; there was something in there. What she pulled out was a purse, which she immediately shoved back in. The loan of a coat was one thing, but a purse was something entirely different. She looked around, but no one was taking any notice of her. She took the purse out again and with her heart thudding in her chest, she opened it. It was stuffed full of notes, loads of them. She wouldn't count them here, she'd wait until she was somewhere more private. There was also a letter, addressed to a Mrs Alana White. Bridie had always hated her name; it sounded like an old person. She had never felt like a Bridie and anyway she hadn't been called Bridie in over ten years, but Alana? Yes, she could definitely live with that. Well, she might as well go the whole hog and change her surname as well.

One of the buses had an advert on the side of it advertising, 'Kennedys super sprung beds. Have the best sleep of your life'.

Bridie Toomey had walked into the bus station without a penny to her name and Alana Kennedy had left wearing a bright yellow coat, with a pocket full of money. She had enough to find herself a boarding house and maybe a job. The life she had dreamed about was gone and she had to find a new one. She picked up her case and walked towards the town.

CHAPTER 5

Nell

Nell Gavin was beautiful. She was beautiful in a way that would break your heart and there wasn't a girl in the county who could hold a candle to her. Her red hair fell in waves around her shoulders and her eyes were the colour of a summer meadow. Yes, Nell Gavin was beautiful, but God love her, the girl was simple and that was a desperate combination, for there were plenty around that would take advantage of such innocence.

Nell was sixteen and her sister Emma, eighteen. They lived with their father in a run-down bit of a farm in the hills above the Blackwater River in West Cork.

Bull Gavin was indeed a bull of a man and you wouldn't cross him if you had a mind to keep your head attached to the rest of your body. They say the farm had been a thriving little business back in the day but when his beloved wife died, Bull had drunk the place into the ground; what few profits he made found their way down his throat.

As far as anyone knew, the sisters had never been to school.

It was said that one of the nuns from the convent had taken it upon herself to venture up the hill to the farm to take Bull Gavin to task, for not only did the girls not attend school, they had never stepped foot inside the church and it was her duty to save their souls.

According to the local biddies, she was warned not to go, but proclaimed to anyone who had a mind to listen that she was on God's business and He would protect her. As it turned out, God must have been looking the other way the day Sister Concepta Aquinas ventured up the hill, for she never managed to venture back down again. Well, that was the story that the old ones spread around town when she disappeared, but the truth was the nun had run off with a young curate and was happily living in sin in Clacton-on-Sea and didn't give a fish's tit about the Gavin girls' souls. But the Irish love a bit of a drama and as it all added to Bull's fearsome reputation, he had no intention of putting them right.

What the people in the town didn't know about Bull was how much he loved his daughters. He knew that they deserved better than a drunken father, who was no good to anyone, but he did the best he could, even though he knew it was never enough. He was proud of Nell's beauty and in awe of Emma's kindness and patience. Every day he prayed to whoever might be listening to rid him of the cursed drink. Oh, he tried, he did, he tried but he couldn't face a world without his wife by his side and his despair would have him racing down the hill to the bar, where for a few hours he could lose himself in the golden liquid that slipped down his throat, taking him gently to a place where he could forget.

Nell saw the world through the eyes of a child, she saw joy in the simplest of God's creations. She could sit silently, totally at peace, watching a snail making its way across the grass.

'Isn't he beautiful, Emma?' she'd say.

Emma would look at the small lumbering grey shell, leaving

a trail of something yucky in its path, and smile at her sister. 'He certainly is, Nell,' she would say.

It was as if all Nell's emotions were heightened, as though she was seeing everything for the first time, in all its freshness and wonder. Her laughter brought happiness to your heart and her tears broke it. Every season held its own special joy for her. The first snows of winter would see her running around the farm, tossing the feathery snow up into the air and letting it fall about her shoulders, her giggles echoing out across the hillside. She'd gather up armfuls of autumn leaves and bring them into the house, where she spread them across the kitchen table, then she'd nudge Daddy, usually from a drunken stupor, and get him to admire them.

He'd stagger across to the table and try to focus on the pile of leaves. 'Now isn't that the grandest display that I have ever laid eyes on.'

'Aren't they beautiful, Daddy?'

'They are almost as beautiful as you, my Nell.'

She loved the warmth of summer that nudged the tiny animals from their sleep. But it was spring that touched Nell's heart as she breathed in the smell of new life. Her complete joy as she witnessed tulips and daffodils, crocuses and forget-me-nots cover the hillside.

One day Emma found her sitting on the grass, with tears running down her cheeks. She sat next to her and held her hand. 'What is making you sad?'

Nell shook her head as if she was trying to make sense of what she was feeling.

'You don't have to tell me, my love. I will just sit beside you until you feel better.'

They sat in a silence that was louder than words.

Eventually Nell sighed, 'Sometimes it's all too much to bear.'

'What is, pet?'

Nell spread out her arms. 'All this,' she said.

'The flowers?' said Emma.

'The world,' said Nell. 'My heart isn't big enough to hold such beauty.'

Emma put her arm around her. 'You have the biggest heart of anyone I know, my darling, and there is enough room in there for the world and the heavens and all the stars in the sky.'

Nell smiled. 'Really?'

'Absolutely.'

'Thank the Lord for that then,' said Nell, grinning.

When the sisters came down the hill and into the town it was noted that despite having Bull as a father, the girls were well turned out and seemed content with their lot.

It was on a fine spring day that Tommy Dunne was cycling down the high street and saw the beautiful Nell Gavin selling eggs on the side of the road.

Tommy Dunne was a bit of a chancer, who had left many a broken heart in his wake and many a mother wanting to drag him up to the priest's house and shame him and his family.

Emma had noticed how Tommy was looking at her sister and even worse was the way Nell was looking at him.

As the weeks and months went by, she noticed that Nell had become secretive, often going off on long walks on her own and coming back all dewy-eyed and dreamy. It didn't take a genius to know what was going on and Emma was sick with worry for her beautiful little sister.

They were sitting on the hill overlooking the farm. There was a warm breeze and Nell was leaning back against a tree with her eyes closed. Emma reached across and held her hand.

Nell opened her eyes and smiled at her sister. 'What?'

Emma smiled back. 'Are you happy, Nell?'

'I think so.'

'You think so?'

Nell started to cry, and Emma cradled her in her arms while she sobbed.

'Now what has brought this on?' she said softly.

'Oh, Emma, I did a bad thing.'

'Did you, my darling?'

'I think it was a bad thing and I didn't like it. I told Tommy that I didn't like it but he said that's what you do when you love someone.'

Emma continued to hold her when all she wanted to do was run down the hill and tear the head off Tommy Dunne, which was nothing to what her father would do if he ever found out.

CHAPTER 6

Emma

Emma couldn't find Nell anywhere. She'd searched the fields and the barns and down by the river where Nell loved to sit, she had searched in all her favourite places, but she was nowhere to be found. Over the months, Emma had watched as Nell's belly swelled and she didn't know what to do. Nell herself never mentioned it, in fact she went about the place as if nothing was wrong. For the first time since her mother had died, Emma was glad that her father spent most days in a drunken stupor; he wouldn't have noticed if Jesus and the twelve apostles had joined him at the breakfast table.

Emma had spent all day in the town selling her eggs and she had missed Nell beside her, but of course Nell couldn't be seen by the busybodies, who would have had the whole of the convent running up the hill like an army of banshees.

Once she'd sold all the eggs, she'd climbed the hill to her home. As she opened the door, she could hear her father snoring his head off upstairs but there was no sign of Nell. That was when she had begun searching for her and now she didn't know where else to look and headed back to the farmhouse.

Bull Gavin was sitting at the kitchen table with his head in his hands when Emma came back in the house. She wasn't alarmed to see him like this, because it's how he looked most of the time.

'I can't find Nell anywhere, Daddy,' she said.

Bull looked up at his daughter. 'Nell?' he slurred.

'Yes, Daddy. Nell, your daughter, or have you forgotten you have one?'

Bull Gavin scratched his head. 'I think, I think, yes, I think I took her somewhere.'

'You think you took her somewhere? Where in God's name do you think you took her?'

'Stop barking at me, Emma, I'm trying to clear my head. Will you get me a glass of something?'

Emma glared at him. 'I'll get you a glass of water.'

'Have you nothing stronger?'

'Jesus, Daddy, I'll pour it over your head if you don't tell me where she is.'

'Wait now, it's coming back to me.'

Emma felt like strangling him with her own two hands but she waited.

'Yes, I remember now. I took her down to the convent, to have a little chat with the nuns.'

'Is that where she is now?'

'I was supposed to go back for her.'

'But you fell into the pub, did you?'

'I must have done, I'll go and get her now.'

'You're in no fit state to go anywhere, especially to the convent – they wouldn't let you in the door. What time did you leave her there?'

'Not long ago, just after you left to sell the eggs.'

'Daddy, I left here at nine o'clock this morning. It's now

almost five o'clock, she's been there nearly eight hours.'

Bull Gavin rubbed at his eyes. 'I'm a useless father, aren't I? I'm a useless drunken bum, who doesn't deserve the pair of you. I'm sorry, Emma, I'll do better, I will. I'll do better.'

Emma walked around the table and put her arms around him. 'I know you will, Daddy. I know you will. I'll go and get her myself, she'll be worried.'

'Tell her I'm sorry.'

'She knows you're sorry, Daddy. I won't be long, put the kettle on – I'm only gasping for a cup of tea.'

Emma hurried through the town towards the Convent of the Blessed Virgin. She pushed open the big iron gates and walked up the long drive towards the main building. Before she could ring the bell, a nun appeared from behind the side of the house.

'Can I help you, child?' she said.

'I've come to collect my sister.'

'Step inside and I will see if the Reverend Mother is available to see you.'

'I don't need to disturb anyone, I just need to take my sister home. If you could fetch her, we'll be on our way.'

'What is her name, dear?'

'Nell Gavin. I'm her sister, Emma.'

The nun pointed to a chair. 'Wait there,' she said.

Emma sat down and looked around. In front of her was a painting of the crucifixion of Jesus that took up nearly the whole wall. There was blood pouring down his side and a crown of thorns on his poor head – it made her feel ill. If the nun didn't return with Nell, she was determined to search every room in the place until she found her. She had a bad feeling about this; she couldn't put her finger on it, but she felt that something was very wrong.

She stood up as the nun walked into the hallway; she was alone. 'Mother will see you now,' she said.

Emma followed her up the winding staircase and along a corridor. She stopped in front of a door, knocked, and gestured for Emma to go in. When she entered the room, she saw a nun standing by the window. She was tall and thin and she had a string of wooden rosary beads around her waist that were attached to a heavy cross that hung down her black skirt.

'Ah, Emma,' she said, smiling. 'I'm glad you came.'

'I've come to take my sister home.'

The nun walked across the room and sat down behind a desk. 'Poor Nell,' she said.

'What do you mean, poor Nell? She is not poor.'

'She is poor in the eyes of Christ, Emma, for she has strayed from the path of righteousness, but she will be looked after now.'

'She'll be looked after at home, Sister, with her family. Not with you.'

'She's not here, Emma.'

Emma could feel her heart thumping out of her chest, she wanted to commit murder. 'Where is she?' she screamed. 'Tell me where she is.'

'She has been taken to the Magdalene Sisters in Dublin, where she will be brought back to the faith and her baby will be found a good Catholic home.'

Emma glared at her. 'You've sent my sister to a bloody laundry?'

'You don't expect the good Sisters to pay for her keep, do you?'

'No one was asking them to pay for her keep, we can give her everything she needs.'

'This is the best solution, Emma, and in time I'm sure that you will come to accept it. Nell can have her baby and come back home with her reputation and her soul intact.'

'You are a cruel and bitter woman and you are no servant of any God that I know.'

'Well, Emma, it pleases me to know that you have a God.'

'Oh, I have a God alright and I didn't need to go to any church to find him, for he has always been in my heart. My God is compassionate and forgiving and I doubt very much that you would have got an invite to the Last Supper.'

The Reverend Mother smiled and it wasn't a smile that reached her eyes. 'I will pray for you,' she said.

'Keep your prayers for yourself, you have more need of them than I do.'

As Emma left the room, she slammed the door behind her, that had the nun who had been eavesdropping outside scuttling off like a little church mouse.

Emma had heard rumours about those places and she feared for her beautiful innocent sister.

She hurried through the town with her head lowered; she was so angry, she had never been so angry. If anyone spoke to her, she feared that she would eat the face off them. She was angry at Nell for being so foolish. She was angry at Tommy for taking advantage of her foolishness and she was angry at her father for caring more for the drink than he did about his own daughters and where was God in all of this?

She had just started climbing when she saw the smoke, thick, grey smoke that billowed across the hillside. She knew at once that it was her home. People were running past her and she started running with them.

The whole house was on fire, flames were shooting out of the roof and through the broken windows. Emma started racing across the field but strong arms were pulling her back. 'Let go of me,' she screamed. 'My daddy is in there, we have to get him out.'

Mrs Coyne, the baker's wife, put her arms around her. 'They've tried, Emma,' she said. 'They couldn't get near the place. It's too late for your daddy but I've a feeling that he wouldn't have known a thing about it.'

Emma fell to her knees; she'd lost her home, and she'd lost her beloved father but she still had Nell and she was going to get her out of that place.

Mrs Coyne helped her to her feet. 'Come home with me, love. Come home with me.'

The whole town had turned out for Bull Gavin's funeral and were surprised to find that his name was in fact William. In life he was a man they had feared, an old drunk who was best avoided if you didn't want your nose broken, but in death, he had suddenly become everyone's friend; they all had a story to tell about him. The pub was packed to the rafters every day and masses were said for his soul, with everyone declaring him to be a gas character and a great man altogether. It was a wonder they hadn't got the Bishop himself down to canonise him. Emma had always known that her daddy was a kind, wonderful man and her heart was breaking at his loss.

Emma had been living above the bakery for two weeks and Mr and Mrs Coyne had been very kind to her. She told Mrs Coyne about her sister being sent to the Magdalene laundry in Dublin; she knew that she could trust her, for she wasn't one of the town gossips.

'I can't leave her in that place, Mrs Coyne. She'll be so scared, she'll think we put her in there.'

'Of course you can't, my love, and my heart is breaking for you. I wish there was something I could do to ease your burden.'

'You've taken me in when I had no one, what more could I ask for?'

'So, you'll be off to Dublin then?'

'I'd go this very minute if I had the bus fare, but I need to find a job first.'

Mrs Coyne walked over to the dresser and came back

holding an envelope. 'The pub did a whip round, Emma, there's more than enough for your bus fare to Dublin and back home.'

Emma's eyes filled with tears. 'People can be kind, Mrs Coyne, it was good of them.'

'Well, that's the least they could have done, considering the amount of money your father spent in there. I'd say he kept that pub going singlehandedly.'

Emma smiled. 'I'd say he did, Mrs Coyne. I'd say he did.'

And now she was sitting on the bus on her way to Dublin. She'd never been further than the farm or the hillside in her whole life, it was all she had ever known. She should have been frightened but every mile was taking her closer to Nell. She wasn't worried about the future, because as long as Nell was safe, they would figure it out together. If she had to go in there with all guns blazing, she would, and woe betide anyone who was foolish enough to try and stop her.

There was nothing to go back for, their home had gone and so had their daddy. Nell was going to be heartbroken when she told her. But Emma was determined to find another home for them, somewhere they would be safe, somewhere Nell's baby would be born. She had no idea how she was going to achieve it but something told her that she would.

As they pulled into the bus station, she began to feel less positive. She was in a strange city, she knew no one and she had nowhere to sleep that night. The place was crowded, she had never seen so many people in her life. She sat down on a bench and watched them rushing past. Perhaps they were hurrying home to families or visiting friends or about to go on adventures. Well, she wasn't going to start feeling sorry for herself, that would get her nowhere. She was young and healthy, and she would survive – after all, she'd been looking out for herself and Nell for most of her life. She could do this, because the thought of Nell in that awful place and her daddy looking down on her would give her the strength she needed. She was the daughter of Bull Gavin, who took no prisoners, and neither would she.

It had been a long journey and Emma was tired and hungry. She stood up and walked across to a kiosk, where she bought a cup of tea and a sandwich, then walked back to the bench. She had to be careful with the bit of money from the pub, but the tea was grand and hot, and the food made her feel better. She was so tired that she could barely keep her eyes open; she would close them for just a minute, then figure out some sort of plan.

When she woke up, there was a woman and a child staring down at her.

'We were worried about you,' said the woman. 'Weren't we, Abby? We were worried.'

'We were,' said the girl.

'Ah sure, look at her,' said the woman. 'She looks like a poor lost little thing, in need of comfort and succour, like yer man at the side of the road that the good Samaritan helped.'

'For heaven's sake, Eliza,' said Abby, 'she's not a man, is she?'

'Maybe not, but she still looks in need of comfort and succour.'

Abby glared at her. 'Have you swallowed the Holy Bible or what?'

Emma listened to the pair of them carrying on a conversation as if she wasn't there and it was such an amusing conversation that she found herself smiling for the first time all day.

'I'm Abby,' said the child. 'And this is Eliza.'

'I'm pleased to meet you both. I'm Emma.'

'Well now, we're friends,' said Eliza.

Friends, thought Emma, and that's when the tears started. All the sadness that she had been holding in was unleashed and she was sobbing like a baby and all because two strangers had shown her some kindness.

They sat down either side of her and each held one of her hands.

'Did you come on the bus?' said Eliza.

Emma nodded.

'And did you come far?'

'From the West of Ireland.'

'Is that a long way?'

'Far enough,' said Emma.

'And where are you staying?'

'Dear God, Eliza, will ya stop interrogating the woman! This isn't the Spanish Inquisition.'

'What's that?' said Eliza.

'I'll tell you another time,' said Abby.

'Am I an eejit?' said Eliza.

Abby smiled at her. 'Not at all, you were just asking out of concern. You're a great girl altogether.'

'I have nowhere to sleep tonight,' said Emma quietly.

'No bed?' said Eliza.

'No bed.'

'That's the saddest thing I've heard all day,' said Eliza. 'Nowhere to lay yer poor head? That's desperate altogether. Do you have a mammy and daddy?'

'They died,' said Emma.

'That's the second saddest thing I've heard all day,' said Eliza. 'Would you like to come home with us? She can, can't she, Abby? Yer woman can come home with us?'

Abby smiled at Emma. 'She can, of course. Would you like to?'

Emma looked up at them. There was something about them that she felt she could trust. They might even help her to find Nell and right now, she would welcome all the help she could get.

Emma nodded and the three of them left the bus station, hand in hand.

CHAPTER 7

Mary Kate

It was cosy and warm in the sitting room as Mary Kate and Moira sat in front of the crackling fire. Mary Kate loved these times when the evenings were getting darker earlier.

The curtains were drawn, the outside world was shut out and inside, the house felt safe and welcoming. It was like being wrapped in a pair of caring arms.

Moira had switched on the lamps and they cast pools of golden light into the dark corners. Flames danced in the hearth, sending warmth into the beautiful room.

Mary Kate stretched out her legs over the rug. She had kicked off her shoes and now she wriggled her toes in front of the fire. She lifted the mug of tea from the table beside her chair and took a sip.

Moira smiled across at her. 'So, what do you think of our new guest?'

'I was going to speak to you about that.'

'Is there something wrong with her? She seems nice enough. Even when Eliza still insists on calling her Banana, she takes it all in good sport. Mrs Lamb's delighted with her, for she eats everything that's put before her. She says it's as if the woman hasn't had a decent meal in years.'

'Well, there might be some truth in that, for I've seen more meat on a sparrow's ankles.'

'So, what's bothering you about her?'

Mary Kate frowned. 'I don't think her name is Alana.'

'Really?'

Mary Kate nodded. 'Well, she's either hard of hearing, or has her head in the clouds. I've called out to her a few times, but she doesn't turn a hair. I don't think her name is Alana at all.'

'Mary Kate Barry, you should be running a detective agency, not a boarding house.'

'But haven't I been right in the past?'

'You have, so what do you want to do about it?'

'I want you to call her name when she can't see you, then I'll know if I'm way off the mark.'

Moira smiled. 'But you don't think you are, do you?'

'There's something about her, Moira. I just can't put my finger on it but I've a mind to find out what it is.'

'And I've no doubt that you will. Now, who else can we slander while we're at it?'

Mary Kate grinned. 'I'll be sure to let you know.'

Moira smiled at her. 'I shall wait with bated breath, my friend.'

'There has been something else bothering me.'

Just then Mrs Lamb tapped on the door and came in. 'Well, I could be overthinking this,' she said, 'for I have a vivid imagination.'

'You're in good company then,' said Moira. 'Come in and get warm.'

Mrs Lamb let out a big sigh and settled herself down on the couch. Darling Mrs Lamb sighed a lot, thought Mary Kate, smiling at her. At first, she thought that perhaps the woman was sad, or worried about something but had learned over the years that sighing was just something she felt the need to do.

Mrs Lamb let out another sigh. 'Someone has been taking food from my kitchen.'

Mary Kate frowned. 'Are you sure, Mrs Lamb?'

'I am. I have a list of everything I have so that I can see when it's running low and when to order more.'

'What exactly is missing?'

Mrs Lamb took a piece of paper out of her apron pocket and began to read. 'On Tuesday, I had six packets of custard creams in the cupboard. Today is Thursday and I have only four left. The peanut butter jar is almost empty, and a loaf of bread has gone missing.'

'I don't understand it,' said Mary Kate. 'No one has ever taken food from the kitchen before, there's only ourselves and the girls here.'

'And the banana,' said Mrs Lamb. 'Don't forget the banana.'

'She hasn't an ounce of flesh on her,' said Mary Kate. 'She doesn't seem the type to be raiding the kitchen.'

'I think I know who the culprits are,' said Moira, grinning.

'You do?' said Mary Kate.

'Eliza and Abby have been making a den down in the shed. I'm thinking the extra food is for a picnic.'

'Well,' said Mrs Lamb, standing up, 'I'm glad that's sorted out but all they had to do was ask. I was thinking of sleeping in the kitchen and catching the thief red-handed.'

After Mrs Lamb had gone, they burst out laughing. 'She sounded as if she had just stepped out of the pages of an Agatha Christie novel,' said Moira.

Mary Kate dried her eyes. 'I'll have a word with them, they should know better than to take anything from the house without asking.'

Moira stood up and shovelled coal onto the fire. 'You said there was something else bothering you, Mary Kate,'

Mary Kate didn't answer immediately.

'Do you want me to guess?'

'I was wondering.'

'Yes?'

'Were you really tired of teaching, Moira, or did you do it for me?'

'Mmm, now there's a question. I'd say it was a bit of both, with maybe a spot of selfishness thrown in.'

'Sure, you haven't a selfish bone in your body, Moira Kent.'

'It seems that I have where you're concerned, Mary Kate. You're the first real friend that I have ever had in the whole of my life. I told myself that I didn't need anyone, that I didn't trust anyone, that I could cope perfectly well on my own. I never once admitted that I was lonely and had been for most of my life. I missed being part of the boarding house. I'd felt useful and needed, it was as if I had found the family that I could only have dreamed of finding and it was all because of you. You saved me, Mary Kate.'

'I'd say we saved each other, my friend.'

'And if it makes you feel better, teaching those children has put ten years on me.'

Mary Kate grinned. 'That's grand then, I'll stop feeling guilty.'

There was a tap on the door and Mrs Lamb poked her head into the room. 'I meant to say, I don't think yer woman's name is Alana at all.'

CHAPTER 8

Bridie and Alana

Bridie was watching Eliza and Abby speaking to the young girl on the bench. She had noticed the girl earlier, because she looked so lost and alone and had considered going across herself but the girls had got there before her.

She had known for weeks that the two girls were following her. They were like a couple of spies, darting behind pillars and squatting behind suitcases. She had found the whole thing rather amusing and sincerely hoped that they had no notion of taking it up as a job, because she feared their career would be very short-lived indeed.

She watched them leave hand in hand with the girl and looked up at the arrivals board.

Bridie came to the bus station every day, and every day she sat and waited. Hoping that the next bus that came in would bring him back to her. He would take her in his arms and they would start their new life together.

It had started slowly, a deep friendship that over the years had grown into mutual respect for each other. She knew that she was falling in love but hardly dared think that he would feel the same. She had been told that she was plain and had never expected anything more than a solitary life but he had loved her, he had loved her with a love that had changed all that had gone before. She saw herself through his eyes, through his words and through his touch. In his eyes she was beautiful and she was wanted. He had lifted her out of her dull grey life and turned it into a world full of colour.

They'd talked late into the night, when everyone else was asleep, about the little cottage where they would live. Maybe it was all just silly talk, lovers' talk, but she had believed in it. The cottage had become so real to her; it had become a home, a home with Stephen, where she could at last find the love and happiness that had alluded her for most of her life. They talked about the garden they would have, wild flowers that would attract the butterflies and the bees. A wooden bench under a willow tree, where they would sit in the shade.

'We must get a dog,' she said.

'What sort of dog?'

'A small one, with big brown eyes.'

'And gnomes,' he'd said, laughing.

'Gnomes?' she'd said. 'You want a gnome?'

'Two,' he'd said, draping an arm around her shoulder. 'A boy and a girl.' He'd kissed the tip of her nose. 'You and me. Mr and Mrs Gnome.'

'The dog must have a name too.'

'Ah yes, every dog deserves a good name. We must put our thinking caps on this very minute.'

But they hadn't, not that day.

They both knew that leaving would bring the wrath of everyone down on their heads but their love for each other had made them brave enough to make the impossible into a reality. They would walk away from all the rules and regulations that had dominated their lives for so many years. It could happen; if she dreamed long and hard enough, it could happen.

The plan was to leave separately, Stephen going first. They would meet at the bus station in Dublin and from there, begin their new lives.

So, what had happened? Why hadn't he turned up? Had he lost his nerve, or couldn't he bear the shame of it all?

He knew she had no money of her own and if it wasn't for the woman who had left her coat on the bench, she would have had nothing. No money for lodgings or food; in fact, she would have been as destitute as the poor souls who slept in doorways.

But Bridie knew the very soul in him, his simple but strong faith and his kindness, not only to her but to anyone in need of a helping hand and he did so quietly. If a halo had been placed on his head, he would have given it to someone in need of such accolades. Stephen was also a gifted teacher, who was adored by the children he taught. He knew who he was and so did she; there wasn't an unkind bone in his body and he had nothing to prove. He would never have let her down like this. Something must have happened.

And so every morning she left the boarding house and went back to the bus station, where she sat on the bench and waited. This was the only place where there was hope, and she needed hope. One day he would sit beside her and they would laugh at the misunderstanding. Wrong bus station, wrong time. She could see it all so clearly: the cottage and the garden, the two gnomes and a little dog called Hope.

CHAPTER 9

Mary Kate

Mary Kate was standing at the bottom of Tanners Row, looking at the pretty houses, with their front gardens and painted doors. When she was a child, it had all looked so different. There had been no pretty houses and no gardens, no electricity, no water and no lavvy, not even an outside one. She walked up the lane and stopped outside the house with the red door: this had been the little cottage where she had grown up. She hadn't known how poor they were, or how her grandparents felt about being saddled with a baby at an age when they should have been free from care, not left to bring up a child. Mary Kate had rarely given a thought to the mother who had abandoned her. Hers was a happy childhood; she was loved and never wanted for anything more than the little cottage, her grandparents, and the friends that she ran the fields and lanes with. Until the day that the mother, who had walked away without a second glance, had gifted her a fortune.

When Mary Kate had been thrown out of her childhood home, she had come to the city looking for work and lodgings.

Those were lonely, desperate years, always on the move, always hoping to find somewhere she would be welcomed, but each boarding house was worse than the last. She lived like this for fifteen years and never thought that things would ever change, but they did.

When Mary Kate had first come into the money, she was all for handing it back – she had never had any money and it scared her. Then she remembered the run-down house that she'd seen in Merrion Square with the FOR SALE sign in the window. The house had been left to fall into disrepair. The beautiful Georgian windows were cracked and broken, the railings rusty with age. This house looked abandoned and unloved, as abandoned and unloved as herself. As she'd stood gazing across the square, Mary Kate could see beyond the peeling paint and years of neglect to the beautiful home that it had once been and could be again. When she walked away that day, the house had stayed in her mind, almost as if it was calling out to her to save it. She now had the means to buy it and turn it into a boarding house for single ladies. A welcoming house, where there was comfort, good food and clean sheets. A boarding house that was nothing like the filthy, bug-infested places that she had endured for so long.

No one in Tanners Row knew that it was Mary Kate who had razed the cottages to the ground and replaced them with homes that were fit to live in, and no one knew that she was their landlady. Her husband Sean had shared her dream of transforming the lives of these people who had lived in squalor all their lives and giving them homes they could be proud of. It had been a labour of love for them both. The money had turned out to be a blessing and not a curse, for the mother she had never known had remembered her and given her this wonderful opportunity to change people's lives for the better. She kept her in her prayers every night.

She was gone now, but fate had brought them back

together. The mother she thought was dead had found her. They had got to know each other and Mary Kate had looked after her until her death. It was one of the happiest times of her life. Another one of her grandad's red-letter days.

She tapped on the door of her old neighbour Mrs Finn, who opened it with a big smile on her face.

'Is it yourself that's in it, Mary Kate Barry?' she said, giving her a big hug. 'Come in, come in, and take the weight off your feet. It's grand to see you.'

Mary Kate smiled. 'It's grand to see you too, Mrs Finn.'

'And it's lovely to see a smile on your face, girl, for I thought I would never see that lovely smile again.'

'It's getting a bit easier, but I miss him every day.'

'I miss him too, Mary Kate, for he was one of the best. It's hard to understand the ways of the Lord that He would take a fine, God-fearing man like Sean Barry when the world is full of gobshites that wouldn't pee on you if you were on fire.'

'Oh, Mrs Finn,' said Mary Kate, laughing, 'you have always had a great way with the words.'

'Ah sure, don't all the Irish have a great way with words?'

'I'd say they do, Mrs Finn,' said Mary Kate, grinning.

'We may have been dragged up without shoes or a decent pair of drawers on our backsides but we always had the gift of the gab and were able to laugh at ourselves.'

'Oh, Mrs Finn, you're a tonic.'

'And you're a sight for sore eyes. Don't ever change, Mary Kate.'

They spent a lovely afternoon reminiscing about the old days. They drank tea and remembered friends that had long gone and babies that had taken their place. When it was time to go, Mrs Finn handed her a grand slab of apple cake, wrapped in *The Irish Times*.

'Something for your belly and something for your mind. Come and see me again, Mary Kate.'

'Oh, I will, Mrs Finn, I surely will.'

Mary Kate decided to walk home instead of taking the bus – there were times when she just needed to be alone with her thoughts. She'd told Mrs Finn that things were getting easier and she supposed that in a way they were. She had the boarding house to keep her busy and she had friends who cared about her. She thanked God for sending Moira to her door when she hadn't wanted to see another person for as long as she lived.

It was when she was alone at night, without Sean by her side, that the pain would wash over her, so intense that she could hardly breathe. There had been times, and may God forgive her, when she had just wanted to go to sleep and never wake up to another day without him. But having decided to live, she was determined to live the very best life she could, because she knew that this was what her beloved Sean would have wanted.

She walked slowly across Merrion Square. She had always loved the changing of the seasons, each one bringing its own special gifts, but this year, spring had only caused sadness. It had, as always, been beautiful, a time of hope and new beginnings, but Mary Kate hadn't wanted new beginnings, her heart was still clinging to old memories. Fresh footprints in their little garden, laying side by side in the iciness of it, staring up at the sparkling Wicklow Hills, their laughter the only sound in a silent white world. Or safe in Sean's arms, listening to the rain beating against the windows of the little cottage where they had been so happy. She held onto these memories like precious jewels and she had no need for new ones. She wanted her old life back, she wanted Sean back, but as she looked at the trees surrounding the square, she felt a kind of comfort. Autumn had always been her favourite season, the softest of the seasons, that seemed to have no need to prove itself.

After the showiness of spring and the heat of summer, it entered slowly, shedding its glorious leaves and letting them fall to the ground, knowing that in time they would return. Maybe this was autumn's special gift, the gift of letting go, showing us that however hard things might be, this letting go still held hope of brighter days.

Mary Kate didn't go up the steps to the red door of the boarding house, instead, she went through the back gate and into the garden – she needed to speak to the girls about the disappearing food.

There was a sign on the shed door that said PRIVATE KEEP OUT. It made Mary Kate smile but she knew that she had to look a wee bit stern for what she had to say. She could hear them laughing and chatting but when she tapped on the door, there was silence.

'I know you're in there, girls,' she said. 'I just need a word with you.'

Still nothing, so she pushed open the door to see three pairs of eyes staring at her. Four counting Guinness the dog.

A young girl jumped up. 'I'm sorry, missus,' she said.

Mary Kate smiled at her. 'No need to be sorry.'

'See,' said Eliza. 'I told you the missus was nice and kind, you've no need to worry there. Isn't that right, Abby? She has no need to worry there.'

'No need at all,' said Abby.

The young girl looked tired and worried.

'How long have you been in the shed, dear?'

'Three days, missus.'

'My name is Mary Kate Barry and you are safe here.'

The girl lowered her head and sobbed. Guinness leaned against her and Eliza held her hand.

They all sat in silence and allowed her to cry.

'Best to let it all out,' said Eliza, as if she was an expert on such things.

When she eventually calmed down, the girl picked up her bag and said, 'My name is Emma Gavin, I'll be on my way.'

Mary Kate shook her head. 'I think that the best thing you can do right now is to come into the house and have a grand hot bath and some clean clothes. And maybe something a bit more substantial than custard creams and peanut butter. What do you think?'

Emma smiled. 'It's very kind of you but I don't want to put you out.'

'Put me out where, child? Sure, where would I be going?'

Emma smiled. 'Thank you so much, you are very kind.'

'She's like the Good Samaritan,' said Eliza. 'Except he was a man, so she couldn't be, could she?'

'No, Eliza, she couldn't,' said Abby, raising her eyes to the ceiling, which had them all laughing.

CHAPTER 10

Mary Kate

While Mrs Lamb was taking care of Emma, the girls sat on the couch, staring at her. Guinness was sitting on the floor beside them, staring at her as well.

'Now,' said Mary Kate, 'I need to ask you a few questions.'

'They won't be hard ones, will they?' said Eliza.

'No, they will be very straightforward. Now, can you please tell me where you found Emma?'

'At the bus station,' said Eliza.

'And what made you bring her home?'

'She looked like a poor lost soul, in need of comfort and succour.'

'Do you even know what succour means?' said Abby to Eliza.

'No, do you?'

'No, but I don't go around using words I don't understand.'

'I think it's a nice word,' said Eliza.

'Then you keep on using it, pet,' said Mary Kate, smiling.

'But tell me, what were you doing at the bus station in the first place?'

Eliza looked across at Abby, who looked the other way. 'I think the good Lord guided us there to bring comfort to a poor lost soul in need of help.'

'He could well have had a hand in it,' said Mary Kate. 'But I'd say there was another reason and I'd like to know what that reason was.'

Eliza's face had gone very red. 'We were following the banana lady.'

'To the bus station?'

'She goes out every day,' said Abby, 'so we thought we'd follow her to see where she went and she goes to the bus station.'

Mary Kate frowned. 'And does she meet someone there?'

'No,' said Abby. 'She just sits on a bench and eats a sandwich.'

'She never gets on a bus?'

'Never.'

Mary Kate frowned. 'That sounds awful odd. There must be nicer places to spend your time.'

'It's a mystery alright,' said Eliza, shaking her head.

Mary Kate smiled at the two girls. Eliza, with her head of fuzzy curls that dwarfed her elfin face, and Abby, whose blonde hair was still as blonde as the day she had taken her from the convent and home to the boarding house. As different in looks as chalk and cheese and yet they had found something in each other that they had both needed. And despite the difference in their ages, they had formed a very special friendship that was a joy to see.

There was a tap on the door and Mrs Lamb came into the room with Emma. 'Your clothes are a bit on the big side, Mary Kate, but at least they are nice and dry. I've put Emma's clothes in the wash.'

'You look grand,' said Mary Kate, smiling at her. 'Sit yourself down.'

'Now, girls, will you take Guinness for a walk while I speak to Emma. I'm sure he could do with one, after being holed up in the shed for three days.'

'We let him out to do his business,' said Abby.

'And we cleaned it up,' said Eliza. 'Didn't we, Abby? We cleaned up the shite.'

'And where did you put it, Eliza?'

'I flung it over the wall, it's grand and clean now.'

'You threw it over the wall onto the footpath?'

Eliza was staring at Abby.

'Don't be looking at me,' said Abby. 'You're the one that did the flinging.'

'I thought I was doing the right thing,' said Eliza.

'Oh, Eliza,' said Mary Kate, shaking her head, 'don't ever change.'

Oh, I won't,' said Eliza. 'I wouldn't know how to.'

Mary Kate smiled at her. 'That's grand then for you happen to be perfect just as you are. Now, on your way out, pop down to the kitchen and ask your mammy to send up two teas.'

'I will, missus, I'll do that right away.'

Emma was sitting on the couch looking around the room. 'You have it lovely,' she said.

'Thank you, but I can't take all the credit – I had the help of friends who have better taste than I will ever have.'

'Well, it's only gorgeous whoever did it.'

Mary Kate smiled. 'It is lovely, isn't it?'

'It really is,' said Emma.

'I'm not going to interrogate you, love, and if you don't want to speak, then that's fine. Your business is your business, but I have a feeling that you need a bit of help, am I right?'

Emma nodded.

'So, would you like to tell me all about it? I'm told that I'm a good listener.'

Emma was looking down at the floor. 'I have to find my sister.'

'Is she lost?' said Mary Kate.

'I know where she is and I'm going to rescue her.'

'Is she in danger?'

'I don't think so but she will be worried and sad and I can't leave her there.'

'Can you tell me where she is, Emma?'

'The nuns have sent her to the Magdalene Sisters here in Dublin, because she's having a baby. But we didn't give our consent, they just sent her there and I have to get her out.'

'You want to take care of her at home?'

Tears were streaming down Emma's face. 'We haven't got a home.'

Just then Mrs Lamb came into the room with a tray of tea and some scones. She could see that Emma was crying, so she placed them on a little table beside Mary Kate and left.

'Was that why the nuns took her, Emma? Because you didn't have a home?'

'Oh, we had a home when they took her away. We lived with our daddy in a little farmhouse above the Blackwater River in West Cork.'

'So, you had a home where you could take care of your sister, but you don't have one now?'

Emma started to cry again.

Mary Kate poured two teas and put three sugars into Emma's cup and sat beside her. 'Take your time, there's no rush.'

'Our home burnt down, with Daddy inside it. They tried to get him out but it was too late.'

Mary Kate held her hand. 'You've been a very brave girl and I'm awful sorry for your loss but together, we shall sort it out.'

'But what if they won't let her go?'

'I have a very good friend. His name is James Renson and if anyone can get Nell out of that place, it's him.'

CHAPTER 11

Emma

Emma was sitting quietly in the back of James Renson's car. She had never been in a car before and even if she had, there was no chance that it would have been as swanky as this one. The seats were so soft you just sank into them and it smelled lovely, sort of like autumn leaves when they went all mushy. Mr Renson was nice, he wasn't all stuck-up, even though he must be desperate rich to own a car like this one. He was whistling a tune that she didn't know and every now and again, he turned around and smiled at her – oh, he was nice, he was, he was nice.

Emma thought that she would be on her own this day, begging the nuns to set her sister free, but someone up there was keeping an eye on her and she liked to think that it was her daddy. She shivered, just thinking of darling Nell shut in that place – it made her feel cold to her bones. Then she felt a hand slip into hers.

Mary Kate smiled at her. 'With God's help and a little nudge from Mr Renson, Nell will be sitting beside you on the journey home.'

Emma's eyes filled with tears, just thinking about holding Nell in her arms again. 'Do you really think so?'

'Oh, I know so. If I have learned one thing in this old life of mine, Emma, it's that you have to keep going, you must never give up, for miracles really can happen. You just have to trust that one day, out of the blue, a rainbow will appear and at the end of the rainbow you will find your red-letter day.'

'Did that happen to you? Did you find your red-letter day?'

'I found it just as I was about to jump into the Liffey.'

'You were going to jump into the Liffey?'

'God forgive me, but I was. I thought there was nothing left for me in this life.'

'But you changed your mind, you didn't jump?'

'I didn't, and it was a good job I didn't, for I can't swim. I would have gone under and what a wonderful life I would have missed.'

Emma smiled. 'I'm glad you didn't jump.'

'So am I, because nothing is as bad as it seems at the time and life has a habit of surprising you when you least expect it. My red-letter day was just around the corner, I just didn't know it. So, trust in yourself, Emma, and love unconditionally, then the love you give away will come back tenfold.

'Oh, I will.'

'And Emma?'

'Yes?'

'Learn to swim.'

They were actually giggling as James Renson drove through the big iron gates and up the drive to the Magdalene laundry.

Emma stared up at the sprawling grey building that looked like a prison. *Hang on, sweet Nell,* she thought, *for I am here. I'm right here, my love, and we'll soon be together again.*

James rang the bell. It seemed to echo through the air as if there was nothing behind the door but emptiness. They waited until eventually they heard the door being unlocked and saw a small nun staring up at them with such a look of terror in her eyes that you'd think she had never seen a human being before in her life.

'Yes?' she said.

James smiled at her. 'Good day to you, Sister. My name is James Renson and I am a lawyer. I would be obliged if you would be kind enough to take us to whoever is in charge of this institution.'

The nun was staring at James as if he had two heads. 'I, I... don't understand.'

'Which bit?'

'Pardon?'

'Which bit don't you understand?'

The nun looked as if she was about to burst into tears. 'I don't know.'

'Then we had best come in while you inform your boss that we wish to speak to her on a matter of great urgency.'

The nun opened the door wider and they stepped inside. There was a young girl down on her knees, scrubbing away at the floor as if her life depended on it – she didn't even look up.

The hallway was bare except for a statue of the Virgin Mary staring sadly down at the polished floor.

The nun suddenly reappeared, it seemed, out of nowhere. 'Mother will see you now,' she said. 'If you'll please follow me. Geraldine, there'll be no floor left at this rate, you've been scrubbing the same bit for the past hour. Away to your room, child.'

The young girl bobbed and scuttled away.

The room they entered was sparse, it had no character. It wasn't a place where you could expect to find pity or comfort, let alone kindness. The only adornments on the walls were pictures of Christ and the Virgin Mary, whose smile was the one piece of warmth against the cold grey stone.

A large desk dominated the room and sitting behind it was a nun. Her chair looked comfortable but the ones in front of the desk were hard-looking. They were also lower, so she would be looking down on whoever occupied them, which meant that they would always be at a disadvantage for they had to look up at her.

James held out his hand. 'My name is James Renson, I am a lawyer.' He pushed a piece of paper across the desk. 'This is a court order to release Nell Gavin from your custody.'

She barely looked at the paper. 'Dear God, man! You make it sound as if we have her imprisoned against her will.'

'Yes, I believe that you might have.'

'Well, you're wrong, Mr Renson, for The Sisters of the Immaculate Conception sent a letter signed by her father, releasing his daughter into our care. It is all perfectly legal and above board.'

'I'd like to see the letter please.'

The nun opened a drawer in the desk, rummaged around and pulled out a piece of paper, which she handed to James.

He looked at it and said, 'There is no signature here.'

'There's a cross,' she said. 'Which is perfectly legal for those among us who are illiterate.'

Emma glared at her. 'My father was not illiterate – he could read and he could write, including his own name.'

'And you are?' said the nun.

'Emma Gavin, Nell's sister.'

'Well, Emma, the nuns have informed me that your present home is not a suitable environment in which to raise an infant. Wouldn't it be better for all concerned for Nell's baby to be adopted into a good Catholic family, who have the means to give the child all the advantages that your family cannot provide?'

Mary Kate saw Emma's eyes fill with tears.

'Nell will be living in my house,' Mary Kate said. 'And whatever the child may lack in so called advantages will be more than made up for in love. And isn't that what God teaches us, Reverend Mother? To love, for He himself was born into a humble home. And when you entered the convent, didn't you take a vow of poverty and turn your back on all worldly things?'

For a fleeting moment, the nun looked ashamed. She pressed a buzzer on the desk, which sent a nun hurrying through the door.

'Please fetch Nell Gavin, Sister.'

'She's at her dinner, Mother.'

'Just bring her here, please. I'm sure these good people can provide her with food; they seem to think that they can provide her with everything else.'

Once the nun had gone, the Reverend Mother started shuffling papers around on the desk as if she was very busy. She had stopped speaking to them.

The door opened and Nell walked slowly into the room. Emma's first instinct was to run to her but as she looked into Nell's beautiful eyes, her heart broke. Her kind, trusting sister, who wouldn't hurt the smallest of creatures, looked defeated. Within these cold walls, it was as if all hope had been destroyed, her very soul had been crushed and her heart broken.

The nun looked up and stared at her. 'It seems you are going home, Miss Gavin. Fetch your things,' she told her.

That was the moment when Emma had seen and heard enough. She placed herself between the nun and her sister. 'She won't be fetching anything,' she said. 'Even if there was a King's ransom in her room I wouldn't take it, for it would carry the smell of this place on its back.'

Emma felt a small hand slip into hers and she squeezed it. Then Nell leaned against her and sighed. 'I waited for you, Emma,' she whispered. 'I waited every day.'

Emma took her sister into her arms and stroked her hair. It felt rough and tangled and it didn't smell like Nell, who carried the scent of the countryside about her as if it was part of her very bones. 'I came as soon as I could, my darling, as soon as I could.'

'I knew you wouldn't forget me.'

'Forgetting you would be like forgetting to breathe.'

'I want to go home, Emma. I want to see my daddy.'

This was not the time to tell her that she would never see her beloved daddy again. 'Of course you do, my love. That is why I am here, to take you home.'

The nun stood up. 'You can't take her just like that, girl.'

'Oh yes I can, and I'll take the face off anyone daft enough to stop me.'

'But there are forms to be filled out.'

'Send them to me,' said James Renson, abruptly. 'Right now, my priority is to get Nell as far away from this place as I can.'

Just as they were about to leave, he reached across the desk and pocketed the bogus court order.

CHAPTER 12

Mary Kate

They drove in silence. There would be plenty of time to talk when they got home and maybe not even then. Mary Kate turned around and looked at the two sisters. Nell had fallen asleep with her head on Emma's shoulder. The poor child looked exhausted but the relief of having her out of that place and in her arms was wonderful. If love could make up for what she had been through then she would heal, Emma would make sure of it.

Her insides burned with anger. She knew that the Magdalene laundries had been in existence for years, she had heard rumours about the cruelty that went on in those places and that wealthy American couples paid for the babies that had the misfortune to have been born there. Was there no compassion for these poor girls who were foolish enough to think that sex was love? And what about the lads in all this, who were able to just walk away, thinking they were great fellows altogether and getting pats on their backs from their mates? Why was there no laundry for them? Why was there no blame attached to them?

Mary Kate felt ashamed that she had known and not given it much thought until now. The Catholic Church was revered in Ireland and no one would say a bad word against it for fear of bringing the wrath of the local priest down on their heads.

Ireland was a poor country. Most people lived hand to mouth and yet they were forced to give birth to child after child when there was no way that they had the means to support them. And yet these women were strong; she admired their strength and their faith and wondered if she could have done it herself.

Mary Kate knew that not all nuns were unkind. It would have been wrong of her to tar them all with the same brush for she had been taught by nuns herself and they were lovely. They glided along the school corridors as if they were on wheels and the girls were in awe of them, including herself. There was no cruelty in the little school she had attended, only kindness. Of all the nuns, Sister Breda had been her favourite. She was very beautiful with lovely green eyes. Of course none of them knew what colour hair she had because it was hidden beneath the white wimple that she wore but it was decided that it was red like Maureen O'Hara's.

The girls made up stories about why she had chosen to become a nun.

Dervla Butler, who could lie herself out of a murder wrap, said that she had it on good authority that Sister Breda had fallen in love with a Protestant feller and shamed her family. Of course no one believed her, you couldn't believe a word that came out of Dervla's mouth – the girl was full of shite.

Sister Breda had taken a shine to her and had wanted her to stay on at school. 'You have a good brain in that head of yours, Mary Kate Ryan. It's a shame to waste it for it was given to you by God Himself. Your mother was clever too, that's where you get it from.'

'You knew my mother?'

'I did and she was a sweet girl, loved by everyone. We may never know why she left but knowing her as I did, I'd say it wasn't because she didn't love you. She would have had her own reasons for going. We may never know what those reasons were, but I'd say she must have been desperate to get away.'

'But why couldn't she have taken me with her, Sister?'

'The thing about leaving a place is fine. If you are travelling to somewhere better, it's a bit of an adventure but I have a feeling that your mother was walking into the unknown because it was safer than staying where she was and that took courage. She didn't abandon you, child, she left you with your grandparents, where she knew you would be safe and cared for. Her parting gift to you was the security of a loving home that she couldn't provide and that was a very unselfish thing to do.'

'I have never thought of it like that, Sister.'

'There is a lot in this life that we don't understand. That's where faith comes in – knowing that God has a plan for all of us, your mother included. We just have to believe in His goodness.'

As they drove into Merrion Square, she saw Abby and Eliza looking out of the window. James had barely parked the car when they were running down the steps.

'Did you rescue her?' shouted Eliza. 'Have you fetched her home? Will I make up a bed? We can, can't we, Abby? We can make up a grand bed, where she can rest her little head.'

'Dear God in heaven, Eliza,' said Abby. 'Will you give them a chance to get their legs out of the car before you start talking about making beds?'

'Well, she'll need a bed, won't she? Everyone needs a bed.'

'But not right now, OK?'

'I'm just trying to help, Abby. You know I like to help and I'm desperate excited to meet her.'

'I know you are, Eliza, but this might not be the right time for excitement – there will be time enough for that later. Anyway, we don't even know if they have her.'

'They have her alright, Abby. I can see a strange head in the back seat and there's bound to be a body attached to it.'

'Oh, Eliza,' said Abby.

'What?'

'Nothing. Just oh, Eliza.'

CHAPTER 13

Moira

Moira had also been waiting for the car to come into the square and praying that they would have the poor child with them. She smiled as she thought of all the waifs and strays that Mary Kate had taken under her wing and it looked as if it was about to happen again.

So far there was only one paying guest in the house and that was the banana. Oh, she must stop calling her that or one day she would let the nickname slip. It was hard to make the woman out – she was pleasant enough, but it was as if she'd put a wall around herself and had no intention of letting anyone in. There was a story there and she could only hope that she was not suffering in silence when herself and Mary Kate were a great pair of listening ears.

She watched as the car came round the corner and Eliza ran down the steps, followed by Abby and Guinness.

Dear Eliza, who at almost twenty-five had the mind and innocence of a child and always would, and darling Abby, the adopted daughter that Moira never dreamed she would have.

Abby was beautiful. She had a wisdom far beyond her years and she was kind. No one knew much about her background, only that she had been abandoned as a baby and found by the monks on the steps of the abbey. The little girl hadn't spoken to anyone except Jessie until she'd felt safe enough to trust again. Mary Kate had gone to the convent to offer one of the orphans a home in the boarding house but Jessie wouldn't come without Abby so she had taken the pair of them. Jessie was now happy running a bookshop with her dear friend Aishling, returning to the boarding house whenever she could.

It was here, behind the red door of Merrion Square, that Moira had found acceptance and love. Mary Kate had broken down barriers, laying bare the pain she had carried all her life. They had become best friends, something she had never known. She was the outsider, the girl who didn't quite fit, the girl who was never invited to parties, the one that no one would remember. But behind the red door she mattered, she counted for something. She had, at last, found herself and in finding herself, she decided that she wasn't half bad – in fact, she was damn awesome.

Moira had thought she had no room in her life for a child, but Abby had crept into her heart and into her very being, and adopting her felt like the most natural thing in the world. She was as much her child as if she had given birth to her, as if the same blood flowed through their veins. What had amazed Moira the most was the way Abby returned her love, for Moira had never been loved by anyone since her little sister had died.

It was here in the boarding house that Moira had found acceptance and love. Mary Kate had broken down her barriers.

She hurried down the stairs to greet them and was relieved to see that they had Nell with them.

'They have her, Miss Moira,' said Eliza. 'She's sitting in the back of the car – at least her head is, I haven't seen the rest of her yet. Isn't that grand altogether? I was telling Abby that we must make up a bed for the poor thing.'

'You're right, Eliza, that is definitely something we must do and I'm sure there will be more to her than just a head. At least I hope so,' she said, laughing.

Moira watched them getting out of the car. Her first thought was *my God, the child is beautiful but so fragile*, she looked like a broken doll. She was leaning into Emma as they walked towards the house. It was as if every bit of strength had been knocked out of her. What on earth had they done to the poor girl?

Nell stumbled on the steps and Emma caught her. 'We're home now, love,' she said gently.

Nell looked up at the house. 'This isn't our home, Emma.'

'Maybe not, my darling, but for now, this is where you will get well. This is where you will grow strong and this is what Daddy would want.'

Moira watched as Nell's eyes filled with tears. 'But I want to go to our home,' she said.

'Look at me, Nell,' said Emma. She took Nell's hand and placed it on her heart, then placed her own hand on Nell's heart. 'This is home, Nell. This is home.'

Moira thought she had never heard anything so beautiful and it seemed to satisfy Nell, who continued to walk up the steps towards the red door.

As Mary Kate walked into the lounge, Eliza went to follow them but Moira took her to one side: 'What Nell needs now is rest and a bit of peace.'

Eliza was nodding her head. 'And a bit of succour. Shall I sit beside her and hold her hand?'

'I think what my mammy means,' said Abby, 'is that it would be better if we made ourselves scarce. Am I right, Mammy?'

No matter how many times Abby called her Mammy, it still

touched her heart and filled her with joy. 'You are,' said Moira, smiling.

'What about Guinness?' said Eliza. 'He's awful good at succour.'

'I think you're right, Eliza. I have always thought so myself. In fact, the first time I saw him, I thought, there is a dog who is good at succour. Now would you be kind enough to fetch a couple of pillows.'

'Is it for her poor head?' said Eliza.

'It is, and while you're at it, could you bring down a blanket for the rest of her body?'

Abby was giggling as she and Eliza headed upstairs.

Moira looked across at Nell – the poor child needed all the help they could give her. She was safe now and the boarding house would do the rest.

CHAPTER 14

Moira

Moira had lit a fire in the room and it was lovely and warm. They watched Nell sleeping on the couch; she looked very peaceful. Emma was sitting beside her on the floor, holding her hand.

She looked across at Mary Kate. 'How can I thank you enough for what you have done for us?'

'Our thanks will be to see you and Nell safe and well – that's all the thanks we need.'

'We have no money,' said Emma. 'We're not able to pay you.'

Moira laughed. 'My dear child, if we had been relying on money, this place would have gone to rack and ruin years ago.' She smiled across at Mary Kate. 'Isn't that right, my friend?'

'I suppose it is,' said Mary Kate.

'I can work for our keep,' said Emma. 'I can cook and I can clean. In fact, I can turn my hand to almost anything – I was brought up on a farm. Daddy was neither use nor ornament but it wasn't his fault, he was a lovely man but addicted to the demon drink.'

'Then you would be a great help here. What do you think, Moira?'

'I think you would be doing us a favour, Emma.'

Emma's eyes filled with tears. 'Then you'll take me on?'

'If you would like to,' said Mary Kate.

'And Nell?'

Mary Kate looked across at Moira, who nodded. 'We would love to have you both, if that's what you would like.'

'Oh, I would, and I won't let you down. I'll work my fingers to the bone for you.'

Mary Kate laughed. 'Well, there'll be no need for that.'

Emma shook her head. 'You don't know what you have done this day. We are strangers and yet you have given us a home and I will be forever grateful to you both.'

Mary Kate smiled. 'Well, the first thing we must do is get Nell seen by a doctor.'

'And then we'll go on a grand shopping spree,' said Moira, grinning. 'We have a baby on the way who will need dressing.'

Just then Eliza and Abby burst into the room. 'A baby?' said Eliza. 'Where is it?'

Mary Kate put her finger to her lips. 'Shush, Nell is sleeping.'

'Is the baby in Nell's tummy?' said Abby softly.

Moira smiled and nodded.

Eliza was staring at the sleeping Nell. 'How in all that's holy did it get in there?'

Moira had her hand over her mouth, trying to stifle the giggle that was nearly choking her.

'Can't we get it out?' said Eliza.

'Come and sit beside me,' said Mary Kate.

Eliza sat down on the couch and Mary Kate held her hand.

'Before you were born, Eliza, you were in your mammy's tummy.'

'I don't think I was, missus. Mammy said she found me in the vegetable patch, in between the carrots and the spuds.'

'Ah well, if that's where your mammy said she found you, then I expect she's right.'

'Anyway, I don't remember being in her tummy. Wouldn't I remember being in there?'

'Do you remember being in the vegetable patch?' asked Abby.

Eliza looked thoughtful. 'Mmm, I don't think so but I'm awful fond of carrots and spuds.'

'I'd say they became your friends,' said Abby, 'and that's why you like them so much.'

'You still haven't told me how to get that baby out of Nell's tummy. And you haven't said how it got in there in the first place.'

Mary Kate and Moira stared at each other, neither of them knowing what to say to Eliza.

Just then the phone rang and Mary Kate picked it up.

Moira knew from the look on Mary Kate's face that whoever was on the other end of the line had shocked her.

'We have to go to the convent, Moira. We have to go right now. I will phone James. Will you be alright here, Emma?'

'Of course.'

'Eliza, go downstairs and ask your mammy to bring up some food for the girls.'

'Moira, go and grab your coat.'

Mary Kate waited in the hallway. Dear God, how was she going to tell Moira the news?

Moira ran down the stairs. She knew that whatever had happened had shaken Mary Kate to the core – her friend looked as white as a sheet. 'What is it?'

'Oh, Moira,' she said. 'That was Sister Luke on the phone, she's had a visit from a woman who claims to be Abby's birth mother.'

CHAPTER 15

Mary Kate

Mary Kate held Moira's hand as they headed towards the convent. James drove slowly through the open gates and up the long drive.

'Can I have a minute before we go in,' said Moira. 'I just need a minute.'

'Of course,' said James, stopping the car.

Moira took a deep breath. 'Will she be in there?'

'We don't know,' said Mary Kate gently.

'I'm not sure if I can face her. I don't even know if I want to. Abby could have died that night she left her and I'm angry. What sort of mother does that to her own child?'

James turned around. 'You don't have to meet her,' he said. 'Just say the word and we'll go back home.'

'What do you think, Mary Kate?' said Moira.

'I agree with James that yes, we can just turn around, but...'

'But what?'

'Knowing you as I do, my friend, I think you might regret it.

We're here now, why don't we see what she has to say? Don't tell me you're not a little curious.'

'OK, but if I'm not comfortable, we can leave, yes?'

Mary Kate smiled at her. 'Of course, my love.'

'So, are you ready?' said James.

'I have one more question before we go in. Can she take Abby away from us?'

James shook his head. 'No, definitely not. You are legally her mother and no one can take her away from you.'

'Are you sure?'

'I'm a lawyer, Moira, and I can tell you without a doubt that the moment that woman abandoned her child, she gave up all rights to her. Now, shall we go in?'

She nodded.

James started the engine and they continued up the drive to the convent.

There was a nun waiting at the door. 'Sister Luke is expecting you,' she said. 'I'll take you to her now.'

As they followed the nun upstairs to Sister Luke's office, they still didn't know if Abby's mother was going to be in there and even James looked anxious, but as they walked into the room, Sister Luke was alone.

She came towards them and hugged Moira and Mary Kate.

'I imagine you must all be shocked,' she said. 'I'm still reeling from it myself.'

'We thought she might still be here,' said Mary Kate.

'I wouldn't have done that to you.' Sister Luke pressed a bell on her desk, which brought a nun into the room.

'Could we have some tea please, Sister?'

The other nun nodded. 'I'll get it right away.'

'Now, sit yourselves down. I'm sure you have lots of questions so I will tell you what I know.'

'I'm sick with worry, Sister,' said Moira.

'I knew that you would be, but I hope that I can put your mind at rest.'

They sat down and waited for Sister Luke to speak.

'Two days ago, a woman turned up at the abbey claiming to be the mother of a baby girl who was discovered eight years ago by one of the monks. They immediately brought the woman here to the convent. As you know, we had very little information at the time. All we knew was that a baby had been abandoned on a cold winter's night, who would have frozen to death if she hadn't been found. We had no idea where she came from, or who her mother was. We tried to find her, we involved the local paper and we put up posters, but no one came forward. In the end, we assumed that she didn't want to be found. Abby was in such a terrible state of neglect that even had the mother tried to claim her, we wouldn't have just handed her over. She was half the weight of a child of her age, which we reckoned was about two years old but she could have been three. There was nothing of the child, she weighed little more than a baby, it was very hard to put an age on her. Another very worrying thing was that she hadn't made a sound, no crying, nothing. And as you know, she spoke to no one except Jessie, not a word.'

There were tears running down Moira's face. 'What kind of a mother would do that to her own flesh and blood? God forgive me but I wouldn't be responsible for my actions if I came face to face with her.'

Just then the door opened and the nun came in with a tray of teas. 'Sister Bernard has just taken these cakes out of the oven and I put a few on a plate before the rest of the sisters pounced on them. I always think that life seems that bit better with a grand slice of cake in your hand.'

Sister Luke looked at the rather short, round nun and smiled. 'Yes, Sister, I'm sure you are right and thank you for your thoughtfulness.'

'Ah sure it's nothing, just a little bit of kindness and that costs nothing.'

When she left the room, they waited for Sister Luke to continue.

'Abby's birth mother is called Norah and she called her baby Alice.'

'Abby is Alice?' said Moira.

Sister Luke nodded. 'Before she came to us, her name was Alice Martha.'

'No surname?' said Moira.

'She didn't say and even if I had asked, she would probably have lied. Abby might have known but as she didn't speak, we had no idea what it was.'

'What did she want?' said Moira. 'Does she want to see Abby?'

Sister Luke shook her head. 'No, that is not why she came.'

'Why then?' said Mary Kate. 'After all this time, why now?'

'Because she wanted to know if her daughter was well.'

'That's all?' said Mary Kate.

'That's all.'

'What was she like?' said Moira, gently.

Sister Luke started to pour the tea. 'I found her to be softly spoken and well turned out but the sadness in her eyes belied the lovely outfit that she was wearing. She could barely look me in the eye. She wasn't asking for forgiveness; she didn't try to justify what she had done and she didn't come across as a victim. She just wanted to know if her daughter was safe and happy.'

'You're making her sound like a saint,' said Moira.

'Not a saint, but not the monster we imagined her to be.'

'Well, I'm sorry, Sister, but I can't forgive her – Abby could have died that night.'

'And I can understand that, Moira, of course I can but I

don't have a choice in the matter. My faith has taught me to forgive, as Jesus himself forgave.'

'Have you always been able to forgive so easily?'

Sister Luke grinned. 'Dear God, no. I was a divel of a young one. I wrote every slight, real or imagined, in a little book. If someone so much as said my hair was sticking up at the back, their name would go into my book and I wouldn't give them the time of day next time I saw them. As you can imagine, it didn't make me popular. When I told my mother that I thought I had a vocation, she laughed so hard, I thought that the poor woman was going to have a heart attack right there in the kitchen and my sisters went round with tea towels over their heads for weeks. I didn't find it funny. My mother said that I'd want to get over myself, my brother said it would do me no harm if I could find meself a sense of humour, and my grandfather said he'd give it a week before I'd be thrown out into the street. But I listened and I followed the rules and I learned. The Reverend Mother had her knees worn out praying that I would soon have the faith to carry out God's work and not question. Have a cake, Sister Bernard makes a grand bit of cake.'

They helped themselves and then Mary Kate spoke: 'Did she tell you about her life?'

'Not at first, I think she was too ashamed but little by little, I eased it out of her and it was not easy to hear.'

'Something has been puzzling me,' said James, who, until now, had kept silent.

'Tell me,' said Sister Luke.

'How did she know that her daughter was taken into the abbey?'

'Because, Mr Renson, she was there.'

'The night that Abby was found?'

Sister Luke nodded. 'I will tell you what I know but let me warn you, it's not a pretty story.'

Mary Kate looked across at Moira. 'Do you want to know?

Because you don't have to. We can leave it in the past and maybe the past is the best place for it.'

'It's not that I want to know,' said Moira. 'But as Abby's mother, I think I should know. Whether we like it or not, it is a part of Abby's life and even though she might not remember it, it will have shaped who she is and I need to understand.'

'You're right, of course,' said Sister Luke, standing up. 'I think that perhaps more tea is needed.'

Once the nun had left the room, Mary Kate turned to Moira. 'Are you sure about this?' she said gently. 'Because if you're not, we can come back another day.'

'I need to know, Mary Kate. This is Abby's story and so it is mine.'

They were all crying by the time Sister Luke had finished speaking.

'My one hope,' said the nun, 'is that Abby was too young to remember. I will pray for you.'

CHAPTER 16

Norah Clancy

Norah pushed open the old wooden gate and walked into the cemetery. She sat on a bench and thought about what had just happened. She had expected to be turned away but instead she had received kindness. There had been no judgement, even though she deserved it and expected it; in fact she had needed it, for there had been no retribution for the sin of neglecting her daughter. The nun hadn't told her where Alice was living, and she hadn't asked. All she had said was that Alice had grown into a beautiful kind girl, who was loved and cared for, and that had been all she needed to know.

Sister Luke had held her hand. 'Don't you think that it's time you forgave yourself, Norah?' she'd asked gently. 'The God I have come to know is not a vengeful God, He knows who you are and He can see into your heart. It was brave of you to come here today and you should be proud. Sure, don't we all deserve a second chance?'

'Maybe not everyone does,' she'd said sadly.

Graveyards had never scared her. It was the living who had broken her heart and her spirit.

She looked over the rows of graves that spread out across the cemetery. Some had pots of fresh flowers, balancing on the earthy mounds, the only colour in this otherwise colourless place. Others were crumbling to the ground, or leaning so far over that it looked as if they were having a private conversation with the grave next to them.

Autumn was coming to an end and only a few leaves still clung to the stark branches of the trees; the rest were carried on the air before settling amid the grey stones.

Norah closed her eyes, feeling the warm breeze touch her face like a gentle hand. And in the silence of that silent place, she let her mind drift back to where it had all begun.

She could barely remember giving birth to her daughter. She'd been roaring drunk when the pains started and had staggered to the nearest hospital. She knew that they had been disgusted with her, for not only was she drunk but she was screaming obscenities at anyone who tried to come near her. She was a nasty drunk and so was Thomas and that was all they had in common, that and their dependence on the booze they threw down their throats every second of every day and night.

They spent their time in a filthy flat in the slums of Dublin with a load of other drunks. They hardly ate and never washed. She lived in a twilight world, amid strangers whose names she never knew. Fights broke out and blood was spilled, and threats were screamed but no one took any notice. Every so often the guards visited and hauled someone up before the judge. For some reason they left her and Thomas alone. Maybe the size of him put them off, for he was a giant of a man and in drink, they were no match for him. They chose to keep their noses from being battered and leave them alone.

Once she'd had her baby, they put her on a ward with a load of women. It smelled nice in there, at least it did until she moved in. The bed was lovely and comfy, the sheets smelled of lemons and the pillows were like laying her head on a cloud. They made her wash and put her in a clean nightie. It was pale lemon with little forget-me-nots all over it. She'd forgotten what it felt like to be looked after and once she'd sobered up and stopped yelling at everyone, the staff were kind to her and the other women were friendly.

A lovely nurse with bright red hair and a face full of freckles showed her how to breastfeed. She would sit on her bed and guide the baby's little mouth onto her nipple but oh, the pain when she started to suck, and yet it was a pain that she bore without complaint, because for once in her life, she was doing something good – she was keeping her baby alive.

'She's a natural,' said the nurse, 'you'll have no trouble with her when you get her home.'

Norah wondered what she would say if she saw the home that she was bringing her back to.

'Now, have you decided on a name?'

Norah looked down at her sweet baby, with her blonde hair and deep blue eyes. 'Alice, after my mother,' she said, smiling.

'I've always loved that name,' said the nurse. 'I wish my mother had named me Alice.'

'What is your name?'

'Martha.'

'Then I shall call her Alice Martha, do you mind?'

'I'm honoured.'

'Allow me to introduce you to Miss Alice Martha Clancy.'

'Welcome to the world, little one,' said the nurse, smiling. 'I wish you a long and happy life.'

She felt so safe lying there, with her little girl in her arms. She breathed in the smell of her and kissed her soft little cheek, it was love at first sight. Norah was fascinated by her – the way her tiny lips kept moving, as if she was telling herself a story and the way she stared up at her with such trust as she sucked at her breast. Most of the other woman on the ward allowed the nurses to take their babies to the nursery so that they could have a rest but Norah wouldn't let Alice out of her sight. 'I love you, little one,' she said, stroking her wispy hair, 'and I promise to take care of you and guard you with my life. I'm going to be the best mummy in the world.'

The next morning, Norah was woken by a commotion in the corridor. She felt her stomach clench as she heard Thomas yelling and swearing. She wanted to snatch Alice up and run far away from him as fast as she could. He burst into the ward, scaring the life out of the women around her. There were a couple of men trying to stop him, but he was roaring drunk and too strong for them. She cowered in the bed as he made a grab for her.

'You're coming with me,' he yelled, swaying all over the place and nearly falling on the woman in the next bed, who was breastfeeding her baby.

'Of course I am, Thomas,' she said gently. 'But first you have to calm down, you're scaring everyone.'

He looked at the woman who he'd nearly fallen on. 'Sorry, missus,' he slurred. 'And if you don't mind me saying, that's a fine pair of breasts you have there.'

Norah got out of bed and went to pick up the baby.

'You're not bringing that with you,' he spat.

Norah was relying on the fact that he didn't have a brain cell in his head. 'We have to,' she said. 'They'll have the guards onto us if we leave her here, it's against the law.'

'Well, don't expect me to look after it. The brat's yours.'

'I'll take care of her, Thomas,' said Norah. 'She'll be no trouble at all.'

'She'd better not be,' he growled. 'Now let's get the feck out of this place.'

As Norah picked Alice up, Martha walked across to her. She took a blanket out of the cot and handed it to Norah: 'It's cold outside, you have to keep her warm.'

'I will, and thank you.'

Martha looked towards the door and whispered in Norah's ear: 'You have to leave him; you know that, don't you? There are places you can go, where you'll both be safe. Promise me you will leave him.'

'I will, I'll leave him.'

Thomas walked back into the room. 'Will ya come on.'

'I'm coming,' she said.

Martha held her hand. 'Promise me, Norah, please promise me.'

Norah leaned in and kissed her cheek. 'I promise, I promise I will leave him.'

She tried, she tried so hard to leave but with a new baby to take care of, Norah felt lost and alone. She had nowhere to go and no one to turn to. She sought help at a local church. They were kind and welcomed her and Alice with open arms. They made her feel safe, but Thomas found her – he always found her and he wore her down with his promises of a better life that she wanted so much to believe, but nothing changed and she felt like a fool for thinking that it would. A fool to think that Thomas could ever be anything more than a pathetic drunk.

She hated herself for the weak woman she was and returned to the only home she knew, the twilight world of filth and booze and hopelessness. She was determined never to drink again. She was a mother now; she had a baby to take care of. Thomas said that one drink would do no harm and that it would relax her. It did, but she didn't stop at one and that was what Thomas was banking on. Her promises to Martha and to her baby disappeared like so many broken dreams.

There were days when Norah forgot she had a baby. One

drunken woman slapped her awake and pressed Alice to her breast. 'Feed your child, you useless cow!' she'd screamed.

How Alice survived babyhood was a miracle, she was a child who was neglected and ignored. If she cried, Thomas yelled at her to shut up and so she learned to be quiet, she didn't even try to speak. She was a sad, lonely little girl, trying to survive in a filthy room full of sad, lonely drunks.

After drinking all day, Norah staggered to the toilet. As she stepped over bodies, she was grabbed by the arm. 'Get yer hands off me!' she shouted.

A woman pushed her to the floor. 'Don't you want to know where your kid is?'

Norah shook her head. 'What are you talking about?'

'Your kid, the one who had the misfortune to land up with you as her mother.'

Norah rubbed at her eyes. 'Alice? What have you done to her?'

'I haven't done anything to her. See that pile of rags in the corner? Well, that's John and he says your kid just walked out of the flat.'

'What do you mean, walked out of the flat? She's just a baby. Why didn't he stop her?'

'Because he can hardly stand up and he's not her bloody minder and why do you care anyway? You've never cared about her before.'

'Of course I care about her.'

The woman grabbed a handful of her hair. 'Who do you think feeds her?'

Norah was trying to make sense of what was happening, but her head was a mess. 'I need a drink,' she said.

The woman shook her. 'Look around the room. We may be a load of lowlifes, we may be the dregs of Dublin, but we still have hearts and we have cared for Alice as if she were our own, because we are all she has. We share what little we have with her, and what we don't have, we take.'

Norah could feel her eyes closing and the woman shook her again. 'I said, look around the room.'

Norah rubbed at her eyes and tried to focus.

'See that young girl over there?'

Nora could feel her eyes getting heavy, all she wanted was drink and sleep.

The woman yanked her head back. 'I said, see that young girl over there? Every morning, she steals milk from doorsteps for Alice and that old woman over there? Well, her name is Bertha. See that doll on the floor? She found that doll in a trash can, it's the only toy that Alice has ever had. Since your child was a baby, that old woman has rummaged through bins for bits of rags to make nappies. Alice sleeps beside her every night because that is where she feels safe.'

Norah struggled to get the woman off her, but she was slapped hard in the face, banging her head against the wall.

'I want you to remember her name, you lousy bitch! It's Bertha, say it.'

Norah's head was throbbing. 'Feck off.'

'I said, say it!' the woman yelled.

'OK, Bertha, Bertha, bloody Bertha! Happy now?'

The woman put her face so close to Norah's that her stinking breath made her retch.

'You bag of shite, you should be down on your knees thanking that poor old sod, because she's the closest thing to a mother that Alice has ever known.'

Norah pressed her hands against the filthy floor and eased herself up. She looked across the room at the old woman and felt sick with shame. 'Bertha,' she said softly.

The woman let go of her and stood up. 'Yes, Bertha.'

Norah picked up the doll and hurried towards the door.

Before opening it, she looked back at the woman. 'Thank you,' she said. 'Thank you all.'

The woman nodded. 'Now go and get your kid and if you bring her back here, I'll knock the living daylights out of you.'

'I won't bring her back,' she said. 'I won't, I promise.'

It was freezing outside, and her feet were bare but she kept running, calling her daughter's name as she ran. What had she done? What if Alice had wandered into the road? If she died, it would be her fault. She couldn't remember the last time she'd prayed but she was praying now. 'I don't deserve your help, God,' she said, 'but please take pity on my little girl and keep her from harm.' She remembered the baby she had held in her arms and promised to love and keep safe. She remembered the sweet smell of her and the softness of her skin. She remembered how she looked up at her as she sucked on her breast and the way her little hands worried at the blanket. She remembered her baby and hated herself for the lousy mother she was. A lousy mother, who had chosen drink over the safety of her child. She wanted to lay down and die.

After nearly giving up, she found herself outside the abbey, just in time to see a monk picking Alice up in his arms and carrying her inside. She was about to shout out but stopped. This was the only gift she could give her, to walk away and let her have a life where she would be cared for. A life where she would be safe. She held the doll in her arms and looked up at the abbey. 'I will always love you, little one,' she whispered. Then walked away from the only good thing she had ever known.

CHAPTER 17

Emma

Nell had taken to following Emma around as she cleaned and polished the boarding house.

Emma sighed. 'Please stop following me, love, I have work to do. And you need to rest.'

Nell frowned at her. 'We've been here ages.'

'We've been here three weeks, Nell.'

'Well, I want to go home, I want to see my daddy. He'll be lonely without us. Who's going to cook his eggs and bacon in the morning and make his old bed and cut his whiskers when they get too long? We must go home now, right this minute. I'll ask Eliza if she would be kind enough to clean the house, but we have to go home today.'

Emma didn't know what to say to her sister. Nell was still in shock after what had happened to her, how could she tell her that they had no home and that their daddy was dead? She knew that there would come a time when she would have to tell her, but it wasn't today.

Emma sat on the bed and Nell sat down beside her.

Emma placed her hand gently on Nell's tummy. 'We have to care for your baby first, my love. It wouldn't be good for either of you to travel all that way just yet.'

'When can we go then? Why are we here anyway? I don't like it here; I want to climb my hillside and watch the boats floating along the river.' Nell started to cry and Emma held her in her arms. 'I just want to go home,' she sobbed.

'I know you do, my love, and we will. One day soon, we will climb the hill together. We will stand at the top and show your baby our beautiful Blackwater River.'

'You promise?'

Emma took Nell's hand and placed it on her heart, then placed her own hand on Nell's heart.

'Home?' said Nell.

Emma smiled. 'Always.'

They could hear Eliza shouting Nell's name.

'We're up here,' Emma called back.

Eliza and Abby came into the room, they were both smiling.

'Abby's mammy has given us money for cakes,' said Eliza.

'For all of us,' said Abby.

'And we wondered if Nell would like to come to the baker's as well, because we don't know which cake she would like. Abby and meself like the apple cake. Don't we, Abby? We like the apple cake?'

Nell looked at Emma: 'Can I?'

Emma nodded. 'I think that the walk will do you good, but don't wander off.'

'Oh, we won't,' said Eliza. 'The last time we did that, they had the guards out looking for us. Do you remember, Abby?'

Abby made a funny face. 'I couldn't forget even if I wanted to, you remind me often enough.'

'Anyway,' said Eliza, 'we're taking Guinness with us. He has a desperate liking for cake himself and wasn't it him that found us last time? He's a grand dog altogether. You've no need to

worry on that score, no need to worry at all. Has she, Abby? She
has no need to worry herself at all.'

Abby didn't answer; she just raised her eyes to the ceiling,
which made Emma smile.

After they'd gone, Emma walked across to the window and
looked out over the square. She was lying to Nell and that was
something she had never done before, but she had no choice.
Her job now was to keep her safe and healthy, for the precious
life that she carried.

Nell had always been a sensitive girl, who cried at every
injured creature she came across, however small. She'd carry
them carefully home in her hands and Daddy would make little
boxes for them. Some survived but most of them died. The hillside was dotted with mounds of earth that Nell would place
wildflowers on. 'So they know someone remembers them,' she'd
say. 'Everyone should be remembered.'

How then could she tell her that her daddy had died?

He was buried in the local graveyard. There'd been no
money for a headstone but one of his drinking buddies made a
wooden cross, on which he'd written, 'Bull Gavin lies here'.
Because of the man's kindness, Emma hadn't the heart to tell
him that her daddy's real name was William. Her daddy had
gone but knowing him as she did, he wouldn't care what they
called him.

Emma had been more like a mother to Nell than a sister,
and there were times when the burden of taking care of her was
almost too much. Her childhood had ended the day their
mammy had died. Emma was seven years old at the time, and
Nell only three. Emma remembered her, but Nell didn't. Emma
remembered her hair as she brushed it in front of the mirror, so
soft and silky, and her eyes, Nell's eyes, that crinkled at the
corners when she smiled. They had been so happy back then;
their home had been full of laughter and love. Daddy spent his
days working hard on the land and taking care of the animals

and his family, but his grief at losing his wife was terrible to see. He had knelt on the ground and howled like an animal, that had Nell clinging on to her. That was when he took to the drink and there had been nothing she could do to make it better.

She watched the girls as they left the house. Eliza and Abby each holding on to Nell as they walked down the steps, as if she was an old one in need of protection, while Guinness ran between them, his tail wagging with excitement. They were both so sweet and she owed them so much.

She could be happy here; she loved the hustle and bustle of Dublin, the crowded pavements, the picture houses, the theatres and the dance halls. There was nothing like this at home, nothing for her anyway. Nell had been content on the hillside, it was a part of who she was – she could sit on top of the hill for a whole morning, just watching the river below her. Nell needed nothing more and Emma knew that she would never settle here.

Was she wrong to keep Nell in the dark about what had happened to their home and their daddy? Didn't she still have a right to know? Nell wanted to go home but Emma didn't care if she never saw the place again. There was no work for her there and no way for her to take care of Nell and the baby. She could make a life for them here, a good life, but there was nothing for them back there.

Emma needed someone to talk to, someone she could trust, someone who would listen to her story and help her decide what to do.

CHAPTER 18

Mary Kate

Mary Kate and Moira were sitting side by side on the couch reading, which they had fallen into the habit of doing on these grey days. The only sound was the howling wind and the rain lashing against the windows. She felt safe and warm and knew how blessed she was to be here in this lovely room, with her best friend beside her. There were still times when she could hardly believe that this beautiful house was hers. For fifteen years, there had been nothing to look forward to, no one to love her or even be her friend. She had missed her grandparents and the little cottage so much that many a night she would cry herself to sleep and pray to God to take her as she slept, so that she need never face another day in this cold, friendless city. As it turned out, God decided that He wasn't in desperate need of her company and instead, she received a letter from a solicitor telling her that her mother had left her a fortune. That letter had changed her life and brought her love.

'I almost feel sorry for her,' said Moira suddenly.

Mary Kate looked across at her friend. 'Sorry for who?'

'Abby's mother.'

Mary Kate stared at her. 'I thought you wanted to murder her?'

'I did and maybe I still do, but the woman I wanted to murder is not the same woman who made sure that Abby was going to be safe that night. She didn't just abandon her, she gave her the chance at a better life and, however bad a mother she was, it must have been heart-breaking.'

Mary Kate closed her book and put it on the table beside her. 'I wonder what, if anything, Abby remembers.'

'I can't remember anything from that age, can you?'

'I've been thinking about that,' said Mary Kate.

'About what?'

'About her age, what if she was older?'

'How much older?'

'Sister Luke said that she was in a terrible state when she was found, so small and thin that it had been hard to know what age she was. What if she was older than two? What if she was three, maybe nearer four? I can remember things from when I was four. I could be wrong but even at ten, Abby is wise beyond her years and always has been. Look at the way she understands Eliza. No one has put into words what is wrong with the poor girl and yet I think that Abby understands and not only that, she has never questioned it.'

'Well, I hope she doesn't remember – I don't ever want her to remember that place.'

'Neither do I Moira, but if she does, she might remember her surname. And without that, we haven't a hope of finding her mother.'

'Jesus,' said Moira, 'will you listen to that rain? The girls will be soaked to the skin and heaven only knows what condition the cakes will be in.'

'Ah sure they're young,' said Mary Kate, smiling, 'and the young don't worry about a spot of rain.'

'It's more than a spot of rain,' said Moira. 'It's a spot of *Irish* rain.'

'And there's nothing like it,' said Mary Kate.

'When I was teaching and it was a wet day, we'd let the children sit in the library and read books.'

'You mollycoddled them, Moira.'

'I'd say the rest of them did, but not me. I wish now that I had. I wish I'd been a bit softer; they might have taken to me, they might even have liked me. I overheard one of the girls calling me the dragon – I was angry when I should have been ashamed.'

'Maybe that's because you were never mollycoddled yourself, my friend.'

'Is that an excuse though?'

'Maybe not, but it's a reason.'

'I think that any kindness I had died with my little sister.'

'So, perhaps you've been protecting yourself ever since. I was raging when Sean died, I was giving our dear Lord all kinds of grief for taking him from me – there are still days when I give out to the poor man.'

'But wasn't it worth it, to have found him and loved him?' said Moira. 'Isn't grief just love, with nowhere to go?'

Mary Kate looked at her friend and started to laugh till the tears were rolling down her cheeks.

Moira began laughing with her, even though she hadn't a clue what she was laughing about. 'What's brought this on?' she said.

Mary Kate dried her eyes. 'Aren't we the deep ones? Chatting away like a pair of old philosophers.'

They were still laughing when there was a knock on the door and Emma came into the room. 'What are you laughing about?' she said, grinning at them.

'Grief,' said Mary Kate, 'we were laughing about grief. Come on in and get a warm.'

'Thanks,' said Emma.

'Is everything OK?' said Mary Kate.

'Everything is lovely and thank you so much for taking us in. It's just that I don't know what to do about Nell.'

'Is Nell not happy here?'

'I think she could be; I know that I am, but she wants to go home, it's all she talks about. I find myself promising her that once she's had the baby, we will go back and she will see her daddy again and her home. I'm lying to her but I don't know what else to do.'

'My grandfather had a saying,' said Mary Kate, 'when truth and kindness collide, always choose kindness.'

Emma smiled, 'That's lovely.'

'You can tackle the truth when Nell is stronger,' said Moira.

'Nell and Daddy were always so close; she was a daddy's girl alright.'

'Weren't you jealous?' asked Mary Kate.

Emma smiled. 'Oh no, we all adored her and looked out for her, especially after Mammy died.'

'You haven't had it easy, Emma,' said Mary Kate gently.

'I've never thought about it like that. We didn't have much but were happy, at least Nell and Daddy were.'

'And you?' said Moira.

'I was lonely. You see, Daddy had the pub and the whisky and Nell had the hillside and the flowers and the animals.'

'And what did you have, Emma?' said Mary Kate, gently.

'Eggs, and I can tell you now, when it comes to deep conversations, they weren't that great.'

'Oh, Emma,' said Mary Kate, grinning.

'It's true, I had eggs, and I don't miss them one little bit.'

'So, you think that you could settle here?' said Moira.

'I know I could, there's so much more to do. I would love to go to the theatre.'

'Do you like music?' said Moira.

'The only music I listened to growing up was when a few fellows gathered down at the pub and had a bit of a session. Daddy used to take me with him sometimes as a treat. I loved those evenings, listening to the fiddles and bodhráns and the sad songs. Daddy said when the Yanks came over, looking for the graves of their dead ancestors, they'd be sitting in the pub roaring their eyes out. It made him proud to be Irish, he said. I loved those dark nights, helping Daddy back up the hill, the pair of us singing the rebel songs at the tops of our voices. Sometimes Daddy would fall over and we'd lay down on the damp grass looking up at the stars.' Emma's eyes filled with tears. 'I miss my daddy.'

'Of course you do,' said Mary Kate. 'And you've been very brave.'

'I'll tell you what,' said Moira, 'there's an Irish club in the town and I've heard the craic is great. We could go there some-time, would you like that?'

'Oh, I'd love it,' said Emma.

'We could all go,' said Mary Kate. 'We could even ask the lady banana to come along, I'd like to get to know the woman.'

'I don't think that any of us really know her,' said Moira. 'Perhaps a few jigs around the room would loosen her up a bit.'

Just then the front door slammed and a bedraggled Eliza and Abby came into the room. Followed by Guinness, who shook water all over the place, before happily flopping himself down in front of the fire.

'What about the cakes?' said Moira.

'We had to eat them in the shop. Mrs Leamy said that they wouldn't survive the journey home. They were grand though.'

'I'm frozen,' said Abby.

'So am I,' said Eliza.

'Well, run upstairs and put on some dry clothes then come down and get a warm,' said Moira.

'It looks like Nell had more sense than to come in here and drench the place,' said Emma.

Mary Kate walked across to the window and looked out over Merrion Square. The lights from the houses shone onto the wet pavement, making it look like a multicoloured river floating past, there was something quite magical about it. She closed the heavy curtains and looked back into the room. 'I love evenings like these,' she said.

Emma sighed. 'It's been so nice sitting here chatting with you both, it feels like...'

'Like what, my love?' said Mary Kate.

'Like a home, it feels like a home.'

Mary Kate smiled at her. 'Oh, Emma, it's your home for as long as you need it.'

'You'll have me crying again, you are so kind.'

Just then, Eliza and Abby bounced back into the room and sat on the floor beside Guinness.

'Isn't Nell joining us?' said Emma, smiling.

'What do you mean?' said Eliza.

'Wasn't she upstairs with you?'

Abby shook her head.

'But she went to the bakery with you?'

'She said she didn't want any cake,' said Abby. 'She said that she wanted to go home.'

Emma felt sick to her stomach. 'Well, she's not here.'

Mary Kate could see the panic in Emma's eyes. 'What else did she say, Abby?'

'She just said that she didn't want cake and she wanted to go home.'

'And is that all she said?'

'I think so.'

'She said that she was going to go home on the bus,' said Eliza. 'Did we do wrong?'

Emma felt sick but she didn't want the girls to feel bad. 'No,' said Emma. 'Of course not.'

'Would you ring for a taxi, Moira?' said Mary Kate. 'Myself and Emma have to go to the bus station.'

'I'll ring now,' said Moira, getting up.

'She's got no money for the bus,' said Emma.

'Well, that's one good thing,' said Mary Kate. 'Because they won't let her on, will they?'

'But what if she's not there?'

'We'll cross that bridge when we get to it. Now grab a coat, Emma, and don't worry, we'll find her.'

CHAPTER 19

Mary Kate

The taxi seemed to take forever, and the driver never stopped talking. They heard about his dead mother, his aunts, his cousins, their cousins, and his poor wife – he didn't say why she was poor, and they didn't ask for fear he'd feel the need to tell them. And if that wasn't bad enough, they got a blow-by-blow account of his dodgy bowels, complete with vivid descriptions. If Mary Kate had been in possession of an iron bar, she'd have whacked him over the head with it.

His last words as he pulled up outside the bus station were, did they want him to wait...? Mary Kate and Emma both said a very definite 'No' at the same time. This didn't put him off though. 'Me name is Paddy Hoolahan,' he shouted after them. 'You can ask for me the next time you want a spin.' If they hadn't been so worried about Nell, they would have been laughing.

The bus station was crowded. Emma started barging through people and jumping over cases with Mary Kate behind her, apologising as she ran.

'I can't see her,' said Emma. 'Can you see her, Mary Kate?'

'Don't worry, she'll be here. We'll find her.'

'I see her,' screamed Emma, suddenly. 'Over there.'

Mary Kate looked across to where she was pointing, and there was Nell, with a face like thunder, sitting on a bench, and sitting beside her was the banana.

Emma ran across and tried to put her arms around her sister but she was having none of it.

'Nell, darling, I've been so worried about you.'

Nell turned away. 'Well, you didn't have to, I can take care of myself. It's all her fault,' she said, glaring at Alana. 'She told the driver man not to let me on the bus.'

Mary Kate smiled at Alana and mouthed, 'Thank you.'

Emma knelt in front of Nell and held her hands. 'I know how much you want to go home and if it was possible, I would take you. You know I would, don't you?'

Nell nodded. 'But why isn't it possible, Emma?'

Mary Kate looked across at Alana. 'Shall we go and find a cup of tea?'

Alana nodded and stood up. 'That would be grand,' she said.

Emma watched them walk away and then sat on the bench beside Nell.

'Sometimes, my darling girl, the path we were travelling gets all tangled up and we have to find another one. The new path will be different and we may not like it but we have to give it a chance.'

Nell frowned. 'I don't understand.'

Emma sighed. She was making a pig's ear of this, talking about old paths and new paths – no wonder Nell didn't have a clue what she was talking about.

'Did our house get all tangled up, Emma?'

'I'm afraid it did, pet.'

'And did Daddy get all tangled up?'

Emma nodded, 'I'm so sorry, my darling.'

'Why didn't you just tell me that Daddy was dead?'

'I didn't think that you were strong enough to hear it and I'm sorry.'

'I'm not a child, Emma, even though people treat me as if I am. I do understand things, I just don't have a need to shout about it. Sometimes I trust people when I shouldn't, like Tommy. I think that is why I prefer the company of the birds and the little creatures because they don't pretend to be something they're not.'

Tears were running down both their faces as she held her beloved sister in her arms. 'Don't ever change, my Nell, not for anyone.'

'I loved my daddy.'

'You can still love him, Nell, and remember all the lovely things he did for us.'

'When he wasn't roaring drunk.'

Emma smiled. 'Yes, when he wasn't roaring drunk.'

'Do you think there'll be in a pub in heaven?'

'Bound to be.'

'I hope so, because that's where Daddy was happy. Just like I was happy on my hillside. Emma?'

'Yes, my love?'

'Is my hillside all tangled up too?'

Emma smiled. 'No, my darling, your hillside is exactly as you left it.'

'Then I must go back, I must say goodbye.'

'That's what we'll do then, we'll go back and we'll say goodbye together.'

Meanwhile, Alana and Mary Kate had found a small café on the other side of the station and were happily drinking tea and munching away on apple cake. They were seated by the window, watching the world and his wife passing by.

'No wonder you like coming here,' said Mary Kate. As soon

as she said it, she put her hands over her mouth. 'Oh, I'm sorry, I shouldn't have said that.'

'Don't worry about it,' said Alana. 'I knew that the girls had been following me and thought they might have mentioned it to you. Please don't be sorry, you've nothing to be sorry about.'

Mary Kate smiled. 'Well, that's awful good of you, Alana.'

Alana stared at her. 'I get the feeling that you have doubts about Alana being my name. Am I right?'

'Well, I'd say you're right there, we did have a few doubts and that was mostly because you never answered to it. You've had poor Mrs Lamb climbing three flights of stairs to tell you that your dinner's ready.'

'Oh dear,' said Alana. 'I must apologise to her.'

'I don't think she's lost any sleep over it.'

Alana grinned. 'I wouldn't make a very good spy, would I?'

'It seems that neither would I, letting the cat out of the bag like that.'

'My name is Bridie, Bridie Toomey.'

'I'm sure you have your reasons for wanting to change it and that's your business and no one else's. If you'd prefer that we called you Alana, that's fine with us. It is after all a lovely name. Not that Bridie's not,' said Mary Kate quickly.

Bridie smiled at her. 'Sure, half of Ireland is called Bridie but I'm used to it, I never really felt like an Alana. I'm sorry I lied to you, Mrs Barry.'

'Mary Kate,' she said. 'Please call me Mary Kate.'

'Thank you.'

'But as far as Eliza is concerned, I think that you will always be known as Banana, whether you want to be or not.'

Bridie laughed. 'I can live with that, for there's no harm in the girl.'

'Can I ask why you chose the name Alana? Was it someone you knew, or did you just fancy a change?'

'I stole it.'

'How can you steal a name? You can call yourself anything, can't you? It's not a crime.'

'Well, I stole a name and a yellow coat and a wad of money.'

Mary Kate didn't know how to respond – was Bridie telling her that she was a thief?

'I've shocked you, haven't I?'

'I suppose you have a bit,' said Mary Kate, doing up the zip on her handbag. Not that she thought Bridie was about to dive into it and steal her money, but it gave her something to do while she took in Bridie's rather startling announcement.

'Do you want me to tell you how it happened?'

'I think you'd better.'

'It's not as bad as it sounds,' she said, launching into the story of the woman who boarded a bus and left her yellow coat on the bench where Bridie was sitting. 'I happened to be freezing cold,' she said, 'so I saw no harm in taking it. Not only was I cold but I was also penniless. It was when I put my hands into the pocket that I found the money. I took it as a sign from God, even though I knew that I wasn't exactly His favourite person at the time. But there, we are told that he is a forgiving feller and I'm hoping he won't hold it against me when it comes to Judgement Day.'

Mary Kate started to laugh, even though she knew it wasn't funny, but it was the way Bridie was telling it, as if finding a grand yellow coat and a pocketful of money was an everyday occurrence. This was the longest conversation she'd had with her and she found herself warming to the woman. She was funny in a very dry way; she liked her, she did – she liked her.

They sat in a comfortable silence, each with their own thoughts. Mary Kate felt that Bridie had more that she needed to share but it had to be in her own time.

Bridie was staring out of the window. 'I suppose you must be wondering why I'm here.'

'Well, I'm thinking that either you have a liking for bus stations, or you're waiting for someone.'

She smiled at her. 'To tell you the truth, I wouldn't care if I never saw another bus station as long as I live.'

Mary Kate nodded. 'So, you are waiting for someone?'

'I don't want to bore you with my problems, Mary Kate.'

'I'm not easily bored, and I find that it helps to get things off your chest. Whatever your story is, it's safe with me and I won't be broadcasting it all over Dublin.'

Mary Kate could see that Bridie was struggling and unsure of letting go of a problem that she must have been carrying on her own for so long.

Mary Kate touched Bridie's arm. 'I might even be able to help. Unless of course you've murdered someone, and then it might be a bit tricky.'

Bridie laughed and it eased the tension between them.

'I was a nun,' she said.

'A nun?' said Mary Kate. 'Well, that was the last thing I thought you'd say.'

'Well, it's the truth and I'm not even sure that I had a vocation, but I persuaded myself that I did. To be honest, I think that I was hiding away from the world. Nothing was expected of me at the convent and it gave me something that I had been yearning for.'

'And what was that?' said Mary Kate.

'Acceptance. I felt accepted and that was all I thought I needed. I was happy there, at least I told myself that I was.'

'So, why did you leave?' said Mary Kate.

'I fell in love.'

'With who?'

'With a priest, and he fell in love with me. It was the most wonderful and unexpected thing that had ever happened. We struggled with it for over five years until it nearly broke us and we knew that we had to be together. The plan was for Stephen to leave first and for me to leave a month later. We were to meet here at the bus station and begin our new life together but you see, he didn't turn up.'

'So, you come here every day?'

'It's where I feel closest to him and where I hope that he will look for me.'

Mary Kate could feel her eyes filling with tears as she listened to Bridie's story. 'I don't know what to say, Bridie, except that I am so very sorry. You must be heartbroken.'

'There are days when I sit here and feel like the biggest fool that ever lived and yet there are days when I know Stephen would never have done this to me and so I wait.'

'Did you return to the convent to make sure that he hadn't gone back?'

'I couldn't, I just couldn't – I was too ashamed.'

Mary Kate reached across and held her hand. 'If you ever need any company, I'd be glad to sit beside you until he turns up, then I'd make myself scarce.'

'Do you know what?'

'What?'

'I feel better. Sharing this with you has made me feel less alone. Thank you.'

'I feel better too,' said Mary Kate. 'Knowing that I won't be harbouring a murderer.'

'Just a thief,' said Bridie.

They were both laughing as they linked arms and walked over to the girls.

When they arrived back at the boarding house, Mrs Lamb brought up bowls of soup for them all. 'This will stick to your ribs and warm you up,' she said, smiling. 'I'm happy to see you back home, Nell.'

Nell smiled at her. 'Oh, but this is not my home.'

'Of course it's not, pet, but isn't it a grand place to lay your head for a while?'

'It is, Mrs Lamb, and I'm grateful.'

'You're a lucky girl. It might not feel that way right now, but you couldn't have landed up in a better place. I'd say that God in His wisdom guided you here as he has guided many a lost soul, myself included, for He knew that you would find kindness behind the red door.'

Nell smiled. 'Maybe it wasn't God who guided us here, Mrs Lamb, maybe it was my daddy.'

'Ah now, I hadn't thought of that, but I'd say that you are probably right. Now, I'll leave you to tuck into the good soup, it will put hairs on your chest.'

'I hope not,' said Emma, grinning.

'So do I,' said Nell.

After Mrs Lamb had left, they did indeed tuck into the soup and it was lovely, even Nell was enjoying it.

The evenings were drawing in and although it was only five o'clock, it was already dark outside, the rain was still battering the windows and it was blowing up a storm. Moira got up and pulled the curtains. She looked around her.

'I love this room,' she said.

'It has seen some things, hasn't it?' said Mary Kate.

Moira smiled at her. 'If these walls could talk?'

'We'd be here all night if they did.'

Emma smiled at her sister. 'It's nice to see you eating, darling.'

'And I think you have a bit more colour in your face,' said Mary Kate. 'You were terrible pale when we picked you up from that awful place.'

'I missed Emma, I thought she'd forgotten me. I thought everyone had forgotten me.'

'I've felt exactly the same in my time,' said Mary Kate, 'so I understand how you must have felt but there you are, you were wrong and so was I. You must be patient, Nell, for good things are waiting beyond the next bend. You may not see them, but they are there.'

Nell's eyes filled with tears. 'They wanted to take my baby. They said they had a lovely couple in mind who hadn't been blessed with a family of their own and would be delighted to adopt mine.'

'Dear God,' said Moira, raising her eyes to the ceiling. 'The cheek of them.'

'I told them that I wanted to go home and that I wanted to keep my baby, but they said that I had sinned against God and that I was a wicked, selfish girl to even think of keeping it.'

'It's themselves that are the wicked ones,' said Moira. 'It makes my blood boil.'

Nell smiled. 'You saved me,' she said.

Emma put her arms around her. 'I would have crossed oceans to save you, my darling girl, and it breaks my heart to know what you have gone through.'

'They weren't all wicked,' said Nell. 'There were some who cared for us and felt sorry for us, there were some who were kind.'

'I think that the kindest people are those who had known suffering themselves,' said Mary Kate.

'Like yourself,' said Moira.

'For heaven's sake, I'm no saint.'

'Well, you're the closest thing to a saint that I have come across,' said Moira.

'Enough now,' said Mary Kate, grinning, 'you'll have me canonised.'

Nell looked across the room at Bridie. 'I'm sorry that I was rude to you,' she said, 'but I wanted to go home.'

Bridie smiled at her. 'Well, if you *had* managed to get on that bus, I would have had to get on with you and as I had no idea where you were planning to go, I wasn't feeling over the moon about it.'

'You would have loved it,' said Nell. 'I could have shown you our chickens and my hillside.'

'Maybe one day you will, and I shall look forward to it.'

'Perhaps we can all go,' said Moira.

Nell looked sad. 'My home and my daddy got tangled up, so there won't be much to see, but my hillside is still there and my creatures and the river.'

'I'm sorry about your home and your daddy,' said Bridie. 'You must be feeling very sad.'

'I am, but I still have Emma and I still have the hillside. We are going back, just to say goodbye.'

'You are a brave girl, Nell,' said Mary Kate.

'I am, aren't I?' she said, which had them all smiling.

Just then, the door opened and Eliza and Abby came in, followed by Guinness, who padded across the room and flopped down in his favourite place in front of the fire.

'You missed some grand apple cake,' said Eliza, looking at Nell.

'I'm sorry that I went off and left you.'

'Ah sure, don't be worrying yer head about that girl,' said Eliza. 'It's not a hanging offence. Is it, Abby? It's not a hanging offence.'

Abby's face looked blank as she responded to Eliza. 'No, Eliza, it's not a hanging offence.'

Abby's response worried Mary Kate – something was very wrong. 'Something's come up,' she said. 'Do you mind if I just have a quick word with Moira?'

'Of course not,' said Bridie. 'Come on, ladies, let's give Mary Kate a bit of privacy.'

'Now what's on your mind?' said Moira, once they had left the room.

'It was the look on Abby's face when she answered Eliza.'

'I saw it too.'

'She's always been so good with her but now I'm not sure.'

'When this was a school, Abby had lots of friends, two, in particular, Marta and Susan. She was very happy there but since it closed, I think she's lonely and maybe losing patience with Eliza.'

'So, what can we do?'

'We need to find a good school. It's not enough for me to teach her here at home, she needs to be with children of her own age.'

Just then Eliza put her head round the door. 'Do you want Guinness to leave as well?'

'He's OK where he is,' said Mary Kate, smiling. 'But it was very thoughtful of you to ask.'

'I'll leave you to it then.'

'Eliza will miss Abby once she goes to school,' said Moira.

'Then we'll have to put our thinking caps on, won't we?'

'And if anyone can do it, we can,' said Moira, grinning.

'Indeed,' said Mary Kate. 'Indeed.'

CHAPTER 20

Moira

Moira, Bridie and Mary Kate had been gardening all morning and they were exhausted and cold.

'I'm too old for this,' said Moira, rubbing her back. 'We need a man!'

'Speak for yourself,' said Mary Kate, laughing.

'I meant a gardener,' said Moira, grinning.

It had started to rain, that fine rain that soaks you to the skin in minutes.

'Enough,' said Mary Kate, standing up.

They hurried indoors. Bridie went downstairs and asked Mrs Lamb to send up some tea. Moira threw some coal on the fire and they made themselves comfortable on the sofa.

'We really do need a gardener,' said Moira. 'We should put an advertisement in the paper.'

'I used to love gardening at the cottage,' said Mary Kate, sadly. 'But I haven't the heart for it now.'

Moira smiled at her. 'I've been thinking about the cottage. It's been a year since you left it and the garden must be a jungle by now but if you're not ready to talk about it, we don't have to.'

Just then Bridie came into the room. She warmed her hands by the fire, then sat down next to Moira.

'We were just talking about my cottage in Glendalough,' said Mary Kate.

'My favourite place,' said Bridie. 'It's where Stephen and I were planning to live. I didn't know you had a cottage there, it must have been lovely.'

'It was,' said Mary Kate, 'but after Sean died, it became the saddest place in the world.'

'I'm so sorry,' said Bridie. 'Life can be shite sometimes.'

'Such language coming from a nun,' said Mary Kate, grinning.

'I don't think I was a very good nun,' said Bridie. 'You wouldn't believe the things I said under my breath, the air would have been blue if I'd let it all out. I must have broken every rule in the book while I was in there.'

'Some things just aren't meant to be,' said Moira. 'I was a pretty awful teacher. I mean, I was OK at the teaching bit, but I just didn't connect with the children. I knew when I left that I wasn't going to be remembered fondly and it has been one of my deepest regrets. I wouldn't have been surprised if there were flags hanging out the windows by the time I got to the end of the drive.'

'Oh, Moira,' said Mary Kate, 'you might not have been the perfect earth mother, but you educated them and I'm sure that one day they will remember that and be grateful.'

'Do you go back and visit your cottage?' Bridie asked.

'Too many memories,' said Mary Kate. 'In fact, it's the happy times that hurt the most.'

'I'm sorry,' said Bridie. 'Have you ever thought of selling it?'

Moira glared at Bridie.

'Oh, Mary Kate, I shouldn't have said that.'

'No, it's alright, because it needs to be spoken about and I've been putting it off. But I couldn't sell it, I couldn't bear to think of strangers living there.'

'Of course you couldn't,' said Moira. 'But I've had an idea, Mary Kate.'

'What's that?'

'Well, what if it was a place where people went for their holidays?'

'You mean rent it out? I'm not ready for that.'

'Not renting it out. I know you wouldn't want that. I was thinking of a holiday cottage for your friends – Colleen and little Rosa, Mrs Lamb and Eliza. I bet Mrs Finn has never had a holiday in her life. James and his wife Erin and what about...'

Moira stopped speaking as Mary Kate put her head down and started sobbing. She kneeled down in front of her. 'Oh, my dear girl, I'm an idiot, a thoughtless, stupid idiot. I'm so sorry, Mary Kate, I'm so very sorry.'

Mary Kate looked up and smiled at her. 'No, Moira, I'm not crying because I'm sad. I'm crying because that is the most wonderful idea. Why hadn't I thought of it myself?'

Moira looked relieved. 'Thank heavens for that – I thought I'd really put my foot in it and I wouldn't have hurt you for the world.'

'It's an amazing idea,' said Bridie. 'If you'll excuse me, I'll be off this minute to pack my case.'

'I think I'll join you,' said Moira, grinning.

Just then Mrs Lamb came in with the tea.

'What would you think about taking a little holiday, Mrs Lamb?' said Mary Kate.

Mrs Lamb looked at Mary Kate as if she had two heads. 'Heavens no, I can't think of anything worse. Beggin' your pardon, Mrs Barry, but I'd rather be boiled in a barrel of pig fat than go on holiday. And who may I ask was going to feed you all while I was off on my little holiday?'

Mary Kate was laughing so much she could hardly get her breath.

'I'm sure we could rustle up a couple of eggs between us,' said Moira.

'No, that wouldn't do at all and what about my kitchen? What sort of state would that be in by the time I got back?' She put down the tray of tea and left the room mumbling, 'Holiday indeed!'

The three women looked at each other and started giggling. 'We'll take that as a "no" then,' said Moira.

CHAPTER 21

Moira

Abby came into the lounge. She had on her good winter coat and woolly hat, but she hadn't a clue where she was going.

'Is it somewhere special, Mammy?' she said to Moira. 'Will I like it? And can Eliza come too?'

'Yes, I'm sure you will like it but today is about you, I'm sure Eliza won't mind just this once.'

'I think she will, Mammy, she doesn't like being left behind.'

Moira smiled across at Mary Kate, who nodded. 'Well, I suppose it will be alright,' she said. 'But tell her to wrap up warm, it's cold outside.'

'Thanks, Mammy, I'll tell her,' said Abby, running out of the room.

'I think it's a good idea for Eliza to know that Abby is going to school,' said Moira. 'I should have thought of it myself.'

'She'll miss her alright, they go everywhere together.'

'And that's why I think it's important for Abby to have her own friends,' said Moira. 'It's not good for her to spend all her time with Eliza. She's the sweetest, kindest soul but she's a woman, not a child, and there are times when I think that Abby forgets that.'

Between them, Moira and Mary Kate had found the perfect school for Abby and hoped that she would love it as much as they did. It was called St Thomas à Becket but lovingly known as St Toms. They fell in love with it from the moment they started walking up the long drive towards the blue door. Either side of the path were what seemed to be small gardens dotted along the verge.

Mary Kate stood still. 'Oh, Moira, it's lovely, isn't it?'

Moira nodded. 'It really is.'

As they got closer to the school they were met by the head-master, who had two small children hanging off him like a couple of excited puppies. 'Off with you now,' he said. 'Go and have a bit of a run around.'

He grinned at them. 'See what a difficult life I have?'

'It sits well on you,' said Mary Kate.

'My name is Cashman,' he said, shaking their hands. 'Let me show you around and then we'll have a chat in my office.'

The school was surrounded by trees, winter bare against the pale grey sky. As they got closer, they could see markings on the rough bark.

'It's become a kind of tradition at St Toms,' he said. 'When a child leaves the school, the last thing they do is carve their initials into their favourite tree.'

'What a lovely thing to do,' said Moira.

He smiled. 'It is, isn't it? I like to think that they have left a small part of themselves here for as long as the tree stands.'

'We saw some gardens on the way up the drive,' said Mary Kate.

Mr Cashman smiled. 'They belong to the children. We offer each child a small plot of land to make a garden. They take great pride in the flowers they grow, while others delight in planting vegetables and the smaller ones just enjoy making mud pies. But I've kept you outside too long. Hot chocolate in my office, ladies?'

'Perfect,' said Moira.

They had been as impressed with the inside of the school as the grounds. The corridor leading to Mr Cashman's office was lined with the children's artwork and not just the best ones. Bits of paper daubed with splashes of paint were also displayed in all their splashy glory.

'When I was at school, the only paintings that went up on the wall were Theresa Duggan's,' said Mary Kate. 'We were only sick of looking at them.'

That was a week ago and unbeknown to Abby, this was to be her first day at St Toms.

The school was on the other side of the park and not too far to walk.

'Is it a surprise for the two of us?' said Eliza.

Moira didn't know what to say. Maybe it hadn't been such a good idea to let Eliza tag along. It felt as if she had two children in front of her and only gave the sweets to one of them. She looked across at Mary Kate and frowned.

'Moira, why don't you walk ahead with Abby and Eliza and myself will catch you up,' said Mary Kate.

Eliza wasn't happy. 'Why can't I go with Abby?'

Mary Kate walked across to a bench and sat down. 'Sit beside me, Eliza,' she said.

Mary Kate held her hand. 'Eliza,' she said gently, 'you do know that you're older than Abby, don't you?'

Eliza frowned but didn't speak.

'You're bigger than Abby, aren't you?'

'Oh yes, I'm bigger.'

'Well,' said Mary Kate, 'the place we're going today is for smaller girls.'

'OK,' said Eliza.

'Are you alright with that, Eliza? Do you understand?'

'Mammy said that there were going to be lots of things in my life that I won't understand but as long as I'm kind and honest, it doesn't matter.'

'You have a very wise mammy, darling.'

'And she's a good cook.'

'Then we are both blessed. Now let's join Abby and her mammy.'

As the four of them got closer to the school, Abby screamed and started running, with Eliza close behind. She couldn't believe it as she stared at her two best friends, Marta and Susan, standing at the door, grinning. The three of them hugged and danced around.

'What are you doing here?' she said.

'This is where we go to school, Abby,' said Marta. 'And it's where you're going to school too.'

'Really? We're going to be together again?'

'We are,' said Marta. 'Isn't it just the best thing?'

Eliza was standing quietly, staring at the girls. Abby looked so happy and she should have been happy for her but it made her feel sad inside.

Abby beckoned her over: 'Come and meet my friends.'

Eliza walked across to them.

'This is Marta and Susan,' said Abby.

'Are you Abby's mammy?' said Marta, smiling.

Eliza looked at Abby and her eyes filled with tears. 'We're friends, aren't we?' she said softly. 'I'm not your mammy, am I?' She glared at the two girls. 'I'm the same as you,' she shouted. 'I'm just a bit bigger. Mammies are old ones, I'm not a mammy.'

'Oh, Eliza,' said Abby, holding her hand, 'please don't cry. Of course you're not my mammy. We're friends, best friends.'

Eliza stared at the two girls and started to walk away. 'See, I'm not her mammy,' she shouted. 'I'm not Abby's mammy. I'm not, I'm not. I'm her best friend. You're silly, you are. I'm going to tell my mammy on you.'

'Where are you going, Eliza?' said Abby.

'I'm going home.'

Marta and Susan looked confused.

'Oh, Abby,' said Marta. 'What did I say to make her so upset?'

Abby watched Eliza walking away and her heart broke. She looked back at her friends. 'It's difficult to explain,' she said softly. 'You have nothing to feel bad about for you have done nothing wrong.' Abby hugged them again. 'I'd better go now but I'll see you soon.'

'Aren't you coming in?' said Susan.

'Not today,' said Abby sadly. 'Not today.'

No one spoke as they walked back down the drive and across the park. They hurried across the square and into the house, where they started calling Eliza's name.

Mrs Lamb came up from the kitchen. 'She's with me,' she said sadly.

They followed her downstairs. Eliza had her head on the table and she was sobbing.

Abby knelt beside her. I know you're feeling sad,' she said gently. 'Marta and Susan didn't mean to hurt you, really they didn't. They're lovely girls.'

Eliza lifted her head and looked at Abby. 'They said I looked like an old one, they said I looked like a mammy.'

'They were just confused,' said Abby. 'Because you seem so grown up for your age and they still have a lot of growing to do.'

Eliza frowned and stared at her and it was as if something in her had changed: 'I look older than you, don't I?'

Mrs Lamb put her hands over her face and busied herself with the kettle.

Abby wiped away the tears. 'What we look like doesn't matter, Eliza. We could be tall or small, or fat or thin but that's just on the outside and the outside isn't the important bit.' She placed her hand on Eliza's heart. 'It's what's in here that counts.

It's who you are on the inside and in there, you are the funniest, kindest person I have ever known.'

Moira and Mary Kate were looking at Abby with such pride. Where on earth did the child learn to be so wise? It certainly wasn't from her awful beginnings.

'Tea?' said Mrs Lamb.

'Tea would be grand,' said Moira.

'I have a very important job for you, Eliza,' said Mary Kate, 'if you'd like it. I was going to ask you at the school, but you'd gone home.'

'I was sad,' said Eliza.

'I know you were, love.'

'What job did you have in mind for her?' said Mrs Lamb, putting cups and saucers on the table.

'I need someone to walk Abby to school every morning and pick her up in the afternoon. It's a proper job, Eliza, and you'll get your own wages at the end of every week.'

Eliza smiled. 'I can do that, can't I, Mammy? I can take Abby to school?'

'I think it would be the perfect job,' said Mrs Lamb.

'You can take Guinness along with you, he'll enjoy the walk.'

'We can chat all the way there,' said Abby. 'And when you pick me up, I can tell you all about my day, we'll have a grand time.'

'And it doesn't matter what I look like on the outside?'

'It never did, my sweet girl,' said Mrs Lamb. 'It never did.'

CHAPTER 22

Cathy

Cathy Doyle learned early on not to get too attached to people. As a foster child she was always getting moved on and she never knew why, maybe she was just unlovable. Once she decided that this must be the reason, she stopped trying to fit in – after all, a bloody sponge fitted in, it was no big deal.

She would be driven to some family, clutching a small bag that held her new knickers and vests. These were provided by the Church with every move. As they travelled along, Mrs Parks would tell her what a lucky girl she was to be going to the Buckleys', or the Quinns' or the Connells'.

'Now, Cathy,' she would say, 'you must try harder to fit in this time. You're such a serious little thing and it would do no harm to put a smile on your face now and again. I thought your last placement with Mrs Tierney would work out for you but she said that she couldn't bear one more morning sitting across from you at the table with a face that would sour milk and Mr Tierney said that they had taken you in out of the kindness of their hearts and they hadn't even got so much as a thank you for their trouble.'

Cathy didn't give a fish's tit what they thought of her because she didn't think much of them either. Mrs Tierney coloured her eyebrows so dark, they looked like a couple of worms crawling across the top of her eyes and Mr Tierney smarmed his hair with margarine that dripped down his face in the hot weather. They also had a horrible son called Albert, who stuck his tongue out at her when he thought no one was looking. They called him their little sweet pea – well, there was nothing sweet about him, or little for that matter. In fact, he looked more like a sausage than a pea. So, all in all, the Tierneys could jump into the nearest lake and take their sweet little pea with them for all she cared.

In the end, it was decided that foster homes were never going to work for Cathy and she was sent back to the orphanage in the west of Cork, which suited her fine. She was happy there, it was the only home she had ever known. Sister Breda, who worked in the kitchen, taught her to cook: 'You have a light touch when it comes to pastry, Cathy, and cool hands. Unlike Sister Ruth, God bless her, whose hands are like a couple of spades and desperate clammy.'

The two of them also shared a passion for books. Cathy loved the winter evenings when they'd sit side by side in front of the big ovens and read to each other. She was the closest thing to a mother she had ever had and she loved her. With every move, it became harder and harder to say goodbye.

She arrived back at the convent and there was Sister Breda and her best friend Nan, standing at the door, smiling. Sister Breda took her little bag full of new knickers and vests and welcomed her inside.

Nan had a gammy leg, which stopped her from being fostered, because the good women of the parish couldn't manage to extend their goodness to a child with a gammy leg.

There were times when, God forgive her, Cathy prayed to have a gammy leg like Nan's so she didn't have to keep getting dragged over the length and breadth of Ireland to strangers who didn't want her.

When Cathy was sixteen years old, Sister Breda took it upon herself to go into the city and get her a job in a library, complete with a little flat over the top.

At last she was free, to just be herself and to hell with fitting in. She said goodbye to Nan, promising to visit, and to dear Sister Breda, who hugged her and gave her the little bag of knickers and vests when what she really wanted was a couple of bras but apparently the Church didn't run to bras. Nan said she thought that was because the nuns didn't like to think that we had breasts.

Cathy loved working in the library. Each book held the promise of villains and heroes and faraway places. When the sun shone through the long windows, the dust mites would float around the room like bits of snow.

She had found her place, she was exactly where she was meant to be and it felt as if she had come home. She threw the bag of knickers and vests into the charity box and started to save up for a bra.

The other girls envied her the little flat upstairs, where they would gather in the evenings for tea and cake. Mostly they chatted about boys, at least the others did. She made friends with Fiona and Carol, who were sisters and longed to have a place of their own just like hers. And sweet Mrs Sweet, who ran the cookery section and mothered her like a baby. She brought in pans of homemade stew and plates of scones, which she shared with her friends.

The antiquarian section was her favourite. It smelled of must and dust and times gone by and voices now stilled but forever ingrained in the very walls of the place; it was like standing in a church. It had a long table that ran down the length of the room, laden with maps and old parchments, yellowed with age and brittle to the touch. It was run by a lovely shy boy called Peter, who introduced her to new authors, opening a world of myths and legends and kings of Ireland and battles lost and won. She skipped the gruesome bits about torture and being hung, drawn and quartered, which sounded desperate painful and not to be dwelled on.

Every Saturday after work the three of them hitchhiked to the Showboat, a dancehall in a town called Youghal beside the Blackwater River. They danced the night away to the fabulous showbands until their feet were hanging off them. They were often walked home by fellers who wanted more than a kiss on the cheek for their trouble.

Cathy had little interest in the country boys, who rolled into the place as drunk as skunks and as ignorant as newly born babies. No, Cathy had no interest in boys until the day she met Greg and that's when everything changed. The dancehall was right on the strand, overlooking the sea. One evening it had been so stuffy in there that she'd made her way down to the beach. He was sitting on a rock, a black outline smoking a cigarette, the white smoke drifting away into the dark night. She'd stood for a while watching him and as if he'd sensed her presence, he turned around: 'It's big enough for two,' he'd said.

She didn't move straight away but stayed where she was.

'I won't bite,' he'd said, laughing, and it was his laughter that had taken her onto the sand and towards the rock.

They sat in silence, looking out over the sea. The only sound was the gentle movement of the waves trickling into the shore and rattling the pebbles.

'My name is Greg,' he said, smiling.

'Cathy,' she said, smiling back at him. 'I didn't see you inside.'

'My dancing days are over,' he'd said. 'I leave all that to the young ones, who have the energy and the inclination.'

Cathy looked at him properly and could see that he was right, for this was not a lad but a man and she should have run a mile, but she didn't, and it had been the undoing of her.

The others knew that she was seeing someone, but she kept this unexpected affair to herself. They had of course tried to get more out of her, until eventually they lost interest. All they knew was that his name was Greg.

On the morning she was going away, there was great excitement. 'Why can't I meet a feller who'd whisk me off to Paris for a couple of weeks?' said Fiona, making a face.

'Because you haven't the charisma that Cathy has,' said her sister, grinning.

When the library closed, Cathy made her way upstairs. Her case was packed and ready, but there was to be no romantic trip to Paris. She was on the night sailing to Fishguard and then by train to London, where she would have an abortion.

From the beginning, Greg had told her that he had a wife and children. 'I'm telling you this,' he'd said, 'because I don't want to lie to you, or lead you on. You're young and you're lovely but I can't offer you any more than this. I will understand if you walk away – in fact, you should walk away. I have fallen in love with you, my darling girl, and I had no right to.'

She hadn't walked away because she had fallen in love with him too and now she was having his baby, a baby that he could never claim as his own. She had assured him that she wanted nothing from him, except the money for the operation and her travelling expenses.

She wouldn't see him again and that was sad. He was married, he had his own family and he hadn't talked her out of having an abortion. In fact, he hadn't suggested meeting again. The words he didn't speak told her that it was over.

Cathy had booked a guest house close to the private hospital where Greg had insisted she went to. She had no ill feelings towards him, it was as much her fault as his. He was a good man, she had loved the time they had spent together and had no regrets. They were never going to walk into the sunset and live happily ever after. She had learned long ago that happy endings were not for her, they were the stuff of fairy tales and she'd never been keen on fairy tales. She would miss him, but she was used to moving on. As a child she had learned to protect her heart and she could do it again.

The owners of the guest house were an elderly couple called Mr and Mrs Roberts and they were lovely. Her bedroom was small but pretty and it was obvious that Mrs Roberts favoured yellow roses. They covered the walls, the curtains and the quilt, it was like sleeping in a garden.

Cathy had been so busy arranging her travel and the hospital and the guest house that she hadn't fully thought about what she was about to do, but in the early hours of the morning, she woke to the awful reality of it all. She was about to end the precious life that was growing inside her. What right did she have to make such a decision? Only God Himself could do that.

She put her hand on her tummy and wept. 'I'm sorry, little one,' she whispered.

The next morning, she walked downstairs just as Mrs Roberts was going into the dining room. 'Now, what can I get you, dear? Are you up for the full breakfast?'

'I'm sorry but I'm afraid that I'm not allowed to eat.'

'May I ask what time your appointment is?' Mrs Roberts said gently.

She knows, thought Cathy, *of course she does. What else would a young Irish girl be doing in London on her own?*

Her eyes filled with tears. 'Three o'clock,' she said.

'Then may I suggest that you wrap up and go for a walk, get a bit of fresh air.'

As she wandered around the unfamiliar streets, she felt that everyone she passed knew what she was about to do and she felt like the worst person in the world. It would soon be Christmas

and the shop windows were full of lights and trees and rein-
deers and the sound of carols that drifted out into the cold air.
She hadn't been looking forward to this season of goodwill to all
men, for she would be on her own in her little flat above the
library. Fiona and Carol had invited her to their house for
dinner, but she said that she would be with Greg that day. She
had told so many lies that she would be spending the rest of her
life in a confessional box.

It had started to snow, flurrying around in the icy breeze
and drifting along the pavements. She was so cold, she could
barely feel her hands; maybe she should go back to the guest
house and rest before she went to the hospital. The shop she
had stopped in front of looked so bright and inviting that she
decided to go in for a while and get warm.

It wasn't until she stepped inside that she realised it was a
toy shop. There was a queue of children waiting to see Santa
Claus. As she looked at them, holding their parents' hands, their
eyes wide with excitement, she had never felt so sad. Her child
would never know that special feeling of waking up on a
Christmas morning, running down the stairs, knowing that
underneath the tree were parcels, just waiting to be opened.
Her child would never know the love of a family, just as she
never had.

She walked round the store and stopped at a counter that
was piled high with teddy bears. She picked up a soft furry one
that had big brown button eyes and a red ribbon around his
neck.

'That's my favourite one,' said the young assistant. 'Those
eyes look real, don't they?'

Cathy nodded and handed over the money. 'Merry Christmas,' said the girl.

'Merry Christmas,' said Cathy.

'I hope your little one loves the bear.'

Cathy smiled and left the shop.

She returned to the guest house, where she said goodbye to Mrs Roberts, who put her arms around her.

'My grandmother had a saying that has stayed with me all my life and helped in many a difficult situation,' she told her. 'She used to say, "if you are not sure about something, don't do it".'

Cathy had tears in her eyes as she picked up her case and walked slowly towards the hospital.

Once it was over, she would head to Dublin, where she had booked two weeks in a boarding house in Merrion Square.

CHAPTER 23

Moira

Moira was on her knees, clearing out the grate. 'We don't only need a gardener, Mary Kate. We need a cleaner, it's too much for Emma on her own. We own the place, we shouldn't be having to clean it. Even Bridie does her share and she's paying to live here. Where is she anyway? I haven't seen her all morning.'

Mary Kate stopped polishing. 'She's upstairs with Eliza and Abby, getting the room ready for our guest.' Then she started to laugh.

'What's funny?' said Moira, smiling.

'You have a blob of soot on your nose.'

Moira grinned. 'Well, that's decided then, we need a cleaner and the sooner the better. What time are we expecting our young guest?'

'What makes you think she's young?' said Mary Kate. 'She didn't mention her age in the letter.'

'I could be wrong, but I can only think of one reason why a woman travels from Ireland to London for an operation, then stays in a boarding house to recuperate for a fortnight. Why doesn't she go home?'

'How do we know she has a home to go to? Our guests seem to have a habit of being homeless.'

Moira grinned. 'They do, don't they? It must be the red door that draws them here. Either that or they've heard what a soft touch you are.'

'Well, if being a soft touch is another word for being kind then I'm happy to be known as a soft touch and if it is, as you say it is, then woman or girl, we will need to be very gentle with her.'

'And we can certainly do that.'

'We can indeed. Anyway, she's coming tomorrow. I told her to get a taxi from the station and we'll pay the driver when they get here.'

Guinness, who had been asleep, started growling.

'What is it, boy?' said Mary Kate. 'Did you have a bad dream?'

The doorbell rang and the growling turned to barking. He ran across the room and started pawing at the door.

'For heaven's sake,' said Moira, holding on to his collar.

As they walked into the hallway, Eliza and Abby came running down the stairs. 'Is it yer woman?' said Eliza. 'The bed's all ready, so you've no need to worry about that.'

Guinness was pulling on his collar and Moira was having a job holding him back.

'What in all that's holy is the matter with him?' she said. 'He'll have the sockets pulled out of my arms at this rate.'

'He's guarding us,' said Eliza.

'From what?'

'It's too early to tell but I'd say that he's definitely guarding us from something.'

The bell rang again and Eliza opened the door, but instead of the girl, they were expecting, it was a man standing on the

doorstep. He was wearing a suit that looked as if it had seen
better days and his hair was in dire need of a good wash but
maybe he was down on his luck and who was she to judge the
poor feller.

Guinness was going mad and managed to pull away from
Moira. He launched himself at the man, who nearly fell backwards down the steps. 'Get that bloody dog away from me,' he
yelled and kicked out at him.

A young man walking across the square could see what was
happening. He ran across and grabbed Guinness before the
man could harm him. 'Leave the dog alone,' he shouted.

'And who the feck are you?' said the man, glaring at him.

'A better man than you are, sir.'

'That animal's dangerous, he needs putting down.'

Moira stared at him. 'There is only one animal here that
needs putting down and it's not the dog.'

'What is it you're wanting?' said Eliza.

'I heard that you were looking for a handyman.'

'Well, I'm sorry for your trouble but the post has already
been filled,' said Eliza. 'Isn't that right, Abby?'

Abby nodded her head. 'And it was only an hour ago, now
isn't that awful bad timing?'

'To hell with the lot of you,' the man growled, turning round
and starting to go down the steps.

Guinness gave another snap at him as he went past. He'd
stopped barking and was wagging his tail, looking very pleased
with himself.

'I told you he was guarding us,' said Eliza.

'And you were right,' said Mary Kate.

'But I told a lie.'

Abby grinned. 'So did I.'

'But sure, it was all in a good cause,' said Eliza.

'What a charming chap,' said Moira. 'I wouldn't want to
bump into him in a dark alley.'

The young man who had come to their rescue was on his knees stroking Guinness, who was licking his face.

'Thank you for stepping in,' said Moira.

'I was heading over here anyway,' he said, smiling.

'You were?' said Mary Kate.

'I was going to enquire about the job, I think it would have suited me fine but it seems that you have already filled the position.'

'Oh, I just said that to get rid of yer feller,' said Eliza. 'He wasn't our type at all.'

The young man smiled. 'Well, in that case I am here to enquire about the job.'

'You'd best come in and I'll tell you what we're looking for.'

'Shall I get some tea?' said Eliza.

Mary Kate smiled at her. 'That would be grand, love, and let me say that I was very proud of the way you handled things out there.'

'I was good, wasn't I?'

'You were and very brave.'

'I'll tell my mammy, she'll be proud of me.'

'Of course she will.'

'I'll help,' said Abby.

'Off you go then, girls, and I think that Guinness deserves a walk, don't you?'

'He does,' said Abby.

Mary Kate smiled and held out her hand. 'My name is Mrs Barry, and this is Miss Kent.'

'And I'm Rooney.'

'Do sit down, Mr Rooney.'

'Oh no, I'm not Mr Rooney. Rooney is my first name, Rooney Cohan.'

'That's an unusual name,' said Moira.

'Well, there's a story there. You see, my mother wanted me to be named Rudolph.'

'After the reindeer?' said Moira, grinning.

'No, the heart-throb, Rudolph Valentino. She sent my father to register my name, but on the way, he fell into the pub. By the time he got to the town hall, he couldn't remember his own name, let alone the name my mother wanted. He just had a vague notion that it began with an R, so he called me Rooney after an old dog he had as a child.'

Moira grinned. 'And what did your poor mother say?'

'Nothing for a fortnight. Now what does the job entail? I can put my hand to most things.'

Mary Kate and Moira were laughing so hard that they couldn't speak.

Eliza and Abby came in with the tea.

'We have an announcement to make,' said Eliza.

'That sounds very serious,' said Moira. 'So, what is this announcement?'

'We have decided that we like yer man and we think that you should give him the job.'

'Well, we shall certainly take your opinion into consideration,' said Mary Kate.

'We'll be off to walk Guinness and by the way, he thinks so too.'

'So, Rooney,' said Mary Kate. 'Can I call you Rooney?'

'I'd prefer it if you did.'

'Can you tell us a little about yourself?'

'I'm twenty-five and I've been working with a team of gardeners on a large estate in Kinsale, but I'm originally from Dublin. My mother has become unwell and I am needed at home, so here I am, looking for a job. I love working outside but as I said, I can turn my hand to most things, so gardener stroke handyman would suit me fine, if that's what you're looking for.'

Mary Kate looked over at Moira, who nodded her head. 'Welcome to our boarding house, Rooney,' said Mary Kate. 'You are exactly what we're looking for.'

Just then, Eliza poked her head around the door: 'Did you get the job, Mr Rooney?'

'I did,' he said, grinning. 'And it was all because of your recommendation.'

'Well, aren't I a great girl altogether?'

'The best,' said Rooney, grinning.

'We'll see you next week then,' said Mary Kate, seeing him out.

'Thank you, Mrs Barry, I won't let you down,' he said earnestly. 'And I have to say, you have a great little guard dog there.'

She closed the door; she was happy with her choice, he was a lovely man.

'He's walking funny,' said Abby.

'Mr Rooney is walking funny? In what way?'

'Not Mr Rooney,' said Abby. 'Guinness.'

'Here, boy,' said Mary Kate. Guinness limped towards her and lay down at her feet. He looked up at her with his big brown eyes as Mary Kate stroked his head. 'What is it, darling? Have you hurt your leg?'

'The bad feller kicked him,' said Eliza. 'Bloody cheek of the man! I've a mind to fetch the guards.'

'I'm not sure the guards care so much about animals,' said Abby.

'Well, they should do, because most of them are better than people. Well, that's what I've found anyway.'

'Oh, Eliza,' said Abby, 'you do make me laugh. I really like being with Marta and Susan, but I like being with you more.'

Mrs Lamb smiled. 'Well, I'd say the pair of you are very lucky to have each other.'

'I couldn't agree more,' said Moira.

'Bloody bloke,' said Eliza. 'May the lamb of God stir his hoof through the roof of heaven and kick his arse down to hell.'

Mary Kate tried to keep a straight face but failed. 'Who in God's name taught you that, Eliza?'

Mrs Lamb wanted the ground to open up and swallow her.

'Me Mammy,' said Eliza, her eyes twinkling.

Moira leaned back against the comfy cushions. Her decision to close the school had been the right one for the boarding house was coming alive again and she knew that there were many adventures ahead for herself and Mary Kate.

CHAPTER 24

Cathy

Cathy leaned against the railings as the great *Innisfallen* sailed towards the green hills of Ireland that emerged from the mist like a beautiful painting. It was cold on deck, but she welcomed the smell of the salty breeze that blew her hair across her face and stung her cheeks. She should have been relieved, maybe even happy, but she was scared and worried and had no idea how her life was going to turn out. She wasn't the same girl that had walked into that hospital and she knew that she would never be the same girl again.

She'd had no idea what to expect but she was met with only kindness. They knew why she was there, of course they did, and yet they were gentle and treated her with a kind of respect that was humbling.

She was put into a room with two other girls, one who looked no older than a child. A woman was sitting beside her, holding her hand, Cathy guessed that it was her mother.

'She's been crying all bloody morning,' said the girl in the next bed. 'She's doin' me head in.'

'I expect she's scared,' said Cathy.

'You're a better woman than me,' said the girl. 'I have the patience of a gnat.'

Cathy smiled. 'I'm sure that's not true.'

'Oh, it's true alright. My poor mother says she must have done something awful in her last life to have landed up with me. My name's Mona, isn't it desperate? My granny said that never has a child been more aptly named.'

'I'm Cathy,' she said.

Just then, a porter came into the room pushing a wheelchair. He went across to the young girl, who started screaming. The mother walked beside her as they left the ward.

'Aren't you scared, Mona?' said Cathy.

'Good God no, I'll be glad to get rid of the little blighter!'

Cathy was shocked at what she'd just heard. 'But you're carrying a precious life inside you, how can you say that?'

Mona laughed. 'The only thing I'm carrying inside me is a bloody great lump on me tit.'

'I thought it was a baby,' said Cathy.

'I wish it was,' said Mona sadly.

'I'm so sorry.'

'I thought my mother would say that I'd finally got my comeuppance, but she hasn't stopped crying since we were told. Is that why you're in here then, because you're having a baby?'

Cathy nodded.

'I'm sorry for your trouble.'

Just then, another porter came into the room and wheeled the chair across to Cathy's bed.

'Good luck,' said Mona.

'Good luck to you too.'

As Cathy looked out over the grey water, she thought about Mona and hoped that with God's help, she would be cured. She'd light a candle to the Blessed Virgin once she found a church and ask her to look kindly on poor Mona, who had made her smile and who had somehow made things a bit easier.

She placed her hand on her tummy. 'I don't know what sort of a mammy I'm going to be, because I never had one of my own to learn from and I'm not going to make you any promises. I learned a long time ago that promises are just words that have a habit of falling flat in mid-air when your face doesn't fit. I don't know where this path will take us, my little one, but I'll carry you in my arms until you learn to walk and then we will stride out together into whatever the future holds for us.'

As they got closer to Dun Laoghaire, she went back inside and collected her case. She had a smile on her face as she followed the crowds down the gangplank because for the first time in her life, she wasn't alone.

As the taxi drove into Merrion Square, Cathy felt sick with nerves. She only had enough money for two weeks bed and board and her fare back to Cork, except that there was nothing to go back to. They were hardly going to let her bring a baby to the library, or even let her work there once her tummy got bigger, and she didn't know what she was going to do.

The driver turned around. 'Here we are, miss,' he said. 'Best little boarding house in the whole of Dublin, this is. There are some places I wouldn't put a dog in but you'll be grand here. I've a mind to book meself in for a few nights, but the missus might not be too pleased.'

He helped her out with her case and put it on the pavement beside her. 'May the day be fair to you,' he said, getting back into the car.

Cathy smiled. May the day be fair to her, that was nice expression. She waved as he drove away and stood looking up at the house. It was the same as all the other houses in the square, but this one had a bright red door and somehow it made her feel better – maybe she'd be OK. She lifted the case and dragged it up the steps. Before she could ring the bell, the door opened and a woman and a young girl were standing there, smiling. There was a black and white dog beside them, who seemed to be smiling as well.

'I'm Eliza,' said the woman. 'And this is Abby, we've been watching out for you. I thought you'd never get here but here you are and isn't that great altogether? Did you come all the way from England?'

'I did,' said Cathy.

'And did you come on a boat?'

'I did.'

'Is England a deadly place?'

'Umm, I don't think so, it didn't feel deadly anyway.'

'I've heard it's full of heathens, did you see any?'

Cathy grinned. 'I don't think so,' she said. 'But then, I wouldn't know what a heathen looks like.'

'They have horns, they're easy to spot,' said Eliza.

'No, I didn't meet anyone like that.'

'Well, that's a blessing, because I've heard he's a fearsome feller altogether.'

'And you'd know all about that, would you?' said Abby.

Eliza ignored her. 'We have your room all ready for you. We've made the bed, so it's nice and clean and the pillows are grand and soft.' She leaned down and ruffled the dog's ears, who thumped his tail on the floor. 'This is Guinness, he's a dog and he lives here too. He must like you because he didn't growl. He growls when he doesn't like people. A feller came here a while ago and Guinness went for him, but as I said at the time, he was just protecting us. He's a grand dog altogether.'

Cathy found herself smiling at the woman in front of her, who seemed to have imparted all this information without taking a breath.

An older woman came into the hall behind her: 'Eliza Lamb, are you intending to leave the girl standing outside for the rest of the day? Wouldn't it be nicer to invite her in before she freezes to death on the doorstep?'

'I'm OK,' said Cathy.

'I get things wrong sometimes,' said Eliza. 'Don't I, Moira? I get things wrong sometimes?'

'You do, love,' said Moira, gently. 'But sure, don't we all?'

'I'm going to run downstairs and tell Mammy that yer woman has arrived, and she needs some tea.'

Moira smiled at her. 'Good idea.'

She turned to Cathy: 'Leave your case there and come and meet Mrs Barry.'

Mary Kate stood up as they entered the room, she walked across to Cathy and shook her hand. 'You are very welcome here, Miss Doyle. And I do hope that you enjoy your short stay with us.'

'Oh, please call me Cathy.'

'Grand so,' said Mary Kate. 'I see you have already met Moira. We run the boarding house together so if you have any questions or worries, one of us will always be around to help you.'

Before she could stop herself, Cathy started to cry. Dear God in Heaven, she'd only just stepped through the door and she was making a show of herself. 'I'm so sorry,' she said. 'I don't know what came over me.'

Moira raised her eyes to the ceiling: another lost soul, what was it that drew them here? Maybe they should put a sign up outside saying FREE LODGINGS, WAIFS AND STRAYS WELCOME. She smiled to herself, because wasn't she one of those lost souls? And didn't this house and the kindness of Mary Kate heal her?

'You're tired, Cathy,' said Mary Kate. 'You've had a long journey and you're recovering from an operation, you're bound to feel a bit low. Could you manage to eat something?'

Cathy hadn't thought about food, but she suddenly felt as if she could eat a horse. 'I think I could,' she said.

'I'll go down to the kitchen and see what Mrs Lamb can rustle up for you,' said Moira.

'You're all so kind,' said Cathy, struggling not to dissolve into tears again.

Maybe Mrs Barry was right, maybe she was just tired. She took a deep breath and looked around the beautiful room. It was lovely here, she felt safe and at peace, but where was she going to go when the two weeks were up?

She'd loved her stay in the boarding house and she didn't want to leave but she had no choice. Everyone had been so kind to her, it seemed as if she'd known them for years. She had felt part of a family and she didn't want to say goodbye. She had become especially close to Nell, who was also having a baby. Cathy hadn't told anyone about her own situation. There was no point, there was nothing anyone could do to change it and anyway she was leaving today, so no one would ever know. She had made the decision to keep the child she was carrying and she didn't regret it. But she had nothing to give her baby, not even a roof over its head. She had never felt more alone. And now she was sitting on the bed, her case on the floor beside her. She hadn't slept all night for worrying. She had nowhere to go and no money to get there, even if she did.

She stood up, took a deep breath and picked up her case. Just then there was a tap on the door. She opened it to see Emma, Nell, Eliza, and Abby standing outside. Even Guinness was there.

'We've come to say goodbye,' said Eliza.

'And to wish you luck,' said Nell.

'And please come back and see us one day,' said Abby.

'It's been lovely knowing you,' said Emma.

Eliza handed her a box. 'It's chocolates,' she said. 'Not the divil ones that would break your teeth but the nice soft ones. It's a going away present.'

'From all of us,' said Nell. 'I'm going to miss you, Cathy, I wish you weren't going.'

'We're all going to miss you,' said Abby.

Cathy had been holding it together, but this was too much and she started to cry.

Nell put her arms around her and led her back to the bed. 'Please don't cry, Cathy, you'll start me off.'

Emma sat beside her. 'You'll be grand once you get back home.'

Cathy lowered her head and didn't answer.

'Abby?' said Emma. 'Run downstairs and get Mary Kate, please.'

'No,' said Cathy. 'I don't want to bother her, I'll just go.'

Emma nodded at Abby, who left the room.

As she continued to cry, Guinness put his paw on her knee.

'He can tell you're upset,' said Eliza. 'I had a desperate earache once and he stayed beside me for days. He's a grand dog.'

'He is,' said Cathy, stroking his soft head. 'I'm going to miss him too.'

The door opened and Mary Kate came into the room.

Cathy stood up. 'I'll be on my way, Mrs Barry, I'm all packed.'

'We'll leave you in peace,' said Emma, ushering the others out of the room.

Cathy sat back down and Mary Kate sat beside her.

'I'm sorry,' said Cathy.

'For what?'

'Everything.'

Mary Kate held her hand. 'Now that's a lot to be sorry for, child.'

'I don't know what to do, Mrs Barry, and I'm scared.'

Mary Kate smiled at her. 'Well now, I think the first thing you can do is unpack that case.'

Cathy looked at her. 'But I have to be out of here today.'

Mary Kate stood up and went across to the window. 'Just as I thought,' she said.

'What?'

'There's no one queuing outside for your bed.'

'But I can't stay any longer.'

'And why is that, love?'

'I only have my fare back to Cork, I haven't the money to stay here.'

'And is that where you're going? Back to Cork?'

Cathy shook her head. 'No.'

'And can you tell me where you *are* going?'

She shrugged her shoulders. 'I don't know.'

'Now put me right if I'm wrong or tell me to mind my own business but I have a feeling that you didn't go ahead with that operation?'

'I couldn't, Mrs Barry, I just couldn't.'

'Then you're a brave girl, it can't have been an easy decision to make.'

Cathy put her hand on her tummy. 'It was the easiest decision I ever made in my life and probably the most foolish. I've nothing to offer a baby.'

Mary Kate smiled. 'Luckily, babies don't need much, just a large amount of love and love costs nothing.'

'But where will I go?'

'You won't be going anywhere.'

'But what about the money?'

'Well, myself and Moira just happen to be looking for a girl to help Emma about the house. What do you think?'

Cathy stood up and put her arms around Mary Kate. 'I think that you are the kindest person I have ever met in my whole life.'

'So, you would like to stay with us?'

'I would love to stay with you. I can clean and Sister Breda at the convent taught me to cook.'

'Then I'm sure that Mrs Lamb will be only delighted. Now put your things back in the drawers, Cathy Doyle, for you are home now.'

CHAPTER 25

Moira and Mary Kate

Mary Kate walked into the sitting room, where Moira was curled up on the sofa, reading. 'We have another guest,' she said, smiling.

'A paying one?' said Moira hopefully.

'Now I can't guarantee that.'

Moira grinned. 'Forgive me if I'm wrong but I was under the impression that running a business was about making a profit.'

'Oh, it's much more than that,' said Mary Kate.

'And do I take it that we are also inheriting another baby?'

'We are,' said Mary Kate, smiling. 'And aren't we lucky?'

Moira shook her head. 'Oh, Mary Kate,' she said, grinning, 'my darling Mary Kate... We'll be running a nursery at this rate.'

Mary Kate smiled at her. 'That's not such a bad idea, my friend.'

'I was joking,' said Moira, pulling a face.

'I know you were,' said Mary Kate. 'But where would

Colleen have gone if she hadn't come here? And Nell and Cathy? What would have happened to them?'

Moira shook her head. 'If we walked through the streets of Dublin this day, we would encounter hundreds of poor souls that need help, but you are one woman, Mary Kate Barry, and however much it would break your heart to walk away, you can't save them all. Somehow, they must find a way to help themselves, just like you did.'

'That sounds awful cold, Moira.'

'I didn't mean it too but it's the truth. I found you and so did Colleen and Bridie, Emma and Nell and Cathy and so many others. We found our way here, we found you, Mary Kate, and that is your greatest gift, my friend. You don't have to go out there looking for people to save, your job is to be here when they all arrive, hauling their baggage behind them. Your gift is just being yourself, and being yourself is enough.'

Mary Kate's eyes filled with tears. 'Are you trying to make me cry?'

'Cry if you want, my darling. I promise I won't tell anyone.'

Just then Eliza and Abby burst into the room.

'Did you know that Cathy is staying here now?' said Eliza. 'She was all for going but she changed her mind, and she isn't leaving us at all, she's staying here. We bought her chocolates, the nice soft ones, not the divel ones that break yer teeth, and she was awful pleased. Maybe she'll give them back now she's not leaving and we can all share them – I love chocolates.'

'Eliza!' said Abby, shocked.

'What?'

Abby glared at her. 'You can't ask for the chocolates back, that would be awful rude. Wouldn't it, Mammy? Wouldn't that be awful rude?'

'I'm sure she didn't mean to be rude,' said Moira. 'You didn't mean to be rude, Eliza, did you?'

'I didn't know that I was being rude. Let's all sit down and talk about it, shall we?'

'Let's not,' said Abby.

Mary Kate and Moira were struggling to keep straight faces but they couldn't keep it up and went into fits of laughter.

Eliza stared at them. 'I don't know what yer laughing about,' she said, 'but it might be rude if I didn't join in.'

Which had them all laughing their heads off again, even Abby.

Mary Kate looked around at these wonderful people who had found her and thought, *Maybe this this is what life is all about, laughter and tears. Just laughter and tears.*

CHAPTER 26

Thomas

Thomas stood behind a tree, where he could still see the boarding house. He lit a cigarette and inhaled deeply. They'd been lying through their teeth – that job hadn't been taken, which suited him fine, because he didn't need it now. He'd found what he came for. As soon as he set eyes on the girl, he'd known without a doubt that it was Alice. She'd grown, but it was her alright. He saw the way they had looked at him, as if he was scum. Well, maybe he was but he was Alice's father and if they thought they'd seen the back of him, they were sadly mistaken.

It had taken two days before he'd discovered that Norah had gone and he was raging and gagging for a drink. The rest of them must have known something but they were either too drunk to remember, or they were keeping it from him. He tore the place apart, punching anyone who dared get in his way. He was a giant of a man and he was taking no prisoners until someone told him where she was.

And then the guards were kicking the door down and

storming into the room. Those able to stand grabbed their filthy blankets and fled. The next thing he remembered was one of them trying to handcuff him. He shook him off and punched him hard in the face. It took four of them to wrestle him to the ground and drag him out of the flat.

Unfortunately for him, he'd punched the guard so hard, he'd broken the man's jaw.

The judge called him a lowlife and a drunken slob, a curse on humanity, who had no right to live among decent, law-abiding people. He felt it was his duty to make an example of him and the bugger sentenced him to six years in jail.

The only thing that had kept him going in there was Norah, who had stuck by him through all those dark days that they had shared together. She had never complained and never blamed him for the mess their lives had become. He had done a lot of soul searching during the long years that he'd been locked up and he didn't like what he found. He was ashamed of the way he'd treated her, she had deserved better, and he would spend the rest of his life making it up to her. It would be different this time – they'd start a new life, a better life, he'd make her proud.

He'd served five years and now he walked the streets of Dublin not only in a straight line but stone-cold sober. The first thing he did was to go back to the flat – there was a chance that Norah might still be there – but the flat had gone and in its place was a row of shops.

It had taken him a year to find her, and it was sheer luck that he'd spotted her coming out of a shop. His heart was thumping out of his chest as he followed behind her. He wanted to run to her, he wanted to call out her name, he wanted to see the look of joy on her face when she saw him, but a niggle of doubt had crept in. It was his Norah, but she looked different. Gone was her beautiful long hair that he had loved so much and it wasn't only her hair that had changed, everything about her was different, even to the way she walked, with her shoulders back and her head held high. He barely recognised the girl who had clutched his hand as they moved silently through the shadows.

Before he'd had time to think, he called her. She turned immediately and the look on her face was not the one he had dreamed it would be – in fact, she looked terrified. He walked closer to her: 'It's me, Norah, it's Thomas. Don't be scared. I don't want to hurt you, I would never hurt you.'

He thought at first that she was going to run but she remained where she was, staring at him. Her voice was cold as she said, 'What do you want?'

'To see you, Norah. I've missed you, haven't you missed me? Aren't you pleased to see me?'

'It's been five years, Thomas. I'm not the same girl I was back then. I have a good life now and I'm happy.'

He glared at her; he was angry; this wasn't the way it was supposed to be. 'Well, I hope it stays fine fer ya,' he said.

'Don't be like that, it's been a long time, you must have moved on too.'

'I've been in prison, I haven't had a chance to move anywhere. I still love you, Norah, and I want us to be together. It will be different this time, I promise you it will. Can't we just try?'

'It's too late.'

'It's never too late. We were good together, weren't we? I took care of you, didn't I? All I'm asking for is a chance, you owe me that much at least.'

Norah shook her head. 'I'm married, Thomas. I've been married for four years and we're happy, *I'm* happy. I'm sorry if you thought there could be a future for us but there isn't and there never will be.'

He felt sick to his stomach as he tried to take in the words that were coming out of her mouth. How could she be married? Why hadn't she waited for him? He had never for one second doubted that she would wait for him and now as he stood looking at the girl he had loved for so long, all he wanted was to hurt her.

'And where does our child fit into this happy little family of yours?' he said.

'What are you talking about?'

'I'm talking about our child. I'm talking about Alice, or have you conveniently forgotten that you have a daughter? Does your perfect husband even know about her, or is she Norah's dirty little secret?'

'What right do you have to question me about Alice? She might be your daughter, Thomas, but you were never her father. It takes a bigger man than you to be a father and God forgive me, a better woman than me to be a mother. The only decent thing I ever did for that little girl was to let her go and I have never regretted it. She deserved to be loved. Every child deserves to be loved but the two people who should have loved her cared more about themselves and where the next drink was coming from than they did for that innocent baby and I will never forgive myself for what we did to her.'

He smiled. 'We can make it up to her, we can get her back. You do want her back, don't you?'

Norah was thinking fast, she had always known how to fool him. 'Of course I do, she's our child.'

Thomas put his hand on her arm, which made her feel sick.

'We can be happy, Norah, just you and me and Alice. I'll find her.'

Just then a car pulled up and a man got out. He was tall and well-built as if he worked out. He stared at Thomas: 'Is everything alright, Norah?'

She turned to Thomas: 'I'll meet you here on Friday at two o'clock, we can talk then.'

Thomas watched as she got into the car, he watched as the

man leaned across and kissed her. He stood in the street staring after her and then made for the nearest pub.

He didn't enjoy the first drink, it felt sour and burned his throat but after the third, he began to feel calmer and suddenly began laughing out loud. An old guy who was propped at the bar started laughing too and a couple of girls began giggling. What an eejit he'd been, what a stupid eejit. He'd believed her when she said she didn't want him anymore, what an eejit. Of course she still loved him, of course she had to pretend – she hadn't been able to run into his arms because she knew her feller was picking her up. They had always joked with each other but fair play to the girl, she'd really got him this time.

He lit up a cigarette and leaned against the wall. She'd almost begged him to get Alice back. Not in so many words but he knew her, he knew the very bones of her. He'd find the girl and bring her back where she belonged, with her family, with her own flesh and blood, and the three of them could go away together, leave Dublin and start a new life. He went back to the bar and ordered another drink and suddenly the world was a better place.

It hadn't taken him so long to find Alice, people talked when you bought them enough drinks. He met an old crone begging on the streets and once he'd said that he'd stand her a round, she quite happily followed him into the pub and boy, did she talk. She said she remembered the child that was left on the steps of the abbey – it had been in all the papers.

'I remember it too,' he'd said. 'Poor little mite, imagine doing that to a baby. I often wondered what became of her.'

'I know what became of her,' she said, staring into her empty glass.

Thomas got her another drink and offered her a cigarette, then waited patiently for her to speak.

'She ended up in the convent with the nuns, I did a bit of cleaning there, that's how I know.' She looked at him and her eyes narrowed. 'Why are you so interested anyway? Why do you care what happened to her?'

Thomas felt like hitting her, instead he smiled. 'It was just such a sad story,' he said. 'For some reason it stayed in my head for all these years. I'd like to think there was a happy ending for the poor thing.'

The woman stared at him, he didn't look like the sort of bloke who cared about an abandoned baby. She decided she didn't like his face, it was a gift she had inherited from her grandmother, may she rest in peace with the angels. She knew a bad'un when she saw one and this was a bad'un alright.

Thomas was getting impatient. 'So, what happened to her after that? Did she stay at the convent?'

'I don't know, you see I'd left by then. All them bells and chantin' and funny costumes done me head in.'

The old cow was lying. He kicked her hard under the table and she yelped. 'Shut up,' he said. 'You tell me where that child is, or you'll find yerself dead in an alley one of these dark nights.'

She glared at him; she had no intention of losing her life over a kid who meant nothing to her. 'She's in a boarding house in Merrion Square.'

'What number?'

'I don't know, as God is me witness I don't know.'

'Really?' he said.

'Well, it's the one with the red door, if that helps.'

He sneered at her. 'It does, now feck off, you smell like a skunk's arse.'

CHAPTER 27

Norah

Since seeing Thomas, Norah had been terrified. Maybe she had always known this day would come, the day that Thomas would find her, but as the years had gone by, she began to feel safe. What a fool she had been.

Liam had asked who the man was that she had been speaking to and she'd told him the truth, she'd told him it was Thomas. What she hadn't told him was that she was meeting him on Friday. He would have stopped her going.

'Maybe we should think about moving away,' he said.

'But you love your work.'

'I love you more and I don't like the sound of this guy. My priority is keeping you safe, where I work is just geography.'

Liam was a wonderful husband and she thanked God every day for him.

From the beginning, Norah had told him everything about her past, leaving nothing out and not making any excuses for her behaviour. She had given him the opportunity to walk away but he hadn't. He'd stayed and they never spoke of it again.

The evening she had run out of the flat in search of Alice would remain in her heart forever. As she walked away from her little girl, her heart was breaking. Alice could have died that night and it would have been her fault. She was no good to anyone, a pathetic drunk who neglected a tiny baby. What sort of mother would do that? A drunken one, that's who.

She remembered how cold it was that night as she ran bare-foot through the icy streets of Dublin, not knowing where she was going and not caring. She ran until she could run no more. The next thing she remembered was waking up in a bed without a clue where she was, or how she got there.

A young man was staring down at her. 'Good morning,' he said, smiling.

She had a hangover from hell and could hardly focus on him. 'Am I in prison?'

'Well, that depends on who you talk to, I suppose,' he said, grinning. 'This is a hospital.'

'Why am I here?'

'You fell over. You have a nasty gash to your head so we'll be keeping you in for observation.'

Apparently, she had looked up at him and said, 'I love you,' then promptly fell back to sleep. She was in there for a week; he visited her every day and she began looking forward to seeing him.

She learned that his name was Liam Flynn and that he was a doctor. He told her about the funny incidents that had happened on the wards. He hated coffee but loved tea and his favourite holiday destination was the Cotswolds in England. Norah realised this was the first time in years that she'd had a proper conversation where she wasn't drunk.

On the day she was being discharged, he came into the room carrying her clothes. 'I hope you don't mind,' he said, 'but I took them home and washed them.'

'You washed my clothes?' she said, grinning.

'Well, they were a bit dirty after your fall. I didn't think you'd want to leave in them.'

'They were dirty before my fall,' she said softly. 'But thank you.'

'You're welcome.'

She smiled at him. 'Do you do this for all your patients?'

'Only the special ones.'

She took a deep breath; she had to know. 'Your wife is lucky to have you.'

'No wife, I'm afraid.'

Norah smiled. 'Oh.'

'So, Norah Clancy, you're leaving us today?'

She nodded.

'I expect you'll be glad to get home.'

She lowered her head and didn't answer him.

Liam put his hand in his pocket and handed her some coins. 'We have a pretty decent canteen here,' he said, 'Go and have a cup of tea and I'll see you in a bit.'

'I'll pay you back,' she said.

As Liam was leaving the room, he turned around: 'Promise you won't disappear on me.'

'I promise,' she said.

As she walked down the stairs, she was smiling because she just knew that against all the odds, her life was about to change.

She had stayed with Liam's sister Jane, who lived in Sandycove, a beautiful seaside town near Dublin. Jane was lovely and treated her like one of the family. Her husband was called Eddie and as nice a man as you could ever hope to meet. They had two little girls: Morgel, seven, and Kiera, four. Norah loved playing with them and reading to them. Herself and Jane became close friends. They shopped together and took turns cooking the evening meals. They took long walks along the sandy beach. Norah loved the feel of the wind blowing through her hair and the taste of salt on her lips. She'd spin round and round, lifting her face to the sky with her arms outstretched, while Jane stood by and laughed. She felt clean, not just on the outside but deep into her very soul. It was as if the pounding waves were washing away all the filth and guilt that she had been living with for so long. This had been the happiest and most wonderful time of her life.

Her dearest wish was that Alice had found a family like this one, where she could grow in love and wisdom and be respected for who she was. Where she would never know hunger or neglect and never, ever remember that terrible room where she had barely survived.

Moving on from that other life hadn't happened overnight. She told herself that she didn't deserve Liam so she pushed him away and she pushed him away, but this lovely, gentle man stayed.

On the day she told him he'd be better off without her, he'd taken her gently by the shoulders and looked into her eyes. 'Is that what you want?' he'd said.

Her eyes had filled with tears. 'No.'

'Then what is all this about?'

That is when she told him her story.

Liam held her hand and listened and when she had finished, he was still holding her hand. Then he took her in his arms. 'Will you marry me?' he said gently.

'Marry you?' she'd said.

Liam had laughed. 'I fell in love with you the first time I saw you, staring up at me from that bed and asking me if you were in prison.'

Norah smiled. 'I remember that bit.'

'How about the next bit?'

'When I said I loved you?'

'That's the bit,' he said, grinning.

'A nurse told me what I'd said. I felt like an eejit and I didn't know how to face you.'

It didn't happen overnight but slowly, slowly, she began to let go of the past. She was now Mrs Norah Flynn, and she wasn't going to let Thomas walk in and destroy everything. She would fight for this wonderful life that she could only have dreamed of. She would fight for Liam, and she would fight for Alice. She had much more to lose than Thomas. She didn't know how, but this time she would fight him and she would win.

CHAPTER 28

Mary Kate

Mary Kate had had doubts about opening up the boarding house again. It had been a kind of adventure the first time. She had loved the assortment of young and old who had found their way through the red door. They all had a story to tell and she had felt part of their lives, they had become the family that she needed so much and their need of her made her feel wanted. They say you should never go back and yet the boarding house was working its magic again. It was giving her a reason to live and to smile and that would never have happened if she had hidden away in the cottage, as she had been determined to do. She didn't want people telling her that time was a great healer. She didn't want to heal, she wanted to scream out her grief; like a woman possessed, she wanted to howl to the moon, like an animal. No pretty little tears for her and it would never have happened if dearest Moira had taken no notice of her weeping and wailing and feeling sorry for herself.

She had grieved for Sean every moment of every day since he had died. She couldn't bear to think of another day without his arms around her. Their love had come late in life, an unexpected gift for them both. There had been times when she'd thought it would have been easier to have never known what love was. Because the price of such love was a heart that was so broken, it was beyond repair.

If she found herself laughing, she would be racked with guilt. How could she laugh when his laughter had been stilled?

One day as she and Moira were giggling over some silly thing, she'd suddenly stopped and put her hand across her mouth.

Moira touched her arm. 'It's allowed, you know.'

Mary Kate moved away from her. 'What is?'

'Being happy, you're allowed to be happy, Mary Kate. He'd want you to.'

'How do you know what he'd want?' she'd said. 'He's not here to ask, is he?'

'No, he's not, but I grew to trust and respect Sean and I know how much he loved your laughter.'

Mary Kate walked across to the window and looked out over the square.

'OK,' said Moira, 'what if things were reversed? What it had been Sean that was left alone? Would you really want him to be continually sad, or would you want him to find what joy he could without you?'

Mary Kate turned around and smiled. 'Why are you always right, Moira Kent?'

'It's just a gift I have, my friend. Think yourself lucky you've got me. And I have a feeling that the Sean Barry that I came to know and love would be up there laughing with you.'

'He would, wouldn't he?'

'He would,' said Moira.

'But I'm allowed a bit of wallowing, aren't I?'

'In small doses.'

So now, there were moments when she didn't think of Sean

and if she did, it was with thanks for the life they had had. She could feel the house wrapping itself around her as if it was saying, 'Welcome home, Mary Kate, I've got you.'

Emma and Cathy had become great friends as between them, they took care of the house and helped Mrs Lamb. Mary Kate would smile as she heard their laughter drifting up from the kitchen. Nell had spent a lot of time with Abby and Eliza and since Abby had started school, she sometimes accompanied Eliza on their daily walks.

And as for Bridie, she had become their dear friend, joining them in the evenings in front of the fire, drinking gallons of tea, eating Mrs Lamb's freshly baked cakes and putting the world to rights. Yes, she was very lucky and often remembered her grandfather telling her that however hard life may seem, there would always be red-letter days for those who looked for them.

Mary Kate often thought about the multicoloured quilt that her grandmother had made. With its blues and reds, soft creams and pale yellows and its greys and browns. She had asked why she hadn't made it all in the lovely bright colours and she had said that you needed the dark to fully appreciate the light. She had been a child at the time and hadn't understood. It wasn't until she was older that she realised her grandmother had been talking about life.

Christmas was only two weeks away and Eliza and Abby kept asking when they were going to get the tree. She knew that she had been putting it off because it could never be the same as that first Christmas when she and Sean had driven out into the countryside and chosen the most perfect tree in the wood. He had held her in his arms to keep her warm and as the snow drifted around them, she had fallen in love with no expectations that he could ever love her in return, but he had.

So today, when Eliza picked Abby up from school, they were all going to choose a tree. Sean had said that there was a knack to picking the perfect one and that he had the gift of spotting it a mile away. Well, today might be a bit different, because Abby and Eliza were doing the choosing and she doubted that it would be quite as perfect as Sean's choice. But a wonky tree chosen through the eyes of love would be the best tree in Merrion Square.

She looked at the clock that stood on the beautiful fireplace and realised that the girls were later than usual.

Moira came into the room, looking worried. 'They should be back by now,' she said.

'I was just thinking the same myself,' said Mary Kate.

Moira walked across to the window and looked out over the square. It was dark and it had started to snow.

Mary Kate came and stood beside her: 'I'm sure they'll be back soon.'

Moira nodded, but she had a feeling in the pit of her stomach that something was wrong.

Abby loved her new school and Eliza loved taking her there and collecting her in the afternoons. Sometimes Moira could hear them laughing together as they crossed the square. She couldn't have loved Abby more if she had given birth to her.

The day she had walked away from Clifton College, she had nowhere to go and no one to go to. She'd felt bitter as she walked down the long drive; she had failed as a teacher and she had no friends.

She never dreamed that she would find her way back home, the home where she had grown up, and if anyone had told her then that she would one day be a mother, she would have laughed in their face. But here she was, mother to the sweetest, kindest little girl in the whole of Ireland and the most beautiful. She must have done something right along the way but she couldn't for the life of her think what it could have been.

'How late are they?' said Mary Kate.

Moira looked at the clock. 'They should have been home

twenty minutes ago.' She peered into the darkness, willing them to appear out of the gloom. 'I wish Guinness was with them.'

Guinness wagged his tail as he heard his name. His leg was bandaged and they were all spoiling him.

Mary Kate looked across at her beloved dog. 'It was because of Sean that she had ended up with this gentle animal. Sean was overseeing the building work on the house and Guinness was there every day. She assumed that the dog was his, but it turned out that it was an old stray. It was Sean who named him Guinness because of his white head and black body. Adopting Guinness had been one of the best decisions of her life – that, and falling in love with Sean Barry.

They sat watching the minutes tick by.

'I think we should call the guards,' said Moira, standing up and going back to the window.

'Let's give it a bit longer,' said Mary Kate.

Nell tapped on the door and came into the room: 'Where are Eliza and Abby?'

Mary Kate shook her head. 'They're not back yet, Nell.'

Moira stared out at the snow. 'This isn't right, Mary Kate, something must have happened.'

That's when she heard the screaming and saw Eliza running towards the house.

Moira and Mary Kate ran outside and Eliza fell into their arms. There was blood streaming down her face.

'Dear God, what has happened?' said Mary Kate.

Eliza stared at her, her face so white against the blood. 'I want my mammy,' she said, sobbing.

'Think, Eliza,' said Moira, 'where's Abby? Where is she? What happened?'

The others had heard the screaming and were running down the stairs.

'Emma, get Mrs Lamb,' said Mary Kate. 'And Bridie, phone the guards.'

CHAPTER 29

Moira

They were all frantic with worry but Moira was in a state of collapse. She couldn't keep still – she was pacing the hallway, going to the window and standing outside, staring over the square.

'I can't just stay here, Mary Kate,' she said. 'I have to go out and look for her.'

'We should wait for the guards, they might have news.'

'I'm going to talk to Eliza, she must remember something.'

'Not now, Moira, the poor girl is in a state of shock. Maybe the guards can get something from her but right now, she's in her mother's arms and that's the best place for her to be. I can't imagine what has gone on and I want to know as much as you do. I want Abby to come home but it's pitch-black out there, what good would come of us tearing around Dublin trying to find her? We need more information, we need something to go on. We'll find her, my love, we'll find her.' But even as Mary Kate said it, she wasn't certain that they would, and she feared for Moira's sanity if they didn't.

The girls were sitting on the stairs, holding onto each other for comfort.

'Emma,' said Mary Kate, 'I want you to phone James, let him know what has happened and tell him to go and get Jessie and bring her back here. Can you do that?'

'Of course,' she said, getting up.

Nell was hanging onto her. 'Don't leave me, Emma.'

'I won't be long and Cathy will look after you.'

Cathy held Nell's hand. 'Of course I will,' she said.

Mary Kate had to let Jessie know. She had been like a big sister to Abby, she had to be told what had happened,

The front door was open and a guard stepped into the hallway. He was a skinny young lad, who looked as if he'd just fallen out of bed. His uniform must have been a hand-me-down from a bigger feller, because it was hanging off him like a sack – she felt a bit sorry for him.

'Thank God you're here,' said Moira. 'You have to find Abby, you have to go now.'

'All we have been told is that a young child is missing,' said the boy. 'What else can you tell us?'

'Abby is eleven,' said Mary Kate. 'She hasn't come home from school and it's not like her.'

'Has she gone missing before?'

'No,' said Moira, 'of course she hasn't.'

'Has there been an upset in the house? Is she in trouble and scared to come home?'

'No,' said Moira, 'she's been taken. Why are you standing there asking a load of stupid questions? Go and find her.'

'They have to ask questions,' said Mary Kate gently.

'I'm afraid we do,' said the guard. 'Was Abby alone?'

'No,' said Mary Kate, 'she was with Eliza. We've tried talking to her but she hasn't been able to tell us anything. Whoever took Abby hit Eliza in the face.'

'So, you really do think that someone has taken her?'

'What else could have happened?' snapped Moira.

'Right,' he said. 'I will need to speak to Eliza.'

Before Mary Kate opened the door, she spoke to him: 'Eliza isn't a child but she acts like one, I don't quite know how to explain it.'

'I have a niece who is the same, I understand,' he said.

When they went into the front room, Eliza screamed.

'It's alright,' said Mrs Lamb. 'This is a good man and he's here to find Abby. Now you need to tell them everything that happened after you collected Abby from school.'

Eliza looked up at the guard: 'Will you find Abby?'

'That's what I'm here for. Now, I know you're very upset but if there is anything that you can remember about today, however small, it could help us to find your friend. Can you do that?'

She nodded.

'You collected Abby from school?'

'Yes, it's my job. I have to make sure she is safe.' Eliza started to cry. 'I tried, I kicked the man in the shin and I tried to get him away from Abby but he hit me. He hit me really hard and then he pulled her into the car.'

'Can you remember what the man was like, Eliza? Was he a big man or a small man?'

Eliza frowned. 'He was a big man.'

'Bigger than me?'

She nodded. 'He was a giant of a man.'

'So, he was very big?'

Eliza nodded again.

'Did he have a beard?'

'His chin was black, but I don't know if he had a beard.'

'And was his hair black as well?'

'I think so, but it was dark.'

The guard smiled at her. 'You are being very brave, Eliza,' he said.

'Yes, I am, aren't I?'

'Now, what about this car you saw? Can you remember what colour it was?'

'It was red.'

'Are you sure about that?'

'Oh yes, red is my favourite colour. Isn't it, Mammy? Isn't red my favourite colour?'

'It is, my love,' said Mrs Lamb.

'That's why I remembered it,' said Eliza.

'I'm afraid I'm going to have to take Eliza down to the station so we can get all this down on paper.'

'Eliza is going nowhere, sonny Jim,' said Mrs Lamb. 'The child is traumatised and she needs to be here with her family.'

'But rules are rules, Mrs Lamb. I am only doing my duty.'

Mrs Lamb glared at him. 'Well, you can go and do your duty somewhere else. Listen, Jimmy Coyne, I knew you when your arse was hanging out your trousers, so don't be standing there telling me about rules. If you need to speak to Eliza again, you can speak to her here and that's my last word on the subject, got that?'

'Yes, Mrs Lamb,' he mumbled.

'Is there anything else you want to ask her before you go?'

The guard knelt down in front of Eliza. 'Now, is there anything else you can remember? Any small little thing that will help us find this man?'

'I can't think of anything else, Mammy. I'm trying hard, but I can't think of anything else.'

'That's alright, my love, you did really well,' said Mrs Lamb.

'Well, if you think of anything, anything at all,' said the guard, 'let us know.'

'We will of course,' said Mary Kate. 'But I think Eliza needs to rest now.'

As Emma let the guard out, a car was pulling up outside.

Jessie jumped out and ran into the house, James Renson came behind her.

'Is there any news?' said Jessie.

Mary Kate shook her head. 'Not yet, darling.'

'I've remembered something,' said Eliza.

'What have you remembered?' said Mary Kate.

'That man called Abby by the wrong name.'

'What did he call her, Eliza?' said Moira.

'He called her Alice.'

Mary Kate and Moira looked at each other: they knew who had taken her.

The waiting was hard but for now there was nothing they could do but wait. Emma brought up a tray of tea but none of them wanted it. The minutes ticked away but it felt like hours. There was a knock on the door and the guard walked into the room.

'I'm glad you came back,' said Mary Kate. 'Eliza has remembered something.'

The guard didn't say anything. He just stood there staring at them all, his face as white as a sheet.

Moira jumped up: 'Have they found her?'

'I don't know how to tell you and I'm awful sorry for your trouble.'

'For God's sake, just say it, Jimmy,' said Mrs Lamb.

'A car was seen going over the cliffs at Howth.'

'Was it red?' said Mary Kate.

'The couple who witnessed it going over said it had been too dark to make out the colour.'

'So, it could have been any car?' said Moira.

'I suppose it could,' said Jimmy.

'It can't be the only car that's ever gone over those cliffs.'

The guard nodded. 'I'd say you could be right there, missus, a fair few have gone over. Mostly suicides. You know, desperate souls wanting to end it all, God love 'em.'

Moira looked ready to punch the poor boy. 'Then why in all that's holy are you frightening the life out of us when it could be any old car?'

Jimmy looked ready to run. 'I was told to.'

'We need to go there,' said James. 'I know Howth very well, it's not far. We need to know.'

'I'm coming with you,' said Jessie.

'You'll need coats, there's a fierce wind up on those cliffs.'

'Will you hold the fort, Bridie? And will you let Abby's school know what has happened?' said Mary Kate.

'I will of course and may God go with you.'

'I'll get some hot food ready for when you come home,' said Mrs Lamb. 'I need something to do before I go mad altogether.' As she was leaving the room, she turned around: 'And you, Jimmy Coyne, should seriously consider a change of career – your bedside manner is shite.'

CHAPTER 30

Mary Kate

It was silent as they sat in the back of James's car, each of them praying that it was not a red car that had gone over the cliff, because anything else was unthinkable. It would be a cruel God indeed who had looked away and let harm come to such an innocent child.

Darling, beautiful Abby, their golden girl who meant the world to all of them, this couldn't be true, it just couldn't. Mary Kate had heard that when a loved one died you knew straight away, you felt them leaving their body. Maybe she was a fool, because in her heart Abby was alive.

They passed North Bull, an uninhabited island sitting in the bay of Dublin, and in the distance, the lighthouse at Howth shone out across the dark waters. It had begun to snow again, thick white flurries of it, sticking to the windscreen; even the wipers weren't dealing with it. James could barely see a foot in front of him. It was dangerous to keep driving so they abandoned the car. Mary Kate and James got out and were nearly blown away by the icy wind. Mary Kate went to help Moira and Jessie.

'I can't,' said Moira. 'I don't want to see anything, I couldn't bear to see anything.'

'You stay in the car, love, and I'll find out what I can. Jessie, please stay with Moira. I'll be back as soon as I know anything.'

Mary Kate and James ran towards the lights. People were gathered in huddles, watching the drama unfolding before them. They were stopped as they neared the cliff edge.

'You can't go any further,' said one of the guards.

'We are the family of the little girl who has been reported as missing,' said Mary Kate. 'We think that she might have been in the car.'

'I'm awful sorry,' he said, 'but it's not safe for you to go any closer.'

'Can you just let us know if the car that went over was a red car?' said James. 'And could you tell us if there is a child?'

'I'll see what I can find out,' he said, walking away.

It was freezing on the top of the cliff, the salty air blowing off the sea stung Mary Kate's eyes and grazed her cheeks. She pulled her coat closer around her and stuffed her hands into her pockets. She was shivering so much that she could hear her teeth chattering. Was Abby down there, cold, alone and afraid? She couldn't bear to think of it.

James took off his scarf and wrapped it around her neck. 'Let's stand back a bit,' he said, 'or we'll both freeze to death.'

It felt like a lifetime before the guard returned. 'It's a red car alright,' he said. 'I'm sorry.'

Mary Kate walked away and fell to her knees, sobbing and retching.

James ran over to her.

'He's killed her, James, he's killed Abby. He's killed our girl.'

James put his arms around her and she sank into him. 'She

wasn't in the car, Mary Kate,' he said softly. 'Abby wasn't in the car.'

'Are they sure? Are they sure, James?'

'There are casualties but no Abby.'

'Oh, James, could she still be alive then? Do you think that Abby could still be alive?'

'We know she wasn't in the car, so let's hang onto that for the moment. I'll stay here and see what more I can find out. You go back to the car, put Moira's mind at rest and get warm. There are a couple of blankets under the seats, wrap yourself up.'

Mary Kate hurried back to the car, her head bent against the snow and the wind. She wrapped James's scarf around her face – she had never been so cold in her life but she had a bit of hope in her heart and for now, that was all that mattered.

Back at the boarding house, they had all remained in the front room. Nell was keeping the fire going and Cathy and Emma had taken over the kitchen to allow Mrs Lamb to look after Eliza. They brought up sandwiches but no one could eat.

Nell had her hand on her tummy.

'Are you OK?' said Emma. 'Do you have a pain?'

'Come and feel,' said Nell, smiling. 'He's turning somersaults in there.'

Emma put her hand on Nell's tummy: 'I think this baby wants to come out.'

'How will he get out, Emma?'

'The same way that Mr Brady's sheep had their babies.'

'But that was awful messy.'

'I suppose it was.'

'And does it hurt? Because those poor things were making an awful racket.'

'I've never had a baby, Nell, but I'd say that once your child is in your arms, you'll forget about the pain.'

'And you'll be with me, Emma?'

Emma smiled. 'I'll be with you, my darling girl.'

'OK then. Well, I hope he's still moving when Abby comes home, she likes to feel him moving.'

'What makes you think it's a boy, Nell?'

'Eliza said it was, she knows about these things. She's very clever, you know. Abby *will* come home, won't she?'

'That's what we're all praying for, Nell.'

'You see, I want her to be with us when we stand on the top of my hillside. I want Abby to be there when we show my baby the Blackwater River.'

'Let's keep that in our minds then until she's home.'

'OK, Emma.'

Just then the phone rang. Bridie picked it up, not knowing what she was about to hear.

There was silence in the room as the others stared at her.

Her eyes filled with tears as she put the phone down.

The others got up and went to her.

Bridie took a deep breath. 'She's safe,' she said. 'Abby is safe.'

They stood in the middle of the room with their arms around each other, crying and laughing and shouting with joy.

'Where has she been?' said Emma.

'All I know is that right now she's at the school. The headmaster is bringing her home, we'll know more then.'

'What about Mary Kate and Moira and Jessie?'

'The guards have informed them and they are on their way home.'

Mrs Lamb came into the room and saw them all crying. 'I heard the phone, it's bad news, isn't it?'

Bridie walked across and held her in her arms. 'She's safe, Mrs Lamb, she's safe.'

Mrs Lamb's eyes filled with tears. 'Abby's safe?'

Bridie nodded.

'God is good,' she said. 'I need to tell Eliza, she'll want to be here, she needs to be here. Oh, and I'll bring tea.'

'I'll tell you what,' said Bridie, 'forget the tea. Let's all wrap up and sit on the steps because I can't settle in here.'

'I don't think any of us can,' said Emma.

'Coats and scarves and gloves,' said Cathy. 'We will welcome her home.'

They were waiting in the hallway as Mrs Lamb and Eliza came down the stairs. Eliza's poor face was black and blue, but she was smiling. 'I knew she'd come back,' she said. 'I get a feeling about these things, don't I, Mammy?'

Mrs Lamb grinned. 'You do seem to, Eliza.'

Bridie opened the front door and the driving snow nearly threw her back into the hallway. 'Gird yer loins, ladies,' she said, laughing. 'It's Arctic out there.'

Mrs Lamb went into the front room and came back with a blanket, which she proceeded to spread over the stone steps. 'I don't mind the top half of me freezing but a frozen bum is a step too far.'

Eliza giggled. 'You said "bum", Mammy.'

'I did, didn't I? I'll have to go to confession now.'

'And then you'll have to say "bum" to the priest.'

'I'm sure the man has heard worse, Eliza.'

They sat on the steps and waited and froze.

'I have this great ball of happiness in my chest,' said Nell. 'I feel like dancing up and down the street.'

Emma pulled a face. 'I'm thinking it's not the done thing in Merrion Square.'

'Well, I think it's a great idea,' said Cathy. 'If nothing else, it will keep us warm and who cares what people think?'

And so they held hands and danced. Even Guinness limped around them, barking and wagging his tail. He seemed to know that something wonderful had happened.

They stopped dancing as they saw a car turning into Merrion Square.

'Now we mustn't overwhelm her,' said Bridie. 'Abby has gone through something unimaginable; she needs peace now and not the pile of us jumping all over her.'

The car pulled up outside the boarding house and a man helped Abby out.

Guinness ran down the steps and stood beside her. She stroked his head and looked up at the house but didn't speak.

Just then, James's car screeched to a halt and Moira jumped out. Tears were streaming down her face as she held Abby. 'You're safe now, my darling,' she said. 'You're home.'

Abby looked up at her and together they walked up the steps and into the house. Mary Kate was about to follow when she noticed that Bridie was still standing on the pavement. 'What are you doing standing there?' she said. 'Come in out of the cold.'

Bridie didn't answer: she was staring at the headmaster. He reached out to her and she walked into his arms. She was laughing and crying. 'Stephen?' she whispered. 'Oh, Stephen.' And as the snow fell about them, they kissed.

CHAPTER 31

Norah

Norah had barely slept. She was meeting Thomas today and she had to get this right. He had never hurt her, not physically anyway, and he was right when he'd said that he had always been there for her but it had never been a healthy relationship. It had grown out of their need for the drink, it had grown out of weakness. Somehow, being together had made it all seem OK – she had needed him as much as he needed her. It was in those rare moments when they were sober that they saw themselves for what they were, a couple of lousy drunks. Thomas was a big man and the rest of the lowlifes had left them alone, even the guards had left them alone. He had been her protection and she had been his warped idea of normality. So, no, she hadn't been afraid of him, not back then anyway but now, he was a threat to everything she held dear. His weakness was loneliness, he couldn't bear to be alone. Even as they slept side by side in a drunken stupor, he would always wrap himself around her, as if he was scared that when he woke, she would be gone. Thomas had controlled her every move and she had let him because she had mistaken control for love. She didn't blame him for her drinking, he hadn't held the bottle to her lips and made her swallow. She just liked the taste of it, she always had. That feeling as it slid down her throat, the heat as it hit her stomach, but most of all she liked the way it made her feel, the way it made everything feel. The world was a better place, a kinder place, and she was a better person.

When she told him that she was married, she might just as well have said: 'I don't need you anymore'. She had watched as his face changed from confusion to anger, as he realised that he had lost control of her, and for the first time she was afraid of him. He would do anything to get her back and it had nothing do with love. He was determined to get her back, even if he had to use Alice to do it.

The one advantage she had over him was that she had a brain in her head that was far superior to his and today she was going to use it and outsmart him. She hadn't protected Alice when she promised that she would and she hadn't walked away from Thomas, even when the nurse begged her to. She had only thought of herself and her needs. This time it would be different, this time she would protect her child by whatever means she had to use, even if it was the last thing she did.

Norah felt sick to her stomach as she drove towards the city. She had put two cases in the back seat of the car where Thomas could see them. She was early, which gave her time to go over the plan. If there was any chance of this working, she was going to have to give the performance of her life. He had to believe that this was what she wanted, a new start.

She closed her eyes and prayed: 'Dear God, I'm just letting you know that I am about to break the sixth commandment. Now, I know killing someone is a mortal sin but I hope that you can make an exception in this case. You see, I have to save Alice and the only way I can save her is to kill Thomas. I promise that I will never kill anyone again. I know it's a big ask but I hope that you can see your way clear to forgiving me, as you forgave Mary Magdalene and the thief on the cross. Oh, and could you be beside me when I do it? Amen.'

The streets were busy with Christmas shoppers, loaded down with bags and parcels, young couples walked along holding hands and children stared into shop windows. There seemed to be a Father Christmas on every corner and carols were ringing out from the stores.

She spotted Thomas leaning against the wall, smoking. He looked out of place on this Christmas afternoon, as if he had no right to be there. They had never celebrated Christmas back then; they probably weren't aware that it *was* Christmas. No tree, no presents, just another alcohol-fuelled day.

She sat in the car and stared across the street at the man she had shared so much of her life with, a life lived in the shadows and the dark corners of the city, but still a life. She had loved him once, just as she had loved the drink. Perhaps love and alcohol weren't so very different, for she had craved both, she had needed both. But she had left him in the darkness and walked towards the light, each step taking her closer to this moment in time. And perhaps as she'd travelled the roads that led to this other life, she had taken a part of him with her, without even knowing it. Maybe once you loved, a little piece of it remained, forever in your heart.

Norah got out of the car and taking a deep breath, she smiled and ran across the road and into his arms. They stood on the pavement like a couple of young lovers, people smiled as they walked past.

Thomas held her away from him and touched her face: 'Oh, Norah, I knew you didn't mean what you said, I knew you still loved me.'

She smiled up at him: 'Of course I still love you, Thomas, but I had to pretend. You do see that, don't you?'

'I eventually figured it out in the pub, but you had me going there for a minute.'

'Perhaps I should take up acting, as I'm so good at it.'

'Perhaps you should, you had me fooled.'

'I'm sorry I said those things, I'm sorry I hurt you.'

'We're together and that's all the matters. You know what we have to do now, don't you?'

'Find Alice?'

'I've already found her.'

'Where is she?'

'Living in some boarding house with a load of tossers. She might need some reining in once she's back with us but we'll have her towing the line in no time at all.'

'Well, I shall leave all that up to you, you're her father and she will have to learn to respect you.' Norah could see him changing before her eyes. He believed her, he trusted her, he thought he was back in control and that was exactly what she wanted.

'I've been watching her,' he said. 'She comes out of school at four o'clock and walks across the park. It will be getting dark by then and that's when we'll grab her.'

Norah felt sick at the thought of what they were about to do. Alice would be terrified, but this was the only way to keep her safe and back with her new family, where she belonged. 'We'd better get on with it then,' she said.

As they got into the car, Thomas noticed the two cases and grinned: 'So where are we going?'

'I have a cousin in Howth, her and her husband run a guest house there. I told her that we needed a fresh start and she offered us work and a room until we got settled. It will give us a bit of breathing space until we decide what to do next.'

'That's great,' he said.

'I've brought some bottles of water and one of them has sleeping pills in it, it will keep Alice calm until we get there.'

'You've thought of everything, haven't you?'

'Oh yes, Thomas, I've thought of everything.'

'You clever girl!'

'Oh no, Thomas,' she said, smiling, 'you're the clever one.'

Norah had convinced him that this was what she wanted. That had been the easy bit – he'd let his guard down, he thought he was in control again. She stopped the car at the edge of the park and he got out.

'Where are you going?' said Norah.

He pointed across the green. 'Over by those bushes, I'll stay out of sight until I see them, then I'll grab her. Leave the back door open so I can get her in fast, then put your foot down.'

Norah smiled at him. 'Don't worry, I'll be ready. Good luck, darling.'

Thomas leaned across and kissed her on the cheek. 'We are going to be so happy, my Norah.'

'Of course we are, Thomas,' she said.

She watched him walk away. Very soon she was going to see Alice and whatever happened this day, she would look on the sweet face of her little girl one last time.

She closed her eyes: 'Dear God, it's me again, Norah. You might remember that I spoke to you this morning. I know that you are up to your eyes, trying to look after the whole world, but right now we really need you, me and Alice really need you. Look down on us, God, and hold us in your arms. And for what I am about to do, I'm truly sorry. Amen.'

The nights were drawing in and there was a mist above the tall trees. In the distance she could just make out the silhouette of a slide and a row of swings. In the light of day, this would be a happy place, filled with the sound of children's laughter. But now there was something forbidding about it. A place where bad things happened, under the cloak of darkness. Suddenly, there was movement at the far end of the park and then a woman and a child emerged out of the gloom. They were holding hands as they made their way across the green. It could have been any child, but her heart told her that it was Alice. Then she saw Thomas running towards them. She wanted to cry out, she wanted to warn them, but she stayed silent. She got out of the car and opened the back door just as he had told her to; she put her hands over her ears as the screaming started.

Alice was kicking and yelling as Thomas dragged her across the grass and almost threw her into the back of the car.

'Put your foot down, Norah, we have to get out of here.'

Alice was kicking the back of his seat. 'You let me out,' she shouted. 'My mammy will be after you.'

'That's your mammy,' he said, pointing at Norah.

'No, it's not.'

'Well, it is, see, and I'm your daddy.'

'I haven't got a daddy.'

'Well, you have now, so shut up.'

Norah wanted to scoop Alice up in her arms and comfort her, but she kept driving. Not long now, and it would all be over.

They hadn't gone far when Thomas told her to pull over.

'I need a slash,' he said. 'There's a garage over there.'

'Would you pick up some food? I'm starving,' Norah asked.

'So am I,' he said.

Norah leaned over and whispered in his ear: 'I'll give her the pills now, so take your time.'

As soon as she saw him go into the garage, she got out of the car and opened the back door.

'I need you to run, Alice, I need you to run as fast as you can.'

'Are you saving me?'

'Yes, darling, I'm saving you.'

'Are you really my mammy?'

Norah kneeled down in front of her. 'I was your first mammy; I have always loved you and I will always love you.'

Abby leaned forward and kissed her cheek. 'Thank you,' she said.

'Now run, darling, run and don't look back.'

Norah watched until Abby was out of sight, then opened the two cases and took out the pillows. She bunched them up on the back seat and threw a blanket over them.

'No bloody food,' said Thomas, getting into the car. 'I hope your cousin's got some for us.'

'Shush,' said Norah, 'she's asleep.'

Thomas didn't even look behind him. 'I need a drink,' he said.

Norah handed him the bottle of water that contained the tablets. She didn't care what happened now. Alice had kissed her, her little girl had kissed her and said thank you.

She started the car and headed towards Howth and the cliffs.

CHAPTER 32

Mary Kate

The boarding house had seen happy times, worrying times and sad ones and the past week had seen them all. Who would have thought that Abby's headmaster was Bridie's Stephen? They were all so delighted for them both and Bridie was so happy. They should have been celebrating but, sadly, because of what had happened to Abby and Eliza, this wasn't the time.

One night when Abby was safely asleep, they all danced in the garden.

Mary Kate had learned long ago that however bad things were, the sun would always rise and the tide would always turn and waiting around the next bend may just be your red-letter day. It seemed that happiness and sadness very often went hand in hand. And perhaps like her grandmother's quilt, we need the darkness to appreciate the light.

Abby had been home for a week and was still in shock. She was barely eating and couldn't sleep alone, so Moira had put an extra bed in her room and slept beside her. She hadn't uttered a word since her terrible ordeal, she hadn't even cried. She seemed to have reverted back to the little girl that Mary Kate had taken from the convent, a little girl who was so traumatised that she would only speak through Jessie, but Jessie didn't live here anymore, she had a life beyond the red door with Aishling and she was happy in the little bookshop that they ran together.

The guards had come to the house and tried to speak to Abby but she had stared at them and turned away.

Moira and Mary Kate were sitting in the front room, watching over Abby, who was asleep on the couch with her arms around Guinness. This sweet dog hadn't left her side from the moment she had come home. He had jumped up onto the couch and snuggled as close to Abby as he could get, pressing his warm body against her side and licking her hand. She had stroked his soft fur and kissed the top of his head. He seemed to sense that his friend was sad and needed comfort.

They had been told that the body of a man had been found dead at the bottom of the cliffs and a woman was in hospital, barely clinging to life. They knew that the man was Thomas but didn't know who the woman might have been.

'She needs to be thrown in prison for what she's done,' said Moira.

Abby suddenly stirred, sat up and shook her head. She put her hand over her mouth, as if she was trying to say the words that were refusing to come out.

'It's alright, darling,' said Moira, going to her. 'You don't have to say anything, you don't have to say anything at all.'

But Abby continued to shake her head and then began stamping her feet.

'You want to tell us something, don't you?' said Moira, taking her hand.

Abby nodded.

'How can we help you, Abby? We want to help you, love.'

Abby put her head down and started to sob.

'Is there anyone you could talk to?' said Mary Kate.

Abby looked up and nodded.

Mary Kate knelt in front of her and held her hand. 'Now, I'm going to say some names and I want you to nod when I get to the right one, OK?'

She nodded.

'Good girl,' said Mary Kate. 'Right, is it Emma? Nell? Cathy? Jessie? Mrs Lamb? Eliza?'

Abby nodded.

'You want to speak to Eliza?'

She nodded again.

'I'll get her,' said Mary Kate, standing up.

Left alone, Abby and Moira sat in silence. It was breaking Moira's heart to see her beautiful girl struggling to communicate again.

Mary Kate and Eliza came into the room.

Eliza smiled. 'Hello, Abby. Mary Kate said that you wanted to talk to me. You can talk to me anytime you want, it's no trouble, no trouble at all. I like talking.'

'Then you're just the person, Eliza,' said Moira. 'Now we'll leave you alone to chat.'

Eliza couldn't sit next to Abby because Guinness wouldn't move, so she sat on the floor.

'What do you want to talk about, Abby?'

At first Abby still couldn't say a word.

'Just take your time,' said Eliza. 'I've all day, I've nothing planned, I'm not taking off on a holiday or anything. Try coughing, it might help to spit the words out.'

Abby coughed, but nothing happened.

'Try harder this time,' said Eliza. 'As if you're choking to death and yer life depends on it.'

Abby coughed again and the words that had been sitting on her tongue fell out. 'I want to go to the hospital, Eliza.'

'Are you ill?'

Abby shook her head. 'I want to see the lady.'

'What lady?'

'The lady that was in the car.'

'With the bad man?'

'Yes.'

Eliza frowned. 'I didn't see a lady, was she bad as well?'

'No, I don't think she was. She saved me and she was kind. I want to visit her in the hospital so that I can thank her.'

'I'm sorry I couldn't save you, Abby, I did try.'

'I know you did, Eliza. You were very brave and I'm sorry he hurt you.'

'That's OK, it didn't hurt that much. It was a bit like in the cowboy films, where they're always punching each other.'

'Well, thank you.'

'You'll need to bring a present.'

'What are you talking about?'

'When you go to see yer woman in the hospital. You have to bring a present, it's the law.'

'I haven't got anything to bring.'

'I'll ask Mammy for a couple of biscuits, that'll do nicely.'

'Now you must tell them what I said.'

'Why can't you tell them yourself, Abby?'

'I don't know.'

'Well, it doesn't matter. I'll be your voice until you find your own one and I'll be glad to do it.'

Abby smiled at her. 'You're a good friend, Eliza.'

Eliza grinned. 'Really?'

'Yes, really.'

'I've never had a friend before.'

'Well, you've got one now.'

'I suppose I'd better come to the hospital with you then, otherwise you won't be able to thank yer woman.'

Abby nodded. 'There is one more thing that I want you to tell them.'

'Fire away,' said Eliza.

'The woman in the hospital was my first mammy.'

'You have two mammies?' said Eliza.

'I have.'

'I've never heard of anyone with two mammies.'

'Neither have I,' said Abby. 'But that's what she said.'

'Ah well, if she said it, it must be true, I mean, she's a grown up, isn't she?'

There was a tap on the door and Moira and Mary Kate came into the room.

'Have you finished speaking, girls?' said Mary Kate.

'Yes,' said Eliza.

'And is it alright if Eliza speaks for you, Abby?'

Abby nodded.

Moira and Mary Kate sat down.

'Wait a minute,' said Eliza. 'I have to get it straight in my head. I've never talked for someone else before – it's a big responsibility, you know.'

Abby raised her eyes to the ceiling, which was something she had always done when Eliza said something daft.

'Take your time, Eliza,' said Mary Kate.

Eliza got up and stood with her back to the fireplace as if she was about to give a speech. Abby was shaking her head.

Eliza cleared her throat. 'Good evening,' she said. 'My name is Eliza Lamb and I will be speaking for Abby until she can speak for herself. So, although the sound will be coming out of my mouth and you can see my lips moving, the words you are about to hear are all Abby's.' She cleared her throat again. 'Abby Bonniface says that she wants to visit yer woman in the hospital to say thank you for saving her.'

'No,' said Moira, standing up. 'No, Abby, I'm sorry but you could have been killed. You are not going to the hospital to visit that woman.'

'One more thing,' said Eliza. 'Abby said that yer woman saved her life and that she was her first mammy.'

Moira looked sad. 'Her first mammy?' she said softly.

'That's what she said.'

Abby beckoned to Eliza and whispered in her ear. Eliza was nodding very seriously to every word she was saying.

'Abby says, if you won't go with her, she will go on her own. Yer woman could be dying, and she needs to thank her and to say goodbye.'

Mary Kate looked across at Moira and smiled. 'Well, it looks like we'll be going to the hospital, my friend.'

Moira nodded. 'Yes, it looks as if we are.'

'I have to go as well,' said Eliza, 'for I am the keeper of Abby's voice.'

Mary Kate stared at her. 'The keeper of Abby's voice,' she said. 'What a wonderful thing to say. You are a very special girl, Eliza Lamb, and you never stop surprising us. You are wise and kind. And we all love you very much.'

Eliza grinned. 'Mammy says I have hidden depths, whatever that means, and anyway, it's easier to be kind than mean, don't you think?'

'Indeed I do,' said Mary Kate. 'And we can all learn from you. You are a beacon of light in a sometimes dark world.'

'You've lost me now,' said Eliza and they all laughed, even Abby.

CHAPTER 33

Bridie

Bridie would be doing something and then suddenly find herself laughing. To think that Stephen had been just down the road all the time. He hadn't let her down, he had gone to the train station instead of the bus station and by the time he realised his mistake he had raced across town, but she had gone.

They had so much to talk about, so many dreams that they had thought were never going to come true. The cottage, the garden, the two gnomes and the little dog called Hope. Silly talk really, they were acting like two skitty young ones but oh, it felt wonderful, every little ordinary thing felt wonderful. It was like being born again; it was like seeing everything for the first time. Life can break you, but it can lift you up and oh, what a lifting this had been.

They wanted to be together but because Stephen lived at the school it would have been frowned upon. Once the school day was over, Bridie would go to his house and make dinner for them both. They would spend their evenings listening to the kind of music that had been denied them for so long and then Stephen would drive her home.

If they could, they would get married straight away. They had wasted so much time already and having found each other, they were desperate to start their new life in a home of their own. Stephen understood that this wasn't the right time. Maybe the religious life that they had chosen had taught them patience.

When Bridie had taken her vows, she thought it was what she wanted. Her mother and her sisters said it was ridiculous, which made her want it even more. But she had struggled and not only was she on her knees every day praying to God to show her the way, but she had the rest of the nuns on their knees too.

She doubted herself all the time. Poverty, chastity and obedience hadn't come easily to her and in a house full of women her tolerance was severally tested. It was hard to be tolerant when you were roused from your bed at five o clock in the morning to stand beside an old nun who was singing off-key at the top of her voice. She would look at her fellow sisters, who seemed so serene and full of the Holy Spirit, while she was thinking how she could get away with murder.

Every Sunday, an old priest would come to the convent and say mass. The poor man was very deaf and nearly dislodged the statue of the blessed Virgin from her pedestal with his booming voice.

One Sunday, he collapsed in the middle of Holy Communion, dropping the Holy Chalice and spilling wine all over the altar. It was said that Johnny Logan was seen licking it up. It was probably just gossip, although knowing Johnny Logan, no one would have been too surprised.

He was replaced by a young priest called Stephen, with his soft voice and kind words, and that is when it had all begun. Loving him had made her a better person, a nicer person; she even complimented the old nun on her enthusiastic singing, which on reflection might have been a mistake as the volume increased dramatically over the next few Sundays.

On the day they were due to meet in Dublin, buses were pulling in and out of the station, but she knew in her heart that Stephen wasn't going to be on any of them. She had no idea where to go, the future she thought was ahead of her had gone and it had taken the best part of her with it. She didn't care where she lived but she was frozen and needed shelter. After walking around for hours, she found herself in Merrion Square and it was behind the red door that she had found acceptance, kindness and friendship.

By the time she left her childhood home, what little confidence she may have possessed had been sucked out of her by indifference and dispassion. Her mother had been a shallow, self-obsessed woman who had taken pride in the beauty and popularity of Bridie's three sisters but had no time for her. She had tried so hard to make her proud, to illicit a kind word here and there, to tell her that beauty was a fleeting thing and that being herself was enough. In the end, she knew that whatever she did, her mother was never going to love her. She would always be the plain one, the runt of the litter – only good enough to take care of her in her old age. In fact, there were times when she felt that her mother was ashamed of her.

It took a long time to realise that she had been grieving almost all her life and she thought that the religious life would help her to heal, but she had been wrong. Grief isn't something you can run away from – wherever you go, however far you travel, you will carry it with you. They say that grief is the price of love, but she was grieving for the love that she had never had.

Mother Superior had always known that she was a troubled soul. One day she called her into her office and Bridie told her story. In fact, until that moment the Mother Superior hadn't really known how damaged she was.

'You carry your sadness like a penance, but you can't go

back and change things. The love you were denied has to come from inside yourself, because you can't rely on anyone else to give it to you. Respect your grief, nurture it, because it is part of who you are and in the end it will make you a stronger person. Love yourself, Sister, for we all deserve to be loved.

But it hadn't been the convent that had given her the peace she craved. It was the boarding house, where the people that she found became the kind of family that she had never had. She could be herself and not be judged or laughed at because of it, being herself was enough. She would wait to marry Stephen until the boarding house was happy again.

CHAPTER 34

Mary Kate

Mary Kate and Moira took a taxi to the hospital with Eliza chatting all the way, which was exactly what they needed, for the pair of them were too wrapped up in their own thoughts to speak. They were both anxious about meeting Abby's birth mother. Moira, because she couldn't bear to think of Abby having another mother before her. She had somehow managed to block out Abby's past life. She hated to admit it, but the truth was, she was jealous. She had known that Norah Clancy existed and she should have talked to Abby about it – the child had a right to know. It would have been kind to tell her that her mother hadn't abandoned her on the steps of the abbey, she had let her go, to give her a better life, because she loved her. She should have told her, but she had allowed her jealousy to cloud her judgement; she had put her own insecurities above that of her daughter. Love wasn't a contest but in her heart that was what she had made it.

No one knew how much Abby remembered from her childhood and Moira couldn't bear to think about it, but it had happened and pretending it hadn't wasn't helping either of them. Moira should have given Abby a safe place to speak and if indeed she still had memories, Moira could have helped her to deal with them. She had let her down and she was ashamed.

Mary Kate was also struggling with it all. The woman in the hospital was the same woman who had neglected a poor defenceless baby, a woman who had put her own addictive needs before an innocent child who needed her protection. This was the woman who had put Abby in danger for the second time.

Liam was sitting beside Norah's bed, holding her hand. He should have known that she was going to do something like this, he felt that he'd let her down. He'd been with her all night and there were times when he thought he had lost her. The doctors had given him little hope that she would survive the fall. She had been found on a ledge halfway down the cliff. It seemed she must have jumped from the car before it went over and that gave him hope, because she hadn't wanted to die, she hadn't meant to leave him. Norah was a strong woman and he was depending on it to get her through.

He stroked her hair that was matted with blood. 'Now you must fight, my darling; you must fight like you've never fought before. If you can't fight for yourself, then fight for us both and for our future. Please don't give up, because I love you and I couldn't bear a life without you. You can do it, my darling, I know you can.'

The next morning, he woke up and looked across at the bed. Norah's eyes were open, not only that but she was smiling at him.

Tears were running down his face as he went to her. She was too fragile to be hugged but he gently kissed her cheek. 'Thank you for coming back to me,' he said.

Norah licked her lips that were cracked and dry. 'I never left you,' she whispered. 'I never left you, my darling.'

Just then there was a tap at the door and a nurse walked in. 'Ah, you're awake, now isn't that grand? I'm sure that your visitor will be pleased too.'

'I don't think that Norah is in any fit state to see anyone,' said Liam.

'Who is it?' said Norah.

'It's a little girl. Her name is Abby, she says she's your daughter.'

'She is here?'

The nurse nodded. 'She's outside, shall I bring her in?'

Norah smiled. 'Yes, please.'

'Are you sure?' said Liam.

'It's my Alice. Alice wants to see me.'

Liam knew that the little girl's name was now Abby, but he didn't correct her because he knew that in Norah's mind, the baby she had given away would always be Alice.

Abby and Eliza came into the room. They stood by the door, staring across at the bed.

'Hello,' said Norah gently.

Eliza stepped forward. 'My name is Eliza Lamb and I am the keeper of Abby's voice. That's why I am here, because I am needed.'

Norah smiled at her. 'It's lovely to meet you, Eliza. Can Abby not speak for herself?'

'No,' said Eliza. 'She's had a shock, you see, but you'd know all about that because you were in the car. Now I didn't know you were in the car because I only saw the bad man and I couldn't save Abby because he punched me in the face.'

'I am so sorry, Eliza, you were very brave.'

'I know,' said Eliza. 'Mammy says I have hidden depths and Mary Kate says I'm a bacon of light.'

'I think you mean beacon,' said Norah, smiling at this lovely young woman. There was something childlike about her that she didn't quite understand. She looked over at Abby, who was still standing by the door. 'Would you come and sit beside me?' she said.

Her daughter nodded and walked over to the bed.

'May I hold your hand, dear? Would that be alright? But you don't have to if you don't want to.'

Abby nodded again and reached across the bed.

Norah wanted to cry but she didn't want to scare her. Abby's hand was so small in hers. She tried to recall that baby hand and the softness of her baby skin, and her heart was breaking.

Eliza cleared her throat. 'Abby wants to say thank you for saving her,' she said. 'That's why we're here. She was worried that you might be a deader before she had a chance to say it.'

Norah and Abby were staring at each other and it felt to Norah as if they were the only two people in the room. 'Do you think that you could speak to me, darling?'

Abby pressed her hand to her mouth. 'Yes,' she said softly.

'Well, would you believe it?' said Eliza, smiling. 'My work here is done, so I'll leave the pair of you to chat.'

'I'll come with you,' said Liam, standing up. 'Is that alright with you, Norah?'

'Yes, my love. Abby and I have a lot of catching up to do.'

After they had left, Norah opened her arms and Abby gently leaned into her.

Norah stroked the silky blonde hair and breathed in the scent of the little girl. Her daughter was breathtakingly beautiful and deserved so much more than she had ever given her. 'I'm sorry,' she whispered. 'I'm so very sorry.'

Abby didn't speak, instead she lifted her hand and stroked her mother's face.

Norah took a deep breath. Oh, to stay like this forever, just the two of them. So many years had passed by, so many years when this lovely child could have been hers. To be given another chance, to love and protect her baby. She closed her eyes and listened to her child's breath against her heart, but she knew that very soon, life would step in and Alice would walk away, back to her other life and her other mother.

She could almost feel the pain of that separation and it was tearing her apart.

Norah hadn't realised that she was crying until she felt a little hand wiping the tears away. She had her baby in her arms again and there was no need for words.

CHAPTER 35

Mary Kate

On a grey windy day, Bridie and Stephen were married in the little church beside the waters of Glendalough, where almost three years before Mary Kate and Sean had made their vows.

They had gathered outside the little church, waiting for Bridie and the girls to arrive. It had been raining all night but as James drove slowly up the drive, a rainbow appeared above the Wicklow Hills.

It had been a simple, beautiful ceremony. The church was packed with friends and pupils from Stephen's school. Not only was the church filled with well-wishers, it was filled with so much love as they all came together to celebrate this very special wedding.

Mary Kate thought that this would be a difficult day for her, but she'd been so wrong. Just looking at the faces of Bridie and Stephen as they promised to love and cherish each other was the most beautiful thing and she was so happy for them both.

James had given Bridie away and Guinness had been Stephen's best man. Abby, in a cornflower blue dress, had been the flower girl, followed down the aisle by Eliza, who wore lemon. Even Guinness was resplendent in a red bow tie around his neck. The girls had taken their duties very seriously, solemnly walking up and down the hall for weeks, holding tea cups in their hands instead of posies.

Bridie had protested that she was too old for a formal wedding gown, but they had taken no notice and marched her off to Clerys, the beautiful department store in the middle of Dublin, where she chose a classic A-line dress in pale ivory. She looked beautiful.

'I can't believe it's me,' she'd said, standing in front of the mirror.

'It's you alright,' said Eliza. 'It's you. Who else would it be?'

Bridie started laughing.

'What's funny?' said Eliza.

'Nothing,' said Bridie. 'Nothing at all.'

Eliza frowned. 'Why were you laughing then, if it wasn't funny?'

'Oh, Eliza,' she said. 'I do love you.'

Eliza had smiled. 'That's alright then.'

After the wedding they returned to the boarding house for a party.

The Christmas tree looked splendid, if a bit lopsided. Not the perfect tree that Sean would have picked but oh, the fun they had choosing it. One evening, in front of a blazing fire, they had gathered in the front room and draped tinsel and baubles over the green branches, even Mrs Lamb had helped, then Moira lifted Abby up so that she could put a fairy on the top.

And now it sparkled in the corner, filling the house with the smell of pine, reminding Mary Kate of that wonderful day in the forest with Sean when they had chosen their own tree and he'd held her in his arms as the snow fell about them. It seemed that the happiest memories were the ones that hurt the most.

The boarding house was full of music and laughter and wonderful food, provided by Mrs Lamb, Emma and Cathy.

In a quiet moment Mary Kate looked around the room at all their friends. There was James's wife Erin and her sister Gerry, who had helped decorate the house when Mary Kate had first bought it. There was Jessie and Aishling, Orla, Colleen, Ashar and little Rosa; even Orla's sister, Polly, had travelled up from Cork to be with them. The staff at Clerys, who had all been so kind to her and Jenny, the sweet young girl, who had made her feel so at ease when she had first visited the solicitors. Back then, she had been a frightened little woman, visiting a lawyer for the first time in her life. Mrs Finn and Duffy were chatting away on the sofa and James was leaning against the marble fireplace, smoking a cigarette.

Each one of them had played a part in this journey of hers, from poverty and loneliness to the boarding house with the red door. She had had no one to care whether she had lived or died but here she was, surrounded by all these wonderful friends.

There was just one beloved face missing – her beloved Sean – and oh, how he would have loved being here with them.

Darling Guinness was stretched out in front of the fire, snoring.

'He must be exhausted,' said Eliza. 'It can't be easy being a best man when you're a dog.'

'I'd say you're right about that, love,' said Mrs Lamb, smiling at her.

Emma put a record on the radiogram and Bridie and Stephen took to the floor. They gazed lovingly into each other's eyes as Frank Sinatra sang 'Young at Heart'.

What a wonderful day it had been. Bridie thought that it couldn't get any better, and then suddenly it did, as Nell clutched her tummy and started moaning. Mary Kate and Moira spent the rest of the night pacing up and down the hospital corridor as if they were the expectant parents and as a pale orange sunrise filled the wintry sky, Nell's son was born.

Eventually a nurse opened the door and beckoned them in.

Nell was sitting up in bed and Emma was beside her. 'Isn't he beautiful?' she said. 'Would you like to hold him?'

Mary Kate carefully took him from Nell's arms. He was staring up at her, his tiny hands worrying at the white towel he was wrapped in. 'Look at him, Moira,' she said. 'He's adorable.'

'He has your eyes, Nell,' said Moira.

Emma held Nell's hand. 'You were so brave, my darling, even though you were in such pain.'

'But wasn't it worth it?' she said, looking across at the baby in Mary Kate's arms. 'For look what I've got.'

'Oh, Nell,' said Mary Kate, kissing her cheek. 'He's adorable.'

'And very smart,' said Moira.

'Have you thought of a name?' said Mary Kate.

'I'm going to call him Bull Gavin,' said Nell, smiling down at her little baby. 'After Daddy.'

Emma, who had stayed by her side throughout the birth, smiled. 'Daddy's real name was William, Nell. Don't you think that's a nicer name?'

'No, Emma, I don't. His name will be Bull Gavin.'

'Welcome to the world, little one,' said Moira.

'And welcome to the Irish Boarding House,' said Mary Kate.

CHAPTER 36

Mary Kate

It was Christmas Eve. Bull Gavin was asleep in his cot by the fire, with Guinness on the floor beside him. This special dog only left him when he absolutely had to and then he was straight back to guarding the baby.

Yes, Nell had insisted that her son be called not only Bull, but Bull Gavin, and no amount of persuading could make her change her mind. His name was Bull Gavin and that was that.

Emma had done her best: 'You can't call him after an animal, Nell, it's not right.'

'What about Cat Forrest down in the village? She's named after an animal, and what about Shrimp Murphy?'

'He wasn't baptised Shrimp,' said Emma. 'It's a nickname his parents gave him because he was on the short side.'

'Well, what about Robin Bolan and Birdie Coogan? They haven't got wings, have they?'

Emma had grinned. 'You win, my darling girl. Bull Gavin it is.'

'Besides,' said Nell, 'Bull is a grand strong name and I think it would make Daddy proud.'

'Then let's hope that he grows up to be a kind, strong man like our daddy.'

'Or a drunk,' said Nell, grinning, which gave them both the giggles.

The name had taken a bit of getting used to but within a few weeks, they couldn't imagine him being called anything else.

Bull Gavin was loved by them all, he only had to make a squeak and someone would pick him up.

'That child will be ruined,' said Mrs Lamb, gently tucking a blanket around him.

'You don't say,' said Mary Kate, smiling.

'Ah, but look at him,' said Mrs Lamb. 'Have you ever seen a finer boy?'

'He's beautiful alright,' said Mary Kate. 'Just like his mammy.'

'Some babies come out a bit on the scrawny side, but Bull Gavin has a good bit of fat on him. Every time I pass the cot, I want to give him a squidge.'

'We all do,' said Mary Kate.

There was no one in the house, apart from herself and Mrs Lamb. The others, at Mary Kate's insistence, had gone into town to see *The Wizard of Oz*.

She was expecting a very special delivery today and only Mrs Lamb was in on the surprise.

'It's a lovely thing you're doing, Mary Kate,' she said.

'Ah sure no, it will benefit us all so there is a bit of selfishness in there as well.'

Mrs Lamb smiled fondly at her. 'You don't have a selfish bone in your body, girl. It would do you no harm if you *were* a bit selfish at times.'

'I have everything I need,' said Mary Kate. 'In fact, I don't know why I hadn't thought of it before.'

It was dark now and the snow was falling like feathers as they all came tumbling into the boarding house, full of the film.

'You should have come with us, Mary Kate,' said Moira. 'It was wonderful.'

'I liked the scarecrow best,' said Eliza. 'That wicked witch was an awful baggage. She tried to set fire to him and him made of straw, me heart was in me mouth.'

Abby still didn't talk much and there were times when Eliza had to step in. 'Which bit did you like, Abby?' said Mary Kate.

Abby didn't speak.

'You don't have to tell us, darling,' said Moira.

Abby put her hand over her mouth, which had become a habit when she wanted to say something.

'Take your time, love,' said Moira.

'I, I liked the lion, because he wasn't very brave but then the Wizard gave him a medal for bravery and he was as brave as Eliza.'

'I don't mind being a lion, Abby,' said Eliza.

They were still all standing in the hallway.

'All we need now,' said Cathy, 'is a good warm by the fire.'

'Not yet,' said Mary Kate.

'But we're frozen,' said Nell.

'I want you all to go upstairs and put on your best clothes,' said Mary Kate, smiling at them.

'Is it a surprise?' said Eliza. 'I like surprises, don't I, Mammy? Don't I like surprises?'

'You do, Eliza,' said Mrs Lamb. 'But right now, you must do as Mary Kate says and put on your best clothes.'

The girls ran upstairs.

'Me too?' said Moira.

'Definitely you too,' said Mary Kate, grinning.

'Now, what are you up to, Mary Kate Barry?'

'You'll see soon enough, Moira Kent.'

Mrs Lamb and Mary Kate sat on the stairs waiting for them.

'My stomach feels like it's full of frogs,' said Mrs Lamb. 'I can't wait for her to see it. Isn't life just wonderful sometimes?'

Mary Kate smiled at her. 'It is, isn't it?' she said.

Eventually they came down the staircase. 'You all look wonderful,' said Mary Kate.

Once they were all there, Mary Kate opened the door. 'You go first, Moira,' she said, holding her hand.

One by one, they stepped through the door. The lights from the tree shone out across the room and in the corner, wrapped in a big red bow, stood a beautiful grand piano. There wasn't a sound as Moira walked over and sat down; she lifted the lid and stroked the keys. There were tears running down her face as she turned and looked at Mary Kate.

Mary Kate smiled at her. 'Happy Christmas, my dear friend, happy Christmas.'

Moira wiped her eyes, placed her fingers on the keys and began playing, Tchaikovsky's *Romeo and Juliet*.

The fire blazed away in the hearth as they sang carols, accompanied by Moira on the piano, and as the snow covered Merrion Square, and the Christmas bells rang out across the city, Mary Kate felt blessed.

CHAPTER 37

Megan

Megan Jones looked nervously at her watch: the train should have pulled out ten minutes ago. She held Charlotte closer. What if they were caught now after all the planning? She lifted Charlotte off her lap and sat her on the seat, then she pulled down the window and peered anxiously along the platform.

She was mad to have left from Paddington station, it was the first place they'd look. She should have caught the bus and put a few more miles between her and the Schwartzes. The station was teeming with people; she rubbed her glasses on the sleeve of her coat and strained to see if there were any police among them.

Satisfied that there weren't, she shut the window firmly and lifted Charlotte back onto her lap. Charlotte immediately snuggled into her and Megan's eyes filled with tears of pure love. She touched the honey-coloured hair – such an unusual colour, she'd thought the first time she'd seen it. Perhaps it would be best to dye it, just till the heat died down. Yes, she'd do that as soon as they were settled. Megan looked at the two cases on the rack in front of her, hers packed hurriedly and Charlotte's more slowly over the last three months. Things that wouldn't be missed but special things that Charlotte loved, her favourite blanket and the soft brightly coloured ball that Megan had given her for her first birthday. She looked down at Charlotte, whose eyes were now closed. She looked so contented and peaceful, it was obvious to Megan that she didn't miss the Schwartzes at all. She, Megan Jones, a childless spinster, was Charlotte's mummy now and she'd never let her down or put her into the care of strangers.

Satisfied that she was doing the right thing, she closed her eyes and let her mind drift back to the Rhondda Valley and home.

Megan had been an only child, born unexpectedly late in life to Gareth and Bronwyn Jones, almost an embarrassment to the fiercely religious couple. Megan felt that her mother never quite forgave her husband for thrusting this unwanted child upon them.

There seemed to have been no colour in Megan's childhood home, a narrow miners' cottage perched on the slopes of the Rhondda Valley. It was always cold, battered by the biting winds that seeped into every crack and through every window frame; her own room at the top of the house seeming to catch most of it. Yet it was in this room that Megan dreamed of a life beyond the valleys to a place of pinks and blues and yellows, the sort of place she saw on the screen of the tiny cinema in the town.

She knew that other children found her odd and she had no friends. She was a plain child, with an almost permanently anxious look on her face, dressed in clothes that her mother had cut down from her own.

She drifted through school, overlooked by children and teachers alike, excelling only at needlework, where her quiet patience produced beautiful pieces of work. Her one friend was

Mrs Davies, the needlework teacher, who brought her in pieces of brightly coloured material that Megan made into a quilt for her bed. It was the one piece of colour in the house, looking almost obscene against the browns and greys.

Megan left school at fifteen and went to work in the local council office. She hated it but it got her out of the house and she could put bits of money away into a savings account for the day she would leave but the days turned into years and she was still there. Her father died and she had to care for her mother, who whined and nagged until she drew her last breath.

When the last of the mourners had left the house, Megan sat alone in the kitchen, then she picked up her case which contained a few clothes and her beloved quilt. Without a backward glance, she left the Rhondda Valley as quietly as she'd entered it.

She caught the train to Cardiff and from there to London. She wasn't frightened – she had waited all her life for this moment and she had left nothing behind that mattered to her.

The first thing she did when she arrived was to buy a paper, then she found a small café and over a cup of steaming hot coffee, she scoured the pages of situations vacant and there it was, between 'Night Club Hostess' and 'Garage attendant'. *Home help wanted, live in. Own room in beautiful house. Tel Knightsbridge 721487.* The couple were called Mr and Mrs Schwartz, and they were American. They sounded to Megan like the heroes and heroines of the films she had watched in the little cinema so many years before. Megan was just what the Schwartzes were looking for: plain as a pikestaff and no chance of any gentlemen callers. They hired her there and then.

The Schwartzes also employed a cook, a couple of maids and a chauffeur. Megan was informed that her job would be to take care of Charlotte, who was eight months old and beautiful – it was love at first sight. She was well paid and was at last able to dress better. Her employers began to wonder if Megan would suddenly become attractive to the opposite sex but they had no need to worry – Megan only had eyes for Charlotte and Charlotte only had eyes for Megan. The pair were inseparable, and Megan felt loved for the first time in her life.

Then came the news that shattered Megan's happy existence: Mr Schwartz was being called back to America to head a new advertising company and Megan wasn't asked to go with them. Mrs Schwartz didn't think that the plain little Welshwoman would fit into the sophisticated lifestyle of New York. She was given three months' notice and a large bonus in appreciation of her wonderful care of Charlotte.

Megan was grief-stricken and unrealistically begged them not to go. She embarrassed them with her tears and pleas, and they wished they had given her shorter notice.

Megan demanded to know who would take over the care of Charlotte and Mrs Schwartz, whose patience was wearing thin, told her that was not Megan's concern – they would find someone.

Megan went to Charlotte and held her close, her tears falling on the honey-coloured hair. She couldn't bear the thought of Charlotte being put into the care of a stranger. It was then that Megan made the decision: she would steal Charlotte and run away, they would start a new life together. Charlotte was Megan's whole world, and she wasn't going to let her go.

She began to make plans; the most important thing was to get out of London. She wouldn't go back to Wales, that's the first place they'd look. Megan's favourite film of all time was *The Quiet Man* starring John Wayne and Maureen O'Hara. It was set in Ireland and she'd fallen in love with the beautiful scenery and its gentle people. They would be taking the night sailing.

Suddenly a whistle blew, and doors were being slammed. Megan opened her eyes as Charlotte stirred in her lap. 'We've done it,' she whispered in her ear. 'From now on, it's just you and me, my beautiful girl.'

Luckily, Charlotte slept most of the way, but Megan stayed awake. She had come too far to let her guard down now. Any minute, the train could come to a halt, and police would be searching the carriages looking for Charlotte. She had to stay alert, even though she was exhausted; she wouldn't rest until they were sailing towards Ireland and safety.

It was crowded on the boat as everyone was going home for the Christmas holidays. Most of the men were rolling drunk, singing rebel songs at the tops of their voices and staggering all over the place. They were bumping into her and she was worried that Charlotte might come to harm.

She picked up her case and went outside but the freezing cold wind took her breath away. She didn't want to go back inside but she couldn't stay out here either.

'Are you lost, love?'

Megan looked up at the young sailor. 'I need to find somewhere warm for the night,' she said. 'You see, I can't go back in there.'

The sailor smiled at her. 'I'd say there'll be some sore heads in the morning, but sure, there's no harm in them.'

'Of course not,' said Megan, wrapping her coat closer around Charlotte. 'It's just that...'

'Follow me,' said the sailor, picking up her case.

Megan followed him down two staircases and along a corridor. He stopped outside a door and beckoned her inside.

'I'm on nights,' he said, 'so I won't be using the cabin – you're very welcome to it if you don't mind the mess.' He opened a cupboard and handed her a blanket. 'This is clean, and it will keep you warm.'

'You've been so kind,' said Megan.

'You remind me of my mammy,' he said, grinning. 'And a

good Irish boy would never see his mammy without a bed for the night. Now sleep well – I'll give you a shout in the morning.'

Cuddled up under the blanket, they slept right through the night and Megan only stirred when the sailor tapped on the door and came into the cabin.

'We're coming into Dun Laoghaire,' he said. 'Did you sleep well?'

'We did and I can't thank you enough,' said Megan. 'Can I ask your name?'

'Eddie,' he said. 'After the daddy.'

'Well, your mother would be very proud of you this day. By the way, my name is Theresa.'

'Then I wish you both well, Theresa.'

She felt quite proud of herself for thinking so fast. No one was looking for a woman called Theresa, were they?

The quayside was crowded with people, welcoming the travellers home. There would be no welcome for her and Charlotte but as long as they had each other, nothing else mattered.

She had decided on Dublin, a city big enough to get lost in. What she hadn't taken into account was that it was Christmas Day: nowhere would be open and the boarding houses would probably be full of visitors, but she'd cross that bridge when she got to it. The hardest part was behind them, and it was time to look forward.

'We can do this, Charlotte,' she said, as she picked up her case and headed for the bus station.

CHAPTER 38

Mary Kate

It was Christmas Day and the bells were ringing out across the city. A wreath of holly hung on the red door and everywhere smelled of pine and the mouth-watering aroma of turkey, wafting up from the kitchen.

Emma and Cathy had been up since the crack of dawn, helping Mrs Lamb with the dinner, while Nell, Eliza and Abby had spent the morning decorating the dining room table. They had put so much foliage on it that there was barely any room left for the plates. The house was full of laughter and music and Mary Kate felt blessed.

'Mary Kate,' said Moira, 'has it occurred to you that most of the boarding houses in Dublin will be empty?'

Mary Kate frowned. 'Now why would they be empty? Sure, it's Christmas Day.'

'Exactly, and the majority of guests will have gone home to celebrate with their families.'

Mary Kate smiled. 'I hadn't thought of that.'

'It seems that it has been the homeless who have found their way to our door.'

'Then aren't we the lucky ones, Moira Kent?'

'We are, Mary Kate Barry.'

Bull Gavin was happily sucking away on a blue dummy, surrounded by so many soft toys that there was hardly room in the cot for himself.

As the morning went on, more of their friends turned up. James and his wife Erin had collected Mrs Finn from Tanners Row to join them for this Christmas Day. Jessie and Aishling arrived, followed by Orla and her lovely fiancé, Donal. The boarding house was bursting at the seams and it was exactly as it should be.

Mary Kate hoped that her beloved grandparents were looking down on her this day and could see her now, surrounded by so many good friends and so much love. She knew that this was what they had wanted for her – not fame or fortune, or fancy clothes, but happiness and peace and love.

She could almost hear her grandfather's voice: 'Red-letter days, Mary Kate. Didn't I tell you that they were just around the corner?' *And you were right, Grandaddy*, she thought. *You were so right.*

'I hope you don't mind, Mary Kate,' said Emma. 'I've said that Rooney can come round this evening.'

'Of course he can, it will be grand to see him. Why didn't you invite him for dinner?'

'Because he has to look after his mammy, but a neighbour has offered to stay with her tonight.'

Mary Kate had noticed that Emma and Rooney had been spending a lot of time together. The weather had been too bad for gardening and so Rooney had been doing odd jobs around the house. Rooney whistled a lot, so you would always know which part of the house he was working in. He was a lovely feller and it pleased Mary Kate to see Emma so happy. She had been like a mother to Nell for almost all her life and she deserved some happiness of her own. Nell didn't rely on her so much these days, for she had found friendships with Abby and Eliza.

These days, Nell hardly mentioned her home or her beloved hillside, which gave Mary Kate hope that she was happy here in the boarding house with her friends and of course baby Bull Gavin, who she adored.

Just then, Eliza came bursting into the front room. 'It's snowing, Mary Kate,' she said.

'Isn't that wonderful?'

'It is, Eliza, it really is,' said Mary Kate.

'Oh, and Mammy said the dinner's ready, so could we all help to bring the dishes up.' As she was about to leave the room, she turned back: 'Imagine that, snow on Christmas Day.'

'Imagine,' said Mary Kate, smiling.

Dish after dish of steaming hot food were brought up from the kitchen and placed on the table.

'Now, girls,' said Mrs Lamb, 'would you be kind enough to put this lovely greenery on the dresser which is rather bare and deserves jollying up, just like the table.'

'Of course we can, Mammy,' said Eliza. 'We can do that, can't we, girls? We can put the greenery on the dresser?'

Abby did her usual eye-rolling but she smiled. 'Of course we can, Eliza,' she said.

'Now,' said Mary Kate, 'who will say grace for us?'

Eliza's hand went up immediately.

'Anyone else?' said Moira. 'Would you like to, Abby?'

Abby shook her head.

'Right then, Eliza,' said Mary Kate. 'And thank you, dear.'

Eliza joined her hands in prayer and bowed her head and everyone else did the same.

'Dear Lord Jesus, thank you for our dinner, which I'm sure will be very nice. We haven't eaten it yet but Mammy is a grand cook, and even if it's rotten, it was very kind of Mammy to cook it for us.'

'Very nice, Eliza,' said Mrs Lamb. 'Now, let us all tuck in before it gets cold.'

'I haven't finished yet, Mammy.'

'Be quick then, love,' she said, smiling at everyone.

Eliza cleared her throat and started again: 'Dear Lord Jesus, thank you for making Bull Gavin, because we all love him very much. Amen.'

'Amen,' said everyone.

The food was delicious and the company perfect. They ate, they drank, they pulled crackers and told silly jokes.

Guinness was lying beside Bull Gavin's cot. Nell had fed the baby and despite all the noise, he was fast asleep. Guinness knew that he wasn't allowed to beg for food but was gratefully accepting any titbits that came his way.

Jessie tapped her glass: 'Aishling and I have some news,' she said.

'Is it exciting?' said Eliza.

Jessie grinned. 'We'll let you be the judge of that, but we think it is.'

'Do tell us,' said Mrs Finn.

'Well, as you know, there's a small café next to our bookshop and now it's up for sale.'

'You want to buy it?' said James.

'We've already put in an offer that's been accepted.'

'Well, anything I can do,' said James.

'Thank you,' said Aishling. 'We were going to ask you.'

'Whenever you're ready,' said James.

'So, are you thinking of running the café as well?' said Mary Kate.

'What we'd like to do,' said Jessie, 'is knock down the wall and have a bookshop-cum- café. It's a dream that Aishling and I have had for a long time and when the café came up for sale, we didn't think twice about buying it.'

'It sounds wonderful,' said Erin.

'And not just that,' said Aishling. 'We want to open up in the evenings and have live music and poetry readings.'

'Books, buns, poetry and music,' said Moira. 'The perfect combination.'

'And I think you're on to a winner,' said James.

'Do you think so?' said Aishling.

'Definitely. It's an exciting project.'

'And you've kept all this to yourselves?' said Mary Kate.

'We had to make sure we got the café before telling you all.'

'The only downside,' said Jessie, grinning, 'is that neither of us can cook.'

'I'm sure you'll have no trouble finding a cook,' said Orla.

'Cathy can cook,' said Mary Kate. 'Not only can she cook, but she worked in a library.'

'What do you think, Cathy?' said Jessie.

Cathy placed her hand on her tummy. 'I'm not sure I can. I mean, I'd love to but I'll have a baby to look after.'

'There's a flat over the top, Cathy, and we'd rather you were in it than strangers.'

'There's enough of us to help out,' said Mary Kate. 'I think it would be a wonderful opportunity for you.'

'Do you think I could?'

'Of course you could, and it will be a great chance for you to meet new people.'

'I could help with the baby,' said Eliza. 'Couldn't I, Mammy? I could wheel it out, like I wheel Bull Gavin out, and I know how to change a nappy. I couldn't feed it though because I don't have milk in my titties.'

As everyone at the table convulsed with laughter, the door-bell rang and Guinness started barking.

Mary Kate stood up and looked out of the window. 'Well, it's not carol singers,' she said.

'I'll get it,' said Moira.

'I'm up now,' said Mary Kate. 'You eat your pudding.'

Mary Kate went into the hallway and opened the door to see a small, anxious woman looking up at her. 'Can I help you, dear?' she said.

'I'm looking for lodgings, missus,' said Megan. 'A small room would do. I've been walking around all day, but I haven't found anything suitable and then I saw an advertisement for this place.'

The poor woman looked desperate and even if there hadn't been a vacancy, Mary Kate would have made her up a bed in the airing cupboard.

'How long were you wanting it for?'

'Umm, forever?'

Mary Kate smiled. 'You've come at the right time, for one of our guests has moved out so the room is vacant and you are very welcome to it.'

'Really?' said Megan.

'If you would like it.'

'Oh, I would,' said Megan, 'but...'

'But what, dear?'

'Would you take Charlotte as well?'

Mary Kate stroked Charlotte's beautiful fair hair. 'How could I resist? She's beautiful.'

Megan's eyes filled with tears. 'You'll take us both then?'

Mary Kate smiled at her. 'Of course, now let's get you warm, but first, come and meet our residents and friends.'

'I don't want to be a bother,' said Megan.

'It's no bother,' said Mary Kate, taking her case. 'What is your name, dear?'

'Megan,' she said. 'Megan Jones.'

Mary Kate took Megan into the dining room. 'We have a new guest,' she said. 'Let me introduce you to Megan Jones and her beautiful little dog, Charlotte.'

CHAPTER 39

Mary Kate

The bookshop and café were completed and everyone from the boarding house had been there to watch Jessie and Aishling cut the ribbon. Cathy's baby was due in two months and she wasn't able to work there yet – Mary Kate and Moira wanted her in the boarding house where they could take care of her.

Having chatted about it, Mrs Lamb volunteered to run the café, while Cathy and Emma took over the kitchen in the boarding house.

Eliza wasn't so happy about it. 'Does that mean me and my mammy have to sleep there? I don't want to sleep there. I want to sleep here with my friends and who's going to wheel Bull Gavin out? I'm not sure about all this at all.'

'Don't you worry, Eliza,' said Mary Kate. 'Once the shop has closed, your mammy will come home every evening.'

'But how will she get home? I don't want her walking through the park, bad things happen in that park.'

'I shall arrange for a taxi to pick her up.'

'Can I help her with the washing up? Mammy says I'm

good at washing up, I've only smashed a few glasses. Then she wouldn't have to come home on her own.'

'Would you like to?'

Eliza nodded. 'I need to look after my mammy.'

'Well, I think that is a wonderful idea and very thoughtful.'

'I know my proper job is to take Abby to school and bring her home, but I'd be too feared to do that again.'

All their concern had been for Abby on that awful night and in the midst of it all, Eliza had been forgotten. Mary Kate now saw, to her shame, that it had affected Eliza more than they had realised and she felt she had let her down. 'Come into my room, Eliza,' she said. 'I think it's time that you and I had a little chat.'

'What are we going to chat about?'

'This and that,' said Mary Kate, smiling.

As they opened the door, Guinness and Charlotte, who were lying beside Bull Gavin, thumped their tails on the carpet but didn't bother looking up. The two dogs had taken to each other from the moment they met. Mary Kate had worried that Guinness might have been jealous of this new addition to the house, but they loved each other and Charlotte followed Guinness everywhere. Megan now walked the pair of them every day.

Mary Kate had always known that this boarding house was special; she knew because of all the rotten ones she had stayed in. No matter who came through the red door, they became part of the family, and she knew this was unusual but she didn't question it. When she decided to buy the wreck of the building, this was exactly the sort of boarding house that she had wanted. Everyone deserved to have warmth and comfort in their lives. A safe place to lay their head, among people who cared about them.

'So, what shall we chat about?' said Eliza, cuddling up on the couch.

'I thought we could talk about the night that Abby went missing. If you don't want to, we shall talk about something else, but I get the feeling that you are still worrying about it.'

'I do get scared at night when it's dark, sometimes I have to go into Mammy's bed.'

'And what does your mammy say about it?'

'She says I don't need to be scared anymore because yer man fell down the cliff and he won't be climbing up again.'

'Did she tell you that he was dead, Eliza?' said Moira gently.

'Mammy said he was diseased but people get better, don't they? He could still come back when he's better.'

Mary Kate smiled. 'I think that your mammy probably said he was deceased, Eliza. And that means he's dead and he won't ever be coming back, not ever again, so you can stop worrying, OK?'

'He's never coming back?'

'That's right, my love, he's never coming back.'

'Well, I'm glad about that, but...'

'Is something else worrying you?'

Eliza sighed. 'I didn't save Abby.'

Mary Kate went across and sat down next to Eliza. 'But you couldn't, could you? Because that man was much bigger than you. Most people would have run for their lives, but you stayed, and you tried your very best to save her. What you did that day was the stuff of heroes. By rights we should have been down on our knees thanking you.'

Eliza's eyes filled with tears. 'I've never been a hero before.'

'You have always been a hero, Eliza. Not every hero wears a cape.'

'But I'm still not rolling Bull Gavin round the park, you can never be sure with deaders.'

'Darling Eliza,' said Mary Kate, 'people don't come back from the dead.'

Eliza got up and as she was about to leave the room she turned around. 'Jesus did,' she said.

Moira was coming in as Eliza was going out. 'Jesus did what?' she said, grinning.

'Came back from the dead,' said Mary Kate.

'And?'

'I feel we've let her down.'

'Both of us?'

'All of us. Not intentionally, but when Abby went missing, we were out of our minds with worry. We were terrified, of course we were. And when she was found, we cared for her, we gave her space to talk about her feelings.'

'But she wasn't able to.'

'But we tried,' said Mary Kate.

'And Eliza got forgotten?'

Mary Kate nodded. 'All this time she thought that "the bad man" as she calls him was still alive and will come back and get her and Abby.'

'Has no one told her that he's dead?'

'Mrs Lamb told her that he was deceased, but poor Eliza thought she meant that he was diseased and that he would get better. That's why she only wheels Bull Gavin round the square. She gets so scared at night that she sometimes sleeps with Mrs Lamb.'

Moira shook her head. 'I feel terrible. All my thoughts were of Abby and I suppose I gave very little thought to what Eliza had gone through.'

'Neither of us did.'

'So that's what you've been talking about?'

Mary Kate nodded. 'I told her that people don't come back from the dead.'

Moira grinned. 'But Jesus did.'

And only Eliza could have thought of it. 'So, we need to keep an eye on her and help her where we can.'

'Of course we will,' said Moira. 'Now is there anything else we should be worrying about?'

'Have you noticed something odd about Megan?'

Moira lifted her eyes to the ceiling. 'Not again, Mary Kate.'

Mary Kate laughed.

'So, what's odd about her?' said Moira.

'I've watched her walking the dogs.'

'And is that a crime?'

'Well, no, but she was acting very strangely.'

'In what way?'

'Looking around her all the time, as if she thought that she was being followed.'

'She's a nervous little thing alright.'

'A couple of days ago, a guard was crossing the square and she actually hid behind a tree.'

'Really?' said Moira.

'Really,' said Mary Kate. 'I think she might be on the run.'

Moira laughed. 'Megan Jones, on the run?'

'Well, what else could it be? She's not even from Ireland, unless someone followed her here.'

'Well, if Megan Jones were in a line-up, she's the last person I'd pick out.'

'I agree, Moira, but something's not right. Do you think that I should say something?'

'You might be opening a can of worms.'

'I might, but if she's scared, she might need our help.'

Moira sighed. 'Well, what do you propose we do about it?'

'I think we should come right out and ask her.'

'Wouldn't it be better if she came to us?'

'Of course it would,' said Mary Kate. 'But if she's running away from something, she's hardly going to tell us.'

'Why don't we join her on her walks? The exercise would do us no harm.'

'That's a great idea. We could watch and observe.'

'Listen to yourself, Mary Kate Barry, you sound like Sherlock Holmes. I've told you before, this ought to be a detective agency, not a boarding house.'

Mary Kate laughed. 'I think that maybe I like solving puzzles.'

The next morning, when Megan came into the front room to collect the dogs, Moira and Mary Kate were all ready.

'Would you mind if we joined you this morning?' said Mary Kate, smiling.

'I'd be glad of the company, Mrs Barry, you never know who you might come across out there.'

Guinness and Charlotte were already pawing at the door. 'Well, these two are raring to go,' said Moira.

It was a perfect spring day as they set off across Merrion Square. The sky was a clear blue and snowdrops were scattered across the grass. 'I love spring,' said Moira.

'Was there somewhere nice to walk Charlotte when you lived in London?' said Mary Kate.

'There was a lovely park,' said Megan. 'We went there every day. Charlotte loved her walks and she was so good, she never ran off.'

'She's a lovely dog,' said Mary Kate. 'You must be very proud of her.'

'Oh, I am,' said Megan. 'I don't know what I would do without her. I love her very much.'

'And it's very obvious that she loves you too,' said Moira.

'I'm very lucky,' said Megan.

'That's how I feel about Guinness,' said Mary Kate, smiling. 'He was a stray when I first saw him and he seemed to take to me.'

'Just like Charlotte,' said Megan.

'Was Charlotte a stray too?'

Megan ignored the question. 'How old is Guinness?'

'Like I said, he was a stray and he wasn't a puppy then. I just hope that we have him for a good while yet.'

'Oh, I'm sure you will, he's as lively as a puppy.'

'It's such a lovely day,' said Moira. 'Why don't we take a walk to the park? We could wander through the woods, the daffodils will be beautiful.'

Megan stopped walking. 'I'd rather not if you don't mind,' she replied. 'I'm not feeling so well. I think I'll just go on home.'

'I'll go with you, Megan. Do you mind walking the dogs on your own, Moira?'

'No, I'm enjoying the fresh air.'

'I have to bring Charlotte with me,' said Megan.

'I'm sure that Moira will take very good care of her.'

'She doesn't like to be parted from me.'

As far as Mary Kate could see, Charlotte looked quite happy to stay with Moira and Guinness, but she didn't say anything.

They didn't speak as they walked back to the boarding house. Charlotte kept stopping and looking back at Guinness, which made Mary Kate feel sad.

They went into the front room and sat down.

'What can I do to help you, Megan?'

'Why do you think I need help?'

The morning sunlight streamed through the long windows and across the room, showing up the dust on the surface of the piano. 'I think I need to get the polish out,' said Mary Kate.

'No one can help me,' said Megan suddenly.

'Perhaps if you could tell me what's wrong, dear. I've found that it helps to share things, even difficult things.'

Megan put her head in her hands and started crying. 'I'm a thief, Mrs Barry.'

Mary Kate frowned. This was the last thing she had

expected to hear. 'But I can see that you are sorry for whatever you have done.'

Megan looked up. 'I'm not, I'm not sorry at all and I'd do it again, I would, I'd do it again.'

Mary Kate was very confused now. 'Was it money you took, dear? Because you needed it?'

'No, it wasn't money, I would never steal money, but I took something that wasn't mine to take.'

'Are you able to tell me what it was?'

'I don't know.'

'Whatever you tell me will go no further than these four walls.'

'And you won't call the police?'

'No, Megan. I assure you that I won't call the police.'

'It was a dog.'

'A dog?'

Megan nodded.

'You stole Charlotte?'

'I did and if you want me to leave, I'll go.'

'I don't want you to leave, Megan, but I *would* like to understand what made you do it.'

Just then, Guinness tumbled into the room followed by Moira. 'You were right about the daffodils, Mary Kate, they are splendid.' Moira sensed a tension in the room. 'Am I interrupting something? Shall I leave you alone?'

'We're just having a little chat, but a cup of tea would be very welcome.'

'That I can do.'

'How would you feel about Moira listening to your story, Megan? Because we have a habit of sorting things out and it would really help me.'

Megan nodded. 'I trust the both of you, so yes, that will be alright.'

Once Moira was back with the tea, she joined them on the

sofa and listened as Megan told her story. By the end of it they all had tears in their eyes.

'You see,' said Megan, 'I was the only one who gave her any attention, I was the only one who loved her, no one else was interested. I couldn't understand why they even had a dog.'

'I would have stolen her too,' said Moira. 'They sound awful.'

'But what I did was wrong, wasn't it?'

'Yes, it was wrong, Megan,' said Mary Kate. 'But sometimes people do the wrong things for the right reasons.'

'So, does that make it alright? Can I stop worrying?'

'I'd say that it was morally right, dear,' said Moira. 'But in the eyes of the law, I'm afraid it was illegal.'

'So, what am I to do? Please don't tell me to give her back.'

'We need advice and I know just the person to go to. His name is James Renson and not only is he a brilliant solicitor, he is also my very dear friend.'

'And he won't turn me in?'

'He definitely won't turn you in. I'll ring him now and see when he can see us.'

CHAPTER 40

Mary Kate

After James had listened to Megan explaining what she had done and why, he sat back in his chair and smiled at her. 'That is a very poignant story, Mrs Jones, and thank you for sharing it with me. You have nothing to fear by telling me this. Everything within these four walls is sacrosanct. It will go no further unless you want it to and I am not here to judge.'

Megan had been crying since the moment herself and Mary Kate had walked into the building.

Jenny, who was sitting behind the reception desk, made them both a cup of tea. 'You have nothing to worry about,' she said. 'Mr Renson isn't a bit scary, is he, Mary Kate?'

'I remember the first time I came through these doors,' said Mary Kate. 'I felt like an imposter – my clothes were all wrong, my shoes were scuffed and my hair looked like a burst mattress. I thought that any minute someone was going to take me by the scruff of my neck and throw me back into the street where I belonged, but Jenny made me feel like a proper lady and Mr Renson couldn't have been kinder. He's a gentleman, Megan.'

'You could have turned up here wearing an old sack and you would still have been a lady,' said Jenny.

And now James was stroking his chin, which he had a habit of doing when he was thinking.

'From everything you've told me, Mrs Jones, your bosses seemed to have had very little to do with the dog. They might even be relieved that they didn't have to take her to New York and go about finding someone to look after her. Now, if they had been devoted to her and were heartbroken at losing her, this would be a different story altogether and I would be advising you to return her to her rightful owners.'

'But I can't do that, Mr Renson. I won't do that.'

'I'm not suggesting that you do. I think that the little dog will have a much better life with you than she could ever have with Mr and Mrs Schwartz.'

'Oh, thank you, Mr Renson.'

'But that doesn't change the fact that a crime has been committed here, albeit a crime of passion, for that is what it is. A crime motivated by love.'

'So, is there anything we can do, James?' said Mary Kate.

'Oh yes, it will just need a bit of thought and a drop of skulduggery.'

Mary Kate grinned. 'Sounds interesting.'

'Well, the first thing we must do, Mrs Jones, is to give you some peace of mind. This has to be resolved but not, I'm afraid, by me.'

'I don't understand, James,' said Mary Kate. 'We don't know anyone else who can help us.'

'But I do. When your mother, Agnes Ryan, first came to me, I couldn't understand how she knew that I was your solicitor. She lived in London and yet she tracked me down. I found out that she had the help of a solicitor by the name of Francis Mallery, who in the words of your mother was the dodgiest solicitor in London. Your mother gave me his details in case I ever needed him. Until this moment I doubted very much that I ever would but he's the only one I know who can help us with this rather delicate situation.'

'But why can't you deal with it, James?' said Mary Kate. 'I don't much like the sound of yer man.'

'Well, you see, if I started making enquiries into the whereabouts of the Schwartzes, they would know immediately that I am a solicitor with offices in Dublin and we don't want that, do we?'

'Oh no, Mr Renson,' said Megan, quickly, 'we don't want that.'

'So, with your permission, I shall contact Mr Mallery and see if he can locate the people you worked for.'

'And then what?' said Mary Kate.

'Well then, we offer to buy the dog.'

'But how much will that cost, Mr Renson?' I'm afraid I'm not a wealthy woman.'

'Don't you worry your head about that, Mrs Jones. You see, we have a special fund for people like yourself.'

'Oh, Mr Renson,' said Megan, 'you are a wonderful man. I have never met such a wonderful man. How can I ever thank you for your kindness?'

'My thanks will be to see you and your little dog happy.'

'You're very kind.'

Just then, there was a tap on the door and Jenny came in, carrying a tray of tea and biscuits.

'You must have read my thoughts, Jenny,' said James. 'This is just what we need.'

'I'm glad,' said Jenny, going out.

James smiled at Megan. 'I note that you have a very lovely Welsh accent. Can I ask which part of Wales you are from?'

'I'm from the Rhondda but I left to go to London.'

'And do you have family there?'

'My parents are dead.'

'And they had a house?'

'Yes, my mother grew up in that house and so did my grand-parents, but I never liked it. I left after my mother's funeral.'

'You just left?'

Megan nodded. 'I couldn't get away quick enough.'

'What about the house?'

'I suppose it's still there. I've never been back, I don't ever want to go back.'

'I'm not prying, Mrs Jones, but did your parents own the house or was it rented?'

'I'm afraid I don't know.'

'Did you ever see a rent book?'

'No.'

'And were you ever sent out to pay the rent? Or do you remember a rent man calling to the house?'

'I don't think so, Mr Renson, not that I can recall anyway.'

'Would you mind if I looked into this? Because if they owned the house, then the house is still yours and could be sold, which would give you a nice little nest egg.'

'Really?' said Megan.

'It's certainly worth finding out, don't you think?'

'I had a good pay-off from the Schwartzes but it's running out. I have to find a job.'

'Well, Mrs Jones, if you could leave details of the house with Jenny, I will find out what I can.'

Megan's eyes filled with tears. 'You would do that for me?'

'If I can be of assistance to a friend of Mary Kate Barry, it will be a pleasure and I will do all I can to help.'

James stood up and shook Megan's hand. 'It has been an absolute pleasure to meet you, Mrs Jones, and hopefully we can get you some peace of mind. May I say that it was very brave of you to leave Wales and travel to London on your own.'

'If I hadn't left, I wouldn't have met Charlotte.'

James smiled at this lovely woman. 'Then it was meant to be, wasn't it? Now, leave everything to me and I will contact you when I have some news. Oh, and Mary Kate?'

'Yes?'

'There is something I want to run past you.'

'Megan,' said Mary Kate, 'why don't you give those house details to Jenny while I have a chat with Mr Renson?'

Mary Kate held the door for Megan, then turned to James.

'You have a vacant house in Tanners Row, at least you will have,' said James.

'Oh no, who's died?'

'No one has died, Mary Kate. Mrs O'Keefe is going to live with her daughter and grandchildren in America. It's where your cottage used to be.'

'Next door to Mrs Finn?'

He nodded. 'So, what do you want to do with it?'

'I do have an idea.'

James grinned. 'Megan Jones?'

'Are you a mind reader now, James Renson?'

'I am when it comes to you, Mary Kate Barry.'

She grinned. 'But I think we must sort little Charlotte out first.'

'And we will. I mean, what could go wrong? We're dealing with the dodgiest solicitor in London.'

Mary Kate laughed. 'Thank you for helping, James. Please give my love to Erin.'

'I'll be in touch, Mary Kate.'

'Oh, he's lovely, isn't he?' said Megan as they left the building. 'I can't believe he's doing all this for me when I'm a nothing but a stranger to him.'

'I don't know what I would have done without him in my

life,' said Mary Kate. 'He's always been there for me, no matter what I've needed. I've been lucky.'

'So have I,' said Megan. 'I could have walked into any boarding house in Dublin, but I walked into yours.'

Mary Kate smiled at her. 'Let's go and visit Mrs Finn. I noticed that the pair of you were getting on fine at Christmas. She's bound to have the kettle on.'

'That would be lovely.'

'Walk or bus?'

'Shall we walk? I'm still trying to find my way around Dublin.'

'You seem so much happier in yourself, Megan, and it's nice to see.'

'Your Mr Renson has put my mind at rest and he didn't even look shocked when I told him that I was a thief.'

'Well, you didn't exactly rob the bank of England. You did what your heart told you to do and I for one am a great believer in following your heart.'

'And you have a big heart,' said Megan.

'As you have yourself,' said Mary Kate.

The sun was warm on their backs as they walked through the park, past Clerys and on to Tanners Row. Mary Kate stopped at the bottom of the lane. 'This is where I grew up,' she said.

'In these lovely houses?' said Megan.

'Oh, they weren't lovely back then, in fact they were falling down. No water or electric, no toilet, just a bucket behind a curtain. Times were hard but sure we were happy enough. You don't hanker after something you've never had and besides, everyone was in the same boat. They were happy times, Megan. I was loved, clothed and fed, what more could I want?'

'What more indeed?' said Megan, smiling.

As they got close to Mrs Finn's house, Mary Kate stopped. 'This was where our cottage used to stand.'

'And it has a red door,' said Megan. 'Just like the boarding house.'

Mary Kate smiled, remembering that it had been darling Sean who had made sure that the door was painted red. It was the only red door in Tanners Row. 'Let's have that tea,' she said.

Mrs Finn was delighted to see them. 'How have you settled in, Miss Jones?' she said. 'And how is that lovely little dog of yours?'

'We've both settled in very well, Mrs Finn. Thank you for asking.'

'Sit yourselves down and I'll put the kettle on.'

'You have a lovely home,' said Megan, looking around her.

'I thank God every day for the angel who made it possible,' she said, smiling at Mary Kate.

Mary Kate returned the smile and changed the subject 'I've just heard that Mrs O'Keefe is off to America.'

'Her daughter has been trying to get her over there for years,' said Mrs Finn, 'but she was having none of it. "I will be buried under Irish soil in the land of my fathers," she used to say till we were all sick of hearing it.'

'What made her change her mind?' said Megan.

'The poor woman's legs went, Mrs Jones. They were like a couple of tree trunks and full of water. In the end she couldn't manage the stairs. It was a choice between the asylum up the hill and America, so she opted for America and I don't blame her – I've heard the food up there is rotten. She used to sit in my garden with the two legs stretched out in front of her and may God forgive me, it would put you off your lunch. Especially when they started leaking.'

'So, when is she leaving?' said Mary Kate.

'The daughter and her husband are flying over next week and taking her back with them. That's if they let her on the plane with those legs.'

'Poor woman,' said Megan.

'It was a shame alright,' said Mrs Finn. 'I promised her that I would do the Stations of the Cross every Easter in memory of her and her two legs and she was delighted with that.'

'You're a good woman, Mrs Finn,' said Megan.

'Sure, it's the least I can do, given the circumstances. None of us know how we're going to end up, do we?'

'I don't suppose we do,' said Megan.

'I'll miss her,' said Mrs Finn. 'She was a good neighbour and we got on great. She has a lovely little dog called Ash but once her legs blew up, she couldn't take him out for walks so I've been taking him and the exercise has done me a power of good.'

'That's an unusual name for a dog,' said Megan.

'Well, Mrs O'Keefe is a great one for the fags. I don't think I've ever seen her without a fag hanging off her lip. Anyway, when he was a puppy, she'd have him in her arms and he'd end up covered in ash so that's how he got his name.'

'Is she taking him to America?' said Mary Kate.

'No, her daughter isn't a lover of dogs so she's leaving him with me.'

'Don't you mind?' said Megan.

'No, we got very close on those walks and I'm happy to have him. How is your little dog, Miss Jones?'

'She's settled in lovely,' said Megan. 'She gets on very well with Guinness.'

'They're never apart,' said Mary Kate.

'And Bull Gavin?' said Mrs Finn.

'A happy baby,' said Mary Kate. 'We're all mad about him.'

'And Cathy? She can't have long to go.'

'We're all keeping an eye on her, Mrs Finn.'

'She's lucky to have you, Mary Kate.'

'It's been lovely to see you, Mrs Finn,' said Megan.

'You're welcome anytime. You must visit again, Miss Jones – we could walk the dogs together.'

Megan smiled. 'I'd like that very much.'

As they passed Mrs O'Keefe's house, Mary Kate knew that she would never get rid of the image of the poor woman's leaky legs.

CHAPTER 41

Isobel

The three Granger girls had just arrived back from their mother's funeral and were now relaxing in the elegant lounge of the beautiful Georgian house where they had spent a very comfortable childhood.

There were in fact four Granger girls. Caroline, who was expecting her second baby any day. Vanessa, who taught in a private girls' school and had a liking for the drink. Beatrice, who was married to a dentist and had four children, whose teeth were so dazzlingly white that it was like looking at four small light-houses. And even though two of them were now married, they were still known as the Granger girls. Then there was Isobel, the youngest, who had not been asked to join them in the lounge, or at their mother's burial, for fear that she would start rearranging the hymn books the way she rearranged everything else in the house.

The three sisters were unanimous in their decision that it was best to leave Isobel at home, kinder somehow, for she would have been out of her depth at such an auspicious event and you'd never know what she might get up to in the church – any chance of solemnity would go straight out the window.

'I thought it was very dignified,' said Vanessa, pouring herself a large glass of wine.

'It was,' said Caroline. 'I think Mother would have approved.'

'And the flowers were very understated,' said Beatrice. 'Mother would never have wanted anything showy. I felt quite ill when old Mrs Logan turned up carrying a bunch of chrysanthemums.'

'The woman has no sense of occasion,' said Caroline.

'She has no sense of style either,' said Beatrice.

'The eulogy will be talked about for years,' said Vanessa, pouring herself another glass of wine. 'And to think that it was the mother superior herself who gave it.'

'A very proud moment indeed,' said Caroline.

It seemed that they had run out of things to say about the understated funeral and sat in a very uncomfortable silence.

Caroline stood up. 'Oh, for heaven's sake, we all know why we're here and we have to talk about it. What are we going to do about Isobel?'

Vanessa had gone red in the face. 'Well, don't look at me,' she said.

'You're the only one without children, Vanessa, you can't expect myself or Beatrice to take her in. She has to have a roof over her head.'

Vanessa glared at her sisters. 'Just because I'm not popping out children like peas doesn't mean I don't have a life. She'll jolly well have to find another roof to put her head under because it's not going to be under mine.'

The room had gone silent and then Caroline spoke. 'OK,' she said, 'but she has to go somewhere, she can't stay here. This house is our inheritance.'

'Well, she certainly can't live here on her own – she can't even boil an egg,' said Vanessa.

'She couldn't stay here even if she could boil an egg,' said Caroline. 'The house will have to be sold and the money split four ways and the sooner the better. I don't know about you two but I have commitments.'

'We all have commitments, Caroline,' said Vanessa.

Caroline smiled. 'So, that's decided then. The house will be sold and Isobel will just have to go into lodgings or something.'

'I'm not sure Mother would have approved of that,' said Beatrice. 'She was very close to Isobel.'

'She spoiled Isobel,' said Caroline.

Beatrice smoothed down her good skirt. 'I know that Mother has passed on but...'

'Dear God, Beatrice,' said Caroline. 'Our mother is dead, she hasn't passed anywhere.'

Beatrice sniffed. 'I just thought that it was much more decorous to say passed on than dead.'

Caroline rolled her eyes. 'Holy mother of God, have you swallowed a dictionary?'

Beatrice's eyes filled with tears. 'I've just lost my mother, Caroline, how can you be so mean?'

Caroline immediately softened. 'I'm sorry, Bea. This Isobel business has my brain mashed.'

'Beatrice smiled at her sister. 'That's OK, I think it has all our brains mashed.'

'Right,' said Caroline. 'Let's all think, there must be somewhere she can go.'

The three girls sat quietly, hoping for a light-bulb moment that would solve everything.

'What about Aunt Maudie?' said Vanessa suddenly. 'Do you think she might take her in?'

'She just might,' said Caroline. 'She's always been very fond of her.'

'Well, they're both a little on the odd side,' said Beatrice. 'I think that maybe the pair of them would rub along fine.'

'I shall write to her immediately.'

'Oh, well done, Vanessa,' said Beatrice. 'Jolly well done.'

Vanessa beamed and headed for the drinks cabinet. She deserved it – after all, it was her that had thought of Aunt Maudie.

Isobel had been sitting on the stairs, listening to her sisters deciding what to do with her as if she was a parcel that they needed to get rid of. She wiped away the tears that were running down her face. She had never felt more alone or more unwanted.

CHAPTER 42

Maudie

Maudie Sullivan put on her good silk coat, shut the front door and stepped into the waiting taxi. She settled herself in the back seat. She had decided long ago that taxis were by far the best way to travel. No hanging about for buses or getting choked to death in a train carriage full of smoke. Maudie had nothing against people smoking; she enjoyed the odd cigarette herself but in the privacy of her own home, where she didn't impose it on anyone else. Yes, taxis were the way to travel.

She smiled as she thought of the letter she'd received from Caroline. It didn't surprise her one bit that her nieces had decided to pass the problem of Isobel on to her, but she was delighted that they had, for she loved the bones of the girl – in fact, she couldn't abide the other three. She had promised her darling sister that if anything happened, she would take care of Isobel. Had Caroline not written, she would have been on her way down to the house in a taxi to bring Isobel home.

Maudie had lived on her own for the past forty years and she wouldn't have wanted it any other way. It wasn't that she didn't like men – she had enjoyed their company from time to time but on her own terms. She had no intention of moving one into her house or into her heart. She had her books, she had a circle of interesting friends and most importantly, she had her independence, which she cherished.

Yes, she had known love, the kind of love where the sky had seemed bluer, where surely the flowers bloomed only for her. She found herself feeling sorry for people who would never have what she had. She had never felt more beautiful, or more desirable and she ate the face off anyone who took it upon themselves to point out that the said Romeo wasn't as perfect as she thought he was. Of course, she ignored them all and put it down to jealousy. What a stupid silly little girl she had been because the man in question had turned out to be a philander and a charlatan who had spread his charms liberally across half the female population of Dublin.

Her heart was broken, she wept and she wailed, she couldn't sleep and she couldn't eat, which turned out to be a bit of a blessing as her mother had commented that she was beginning to look like the side of a house. She wrote romantic poetry badly and sent heartfelt love letters, begging him to come back to her. In giving her all to him, she had lost herself and declared to anyone who had a mind to listen that her life was over and what was the point in living?

Her mother had lost patience with her. 'I endured thirty-six hours of labour pushing you out,' she said. 'I was stitched up like a patchwork quilt, it was like passing a block of flats. The nurses had changed shifts three times before you decided to make an appearance and in the end the doctor had to haul you out with a pair of tongs. You came out with a head like a triangle, you looked like something from outer space – I was only mortified. When I rolled you out in the pram, I had to keep you in a bonnet for fear of scaring the neighbours. They told me I'd had a natural birth. Well, believe me, girl, there was nothing natural about it and now you're telling me you want to jump into the Liffey and end it all for some lowlife gobshite who has his brains in his trousers. Cop on to yourself, Maudie Sullivan, because you have us all demented with your goings-on – it's like living in a feckin' morgue. Even the cat has moved next door.'

Maudie ran upstairs followed by her sister Beth. She sat on the bed and Beth sat next to her and put her arms around her shoulders. 'Please don't be sad, Maudie, I hate to see you so sad.'

Maudie wiped the tears that were running down her face. 'It's just that my heart is broken and no one cares.'

'I care and I wish I could help you but I don't know much about broken hearts. Maybe I don't feel quite as strongly about love as you do.'

'Don't you want to fall in love then?'

'Not the kind of love you're talking about, it sounds exhausting. I just want to find a decent man who'll take care of me. I would like a house of my own, somewhere to grow flowers and perhaps a little dog, but most of all I want to be a mother. I sound terribly boring, don't I?'

'If that's what you want, Beth, then it's what I want for you too. I have a feeling that you will have an easier life than me.'

'What do you want, Maudie?'

Maudie lay down on the bed and stared up at the damp patch on the ceiling. 'Everything,' she whispered.

Beth lay down beside her. 'Be more specific.'

'I want to travel, I want to try new things, even dodgy things.'

'Oh, Maudie,' said Beth, grinning.

'I want music and dissolute nightclubs down dark alleys. I want to lay down with beggars and wake up with princes. I want to experience everything that life has to offer, even if I lose my way in the process. I want to climb mountains and dive into azure seas.'

'But you can't swim,' said Beth, laughing.

'I'll learn. I'll listen, and I'll learn. I'll grab everything that life throws at me. I'll taste the sweet and spit out the sour, but most of all, I want to find out who I am without someone else deciding and when I tire of it all, I shall come home and spoil your children.'

The sisters lay side by side, holding hands. 'I love you, Beth,' said Maudie.

'And I love you too,' said Beth, closing her eyes.

That night Maudie had slept like a log and in the morning sat down to a grand fry-up. Her mother had been delighted.

'Now, Maudie,' she'd said, 'when you've finished eating, you can run upstairs and bring down the sackcloth and ashes so that I can pop them in the wash.'

That had the pair of them laughing and she knew that she was going to be OK. Not only OK, but she made a promise to herself never to let a man take control of her ever again.

Over the years, she'd watched her friends marry and have children. She'd roll the screaming babies around the park to give their poor mothers a bit of a break, then go home to her beautiful peaceful house and listen to Vivaldi or Bach. She was godmother to four of them. She took them to a pantomime every Christmas and always bought them a good book for their birthdays.

As the taxi pulled into the bus station, she saw Isobel looking anxiously around her. Maudie asked the driver to wait while she walked over and took her niece into her arms.

'Let's go home,' she said.

That evening, they snuggled up on the cream velvet couch in front of a grand fire.

'Auntie?' said Isobel.

'Now that's a good place to start,' said Maudie.

'Start what, Auntie?'

'Your education, Isobel.'

'I don't have to go to school, do I?'

'School is not the kind of education that I have in mind, what I have in mind is something much more valuable. I was taught Algebra as a young one and I've never had an overwhelming desire to use it since. We shall start tomorrow and we shall begin by dropping the auntie bit.'

'But why?'

'Because, my darling girl, we shall be equals. We shall respect each other's views and opinions and you will learn.'

'What will I learn, Aunt – I mean Maudie?'

'You will learn about life, Isobel. We shall go to the theatre and to concerts, we shall read the classics together and we will follow the latest trends in fashion. I have you booked into my hairdresser's tomorrow.'

'Maudie?'

'Yes, dear?'

'What will happen to me when you die? Where will I live?'

'Oh, you'll be long gone before I give up the ghost.'

'But aren't I going to live here forever?'

'Heavens no, that wouldn't suit either of us.'

Isobel's eyes were filling with tears. 'Wouldn't it?'

'Oh no. The last thing you will want is to live with an old goat like me. Once we have finished your education, my sweet girl, you will be ready to fly and I shall be right behind you and so will your mother. Think of it as an adventure, the best adventure of your life, and oh, Isobel, we shall have such fun, you and I.'

CHAPTER 43

Mary Kate

Mary Kate watched Emma and Rooney's friendship gradually turn into something deeper and it touched her heart to see it. Emma had spent her life taking care of her little sister Nell and it was wonderful to watch her maturing and finding a life of her own. Maybe, as Moira had said, she couldn't help everyone, but those who found their way to the red door became like a family and, rightly or wrongly, she felt responsible for their happiness.

Rooney was a gentle boy and a kind one. He was a boy who took care of his mother and was fond of Nell. Bull Gavin's little face would break into smiles whenever he saw him, holding up his arms for Rooney to pick him up and spin him around the room; even Guinness adored him. It was early days for these two young people but Mary Kate had no doubt that this was a relationship that would last the course of time. She knew that Emma would be safe with him, and she wished them both all the luck in the world.

Mary Kate put on her coat and picked up the flowers as Emma came into the sitting room.

Emma smiled at her. 'Going somewhere nice?'

'I'm taking the bus to Glendalough to visit my husband's grave,' said Mary Kate.

'Oh, I'm sorry.'

'Please don't be sorry, Emma. I know he's not there, but it's where I feel closest to him.'

'Nell never mentions her daddy,' said Emma. 'And I don't speak of him. Even if he was closer, I still don't think Nell would want to go back and until she asks to, I let it be. I am only ever as happy as Nell.'

'You're her protector, Emma.'

'I always have been and I suppose I always will be.'

'She is lucky to have you, dear.'

'We are lucky to have each other.'

'She does seem happier these days and it's lovely to see,' said Mary Kate.

'She has Bull Gavin and who wouldn't be happy with that little feller around?'

Mary Kate smiled, thinking of the little boy who they all doted on.

'Does it make you sad to visit his grave, Mary Kate?'

'It's not just the grave, Emma, it's the place that I go back to. It was in the church at Glendalough where Sean and I were married, it's where we found our little cottage and it's also where I buried my mother. You could call it a kind of pilgrimage that I feel the need to make now and again and today is one of those days.'

'Would you like some company?' said Emma. 'Say if you don't, I won't be offended.'

'I'd like that very much, Emma, very much indeed.'

'That's grand then,' said Emma. 'I'll get my coat.'

As the bus left the city and drove towards the countryside, Mary Kate felt that familiar feeling of going home. She didn't try to block the feeling out for it was a huge part of her life, the loveliest part, and it wasn't easily forgotten. Grandad had said that you must leave the past behind and move on but she realised now that he hadn't meant the memories. He had meant journeying from one part of your life to another. When she had left the little cottage where she had grown up and been so happy, it was only the walls and bricks that she was leaving, she carried her memories with her and she didn't need a huge bag to carry them in. It was the same when she left the cottage she had shared with Sean.

Bricks and mortar, Mary Kate. Bricks and mortar.

The bus dropped them off a short distance from the church. Emma stood still, looking up at the beautiful Wicklow Hills. 'Oh, Mary Kate,' she said, 'it's so beautiful.'

'It is indeed.'

'But doesn't it make you sad, coming back?'

'I'm at peace with it now – well, maybe not entirely, but I'm getting there. It helps having you with me.'

'I can always come with you if you want me to.'

Together, they walked up the narrow track that led to the church, under the wooden lychgate and into the graveyard. There was a soft breeze that moved gently through the trees. The air was warm and the hills, which were sometimes wreathed in mist, were clear and enchanting.

Mary Kate separated the flowers into two bunches and laid half on Sean's grave. She usually had a chat with him but not today as Emma was beside her. Instead, she said a silent prayer to the man she had loved and still loved so much.

They walked between the grey stones and Mary Kate stopped at her mother's grave. 'Agnes Ryan,' she read. 'Beloved mother and friend.'

'Whose friend was she?' said Emma.

'She was mine. I had never known her growing up but we became friends, the best of friends, and that's still how I think of her. A friend who I grew to love and respect.'

Mary Kate laid the rest of the flowers down and they went back to the bus stop.

'Would you like to see my cottage, Emma?'

'I'd love to, as long it doesn't make you too sad.'

'Like I said, it's easier with you beside me.'

The bus dropped them off and they walked down the lane towards the cottage.

Emma stood at the gate, looking at it. 'Oh, Mary Kate,' she said, 'it's magical, like something out of a fairy tale.'

'It was love at first sight.'

Emma looked up at the Wicklow Hills that rose above the cottage: 'Nell would love it here.'

Mary Kate opened the gate and they walked into the garden. 'Believe it or not, Sean and I had it looking lovely.'

'It could be again,' said Emma.

'If I could find someone to do it.'

'Rooney and I would be glad to do it, we really would. We could bring Nell and Bull Gavin with us, they'd love it.'

Mary Kate looked around the garden. These young ones would bring it alive again. How wonderful would that be?

CHAPTER 44

Isobel

Isobel was standing outside the hairdresser's with Maudie, peering through the window. She felt sick with nerves for she had never been in such a place before.

'Straighten those shoulders, Isobel,' said Maudie. 'You are every bit as good as the next person, better than most, and you are in for a treat.'

Maudie was greeted like a long-lost friend and they stepped through the door. 'Lovely to see you, Mrs Sullivan,' said the girl behind the desk. 'And this must be the niece you spoke so highly of.'

Maudie nodded. 'This is Isobel, and I want you to take very good care of her.'

'Oh, we will, Mrs Sullivan. We most certainly will.'

The room smelled of spring flowers that reminded her of the meadows behind the house where she would walk with her mother. Her sisters must have been with them but she could only remember the two of them, it seemed always to have been just the two of them. Her small hand enclosed in her mother's and the smell of the wildflowers on the cool breeze.

It was cold outside but inside the salon, it was lovely and warm and filled with chatter and laughter, low lights and soft music. She felt less anxious and smiled at Maudie, who squeezed her hand.

'I'll be waiting right here,' she said, sitting down in a chair by the window and picking up a magazine. 'Now go and enjoy yourself.'

A young girl came across and draped a cape around her shoulders before leading her towards a row of basins.

'My name is Sophie,' she said warmly. 'I will be washing your hair today. We had some new shampoo in just this morning and it smells only gorgeous. It's called "Summer Meadows". Isn't that a lovely name? I'd get some myself, but it's desperate expensive. I'd have to find a rich man to afford it. You don't know any, do you?'

'I don't think so,' said Isobel. 'But then, wouldn't it be more satisfying if you saved up and bought it yourself? That way you wouldn't feel obligated to anyone.' She knew as soon as the words left her lips that she had said the wrong thing again. Caroline said that it would do no harm if she could manage to engage her brain before opening her mouth. Luckily, Sophie didn't seem in the least bit offended.

'You're probably right, miss, but there's no harm in dreaming, is there?'

Isobel smiled at her. 'I have a habit of saying the wrong thing at the wrong time.'

'And I have a habit of talking too much. I'm usually told to put a sock in it. My mammy says it's a wonder they keep me on.'

'Well, I'm glad they have, for you have put me at my ease.'

'Ah, that's nice, miss.'

Isobel sat down and leaned her head backwards over the sink.

'I'd only die to have lovely thick hair like yours,' said the young girl. 'You must be the envy of all your friends.'

Isobel had never had any friends that would be envious, it was only her mother who had ever remarked on her hair. Every night before she went to bed, she would sit her down in front of the dressing table mirror, then she'd pick up the special silver brush and gently run it through her hair. 'You take after me for the thickness of it,' she would say. 'Your sisters missed the boat on the hair front.'

Isobel had often wondered why her mother seemed to take more notice of her than of her sisters. Perhaps it had been because she was the youngest – either that or she felt sorry for her. She closed her eyes as Sophie massaged the sweet-smelling shampoo into her hair. It was all perfectly lovely; she could have quite happily stayed there all day. She wondered what her sisters would say if they could see her now.

After her hair had been washed, it was cut and styled.

'A bit shorter, dear,' said Maudie, who was standing behind her.

'Isn't it short enough?' said Isobel as she watched in horror as strand after strand fell around her shoulders and onto the floor.

Maudie smiled. 'You just wait and see, darling. Once it's been coloured, I promise you are going to love it.'

'Coloured?'

'Don't look so shocked. Did you really think that this was my natural hair?'

'Isn't it?'

Maudie laughed. 'Darling girl, I went grey years ago.'

Isobel stared at her. 'Really?'

Maudie put her finger to her lips. 'But don't tell anyone.'

'Oh, I won't,' said Isobel, smiling.

'Good girl.'

Isobel looked at her reflection in the mirror. Soft golden

waves fell about her shoulders and framed her face in a way that the long mousy locks never had. She moved her head and felt her hair swish against her cheeks.

Was that lovely girl in the mirror really her?

Maudie had tears in her eyes as she looked at her beloved niece. 'You'll do, Isobel Granger,' she said. 'Oh yes, you'll do.'

That was yesterday and last night she had hardly slept because today was the reading of her mother's will and she didn't want to go. She wouldn't understand what was being said and she was worried about seeing her sisters again.

She slipped the soft grey dress over her head. 'There's nothing like the feel of silk against your skin, Isobel,' Maudie had said. 'I don't think of it as a luxury but a necessity, like a good face cream, but we will get onto that another day.'

Isobel added a pale cream jacket to the outfit and went into the lounge. Maudie looked up and smiled at her: 'Give me a spin, dear,' she said.

Isobel did as she was told and spun around.

'You look beautiful, my darling. Ready to face the inquisition?'

Isobel grinned. 'Do I have a choice?'

'Not really,' said Maudie, laughing.

Just then the doorbell rang. 'That will be our taxi,' she said, picking up her handbag.

It wasn't far to the centre of Dublin but Isobel wished it was miles away. She would say the wrong thing, she just knew she would – she always said the wrong thing. She felt a hand slip into hers and turned to Maudie: 'I don't think that I can do this. Do I have to be there?'

Maudie smiled at her. 'I'm afraid you do, in fact you are today's star turn and you won't want to miss that.'

'Do I have to speak?'

Maudie shook her head and smiled. 'But you may have some questions.'

'I won't have any questions,' said Isobel, quickly. 'I definitely won't have any questions.'

'As you wish, my darling girl, as you wish.'

Maudie leaned forward in her seat. 'Stop here, please,' she said.

'Is this the place?' said Isobel.

'Not quite,' said Maudie. 'It's just along the road.'

'Then why are we stopping?'

'Patience, child.'

They sat in silence and then Maudie spoke: 'There they are.'

'Who?'

'Your sisters, standing on the steps. Patrick, would you mind taking us round the block, please?'

The driver started the engine and pulled away. 'The scenic route, Mrs Sullivan?'

'Always, Patrick.'

'Aren't we going in?'

'Of course we're going in,' said Maudie, smiling, 'but we are going to be fashionably late.'

Having driven around the block, Patrick helped them out of the car: 'I'll wait for you here,' he said.

At the top of the steps, Maudie stopped. 'Now listen carefully, Isobel, for this is important.'

'I'm listening.'

'I want you to walk in there as if you own the place. No shuffling and no looking down at the floor. Can you do that?'

Isobel took a deep breath. 'Yes, Maudie, I believe I can.'

'OK, let's do it,' said Maudie, opening the door.

Isobel wasn't sure what she had been expecting, but it wasn't this lovely room with soft sofas and low tables. If she had imagined anything at all, it would have been a courtroom, where she'd have to swear on the Bible to tell the truth the whole truth and nothing but the truth. This was more like someone's front room and she began to relax.

She had been so busy looking around that she hadn't noticed her three sisters staring at her: 'Oh, hello, Caroline, hello, Vanessa, hello, Beatrice,' she said, smiling.

'Isobel?' said Caroline. 'Is that you?'

'Don't be ridiculous, Caroline,' said Maudie. 'You know perfectly well it's Isobel.'

'But she looks, umm, she looks…'

'Different,' said Vanessa.

'I think you look lovely,' said Beatrice.

Isobel smiled. 'It's all Maudie's doing.'

'Well, it suits you. I love your hair.'

'Thank you, Beatrice. I could introduce you to my hair-dresser if you like, she's very nice.'

While this was going on, Maudie was looking at the three girls. This was exactly the response she had wanted. They hadn't allowed their sister to attend her own mother's funeral and she found that very hard to forgive.

Just then, the door opened and Tim Bennett, the family solicitor, came into the room and sat down in front of them.

'Good morning,' he said, taking a seat. 'First, I would like to say how very sorry I am for your loss. I have known your mother for many years. She was a great lady, kind and wise, and it has been a privilege to call her my friend. She loved her family and was very proud of you all.'

He shuffled some papers on the desk and then looked up. 'So, we are here today to read the last will and testament of Anne Marie Granger.

'Your mother came to see me a year ago with the intention of writing a new will.'

'A new will?' said Caroline. 'Why did she need a new will?'

'It's not unusual, Caroline – things change, situations

change, and she felt the will needed updating. Her old will was made before she was blessed with grandchildren.'

'Oh, I see,' said Caroline, looking satisfied with this explanation.

Tim took a sip of water before carrying on. He knew that what he was going to say next was not going to go down very well: 'Your mother's main asset is the house in Fitzwilliam Drive where you grew up and she has left this to her daughter, Isobel.'

There was complete silence then Vanessa stood up: 'What do you mean, she has left it to Isobel?'

'That was her wish, Vanessa, and she was very clear about it. Her wish was that the house was to be left to Isobel.'

'What about us?' said Beatrice.

'The contents of the house are to be divided equally between yourself and your two sisters.'

'This isn't fair,' shouted Caroline. 'I want this will to be annulled.'

'Your mother was of sound mind when she came to see me. Her signature was witnessed by myself and my colleague. It is perfectly legal and above board and there is no question that it can be revoked. Those were her wishes and I would hope that you can respect them.'

'Well, we can't,' said Vanessa. 'Well, I can't anyway.'

'And what about her grandchildren?' said Caroline. 'Or did she forget she had any?'

'A very generous trust fund has been set up for them. They will be able to access their inheritance when they reach the age of maturity, which in this case is twenty-one.'

'What about me?' said Vanessa. 'I don't have any bloody children.'

'As I said, Vanessa, the contents of your family home are to be divided equally between the three of you.'

'What if I don't want a load of old furniture?'

'That is entirely up to you, dear.'

Caroline glared at Maudie: 'And I assume that you knew all about this?'

'Then you assume wrong. I am as surprised as you.'

'Really? Isn't that why you were so quick to offer my sister a home? Because you knew that she was going to be wealthy?'

'In case you've conveniently forgotten, I offered her a home at your request, Caroline, because the rest of you couldn't or wouldn't.'

Caroline turned on Isobel: 'And what about you? Sitting there with your new hairstyle and fancy clothes. Don't you have anything to say?'

'As a matter of fact, I do,' said Isobel. 'I also think that our mother's decision to leave the house to me is unfair on the rest of you. After all, you have as much right to the family home as I do. The reason I haven't spoken out is because I had pretty much decided to split the house four ways.'

'Well, that's more like it,' said Vanessa, looking delighted.

'It's the right thing to do,' said Caroline.

Isobel looked at each of her sisters in turn: 'But I've changed my mind. Our mother, for reasons of her own, wanted me to have the house and I intend to honour her wishes. The three of you are rude and greedy, you have never shown me one moment's kindness in my whole life, and I owe you nothing.'

'That is not true,' said Caroline.

'Oh, but it is,' said Isobel.

Tim Bennett looked at the three sisters: 'I would suggest that you make an appointment to view the house and decide which pieces you would like. I would also suggest that you make it sooner rather than later so that we can finalise things.'

Caroline glared at him. 'You expect us to make an appointment to visit our own house?'

'It's not your house anymore, Caroline. As from now, the house belongs to Isobel.'

'Well, I can assure you, Mr Bennett, that you won't be hearing the last of this. Isobel has been an embarrassment to this family since the day she was born. Our mother indulged her when by rights she should have put her in an institution years ago. No judge in the land will uphold this will and I shall make sure it's dismissed and the house returned to my sisters and myself.'

The solicitor smiled at her. 'As you wish, Caroline, but you will be wasting your money.'

'What about her old will?' said Vanessa.

'Your mother always intended the house to go to Isobel.'

'Then why did she change it?' said Beatrice, glaring at him.

'I have already explained why your mother updated her will. It was to include her grandchildren and she has done that.'

'And we're supposed to believe that, are we?' said Beatrice. 'Well, I for one want to see the original will.'

'We all do,' said Caroline.

'As you wish. I shall make sure that each of you receive a copy of both wills and my hope is that you can then see for yourselves that this has always been your mother's wish.'

Isobel's eyes filled with tears as she listened to her sisters. They might not have had much time for her but until now, she hadn't realised how much of an embarrassment she had been to them. They were her sisters and she had loved them and looked up to them when all the time they wanted to shut her away in an institution. Between them, they had broken her heart.

'I think it's time to go, dear, don't you?' said Maudie softly.

Isobel nodded and stood up. 'Thank you for everything, Mr Bennett,' she said.

Tim Bennett smiled at her. 'It has been my pleasure, Isobel, and I wish you a very happy life because that was all your mother wanted for you.'

'Are you ready, Maudie?' she said.

'Oh yes, my darling,' Maudie said, smiling. 'I've never been more ready.'

CHAPTER 45

Isobel

Isobel and Maudie were sitting at the kitchen table, eating French toast drizzled with maple syrup.

'This is delicious, Maudie, we never had this at home.'

'Your darling mother wasn't very imaginative when it came to food on account of her never setting foot outside of Dublin. The Irish have a tendency to be suspicious of anything they can't pronounce.'

'I'd like to learn,' said Isobel.

'And you will, dear. I shall arrange for you to attend a course on French cuisine.'

'So that I could be a cook?'

Maudie visibly shuddered. 'No, Isobel. What you learn will be purely for entertainment purposes. No, dear, I have something else in mind for you. Let's go into the hallway – I want you to look in the mirror.'

Isobel followed Maudie and stood in front of the long mirror that took up most of the wall: 'What am I supposed to be looking at?' she said.

Maudie smiled. 'Yourself. Now what do you see?'

'I suppose I see me.'

'Shall I tell you what I see?'

Isobel grinned. 'I think you are going to anyway.'

'I see a beautiful young girl.'

'But I'm plain Maudie, everyone says I'm the plain one. It's my sisters who are beautiful.'

'Your sisters are pretty, not beautiful, and pretty doesn't last, there's no depth to it. What you possess, dear, will never fade. Look again.'

Isobel shrugged her shoulders. 'Just plain old me.'

'Look at those cheekbones, girl. What I would have done for cheekbones like that when I was your age! And you have lovely eyes.'

'Really?'

'You have your mother's eyes, Isobel, and your father's height.'

'But I'm lanky. My sisters used to call me the beanpole of the family.'

'You are not lanky, dear, what you are is statuesque.'

'Golly.'

'Your sisters, bless them, came up short.'

Isobel grinned. 'You make me sound wonderful and it's nice to hear but I think you might possibly be humouring me.'

'Balderdash!' said Maudie. 'I have never felt the need to humour anyone in my whole life.'

'So, what's having cheekbones and being statuesque going to do for me? I mean, they haven't helped much so far.'

'You will be a model, Isobel.'

'I couldn't possibly be a model.'

'Don't look so alarmed, dear. I wasn't suggesting carting you off to the runways of Milan after lunch.'

Isobel grinned. 'You are marvellous, Maudie.'

'And you, my darling girl, are quite spectacular.'

'I know you only want the best for me and I am so grateful but I don't think that I want to be a model – I couldn't bear to have all those strangers looking at me.'

'They won't be looking at you, dear, they will be looking at the clothes. You will merely be a clothes horse.'

Isobel started giggling, which set Maudie off. They flopped down on the sofa and put their arms around each other.

'Well, of all the things I thought I might be,' said Isobel, 'a clothes horse was not one of them.'

'Of course it wasn't, darling, but I have made up my mind and I very rarely change my mind once it's made up. You shall be a model, Isobel.'

Isobel jumped up, took a book from the bookcase and started walking up and down the lounge, balancing it on her head.

'Look at me, Maudie, I am Queen of the Runway.'

Maudie smiled at her. 'You will be, if I have anything to do with it.'

Isobel looked at her beloved aunt. 'Now why am I beginning to believe you?'

'Because you know that I know best.'

'Do I have any say in it all?'

'Mmm, probably not, dear,' said Maudie grinning.

The fire blazed in the hearth as Maudie and Isobel cuddled up on the beautiful velvet sofa. Isobel loved it here – she had never felt so happy, or so loved, and she wished she could stay for ever but she trusted the plans that Maudie had in mind for her.

'You said I had a lot to learn, Maudie. What sort of things?'

'Where on earth to start?' said Maudie.

'At the beginning,' said Isobel.

'Well dear, I shall start by telling you some of the things that I learned in this old life of mine.'

'Yes, please,' said Isobel, leaning back against the soft cushions.

'When you are invited to a party or a meal, drink the wine but only drink enough to keep your dignity, even when those around you lose theirs. You will wake up the next morning and enjoy the memories of your night out and not wonder whether you might have spoken out of turn or flirted with someone's husband. Plenty of people love the sound of their own voices, so be the listener and believe me, Isobel, your silence will be the loudest thing in the room. Never let others define who you are, this is your journey and no one else's. If someone hurts you, hold your tongue – you don't know what journey they might have been on. If they continue to hurt you, walk away. Never meet anger with anger for that will create chaos. Be the voice of reason, even when others are unreasonable – they have to live with their anger, not you. Focus on yourself but be mindful of those in need and when truth and kindness collide, always choose kindness. Lesson over.'

Isobel was hanging onto every word, taking in all Maudie's advice, wanting to be as wise and as kind as she was. 'How on earth did you learn it all?'

Maudie giggled. 'I learned all that, my dear, from drinking too much wine, speaking out of turn and flirting with other people's husbands. I loved the sound of my own voice and listening was the furthest thing on my mind. If someone hurt me, I'd bear a grudge for years and never forgave them. I let others define who I was because I wanted to fit in and believe me, fitting in is not all it's cracked up to be. I met anger with anger and caused chaos and I was never the voice of reason. I told the truth and forgot to be kind. What I bring to you now, Isobel, are my own mistakes.' Then she winked. 'But oh, I did have a wonderful life.'

Isobel grinned. 'And there was me thinking that you were some kind of angel.'

'I sincerely hope not, dear. I find all that sweetness and flapping of wings rather nauseating. Besides, Lucifer happened to be an angel and he didn't exactly spread sweetness and light around the world, did he? Now is there anything else you want to know?'

'Well, there is something that has been on my mind.'

'You can say anything to me, Isobel.'

'Well, I know you said that I wouldn't be living with you forever?'

'That's right, dear.'

'The thing is, I don't want to live on my own in the house where I grew up.'

'I wouldn't want to live there either – it's a barn of a place. I think that your mother would have preferred something a bit cosier.'

'Really?'

'I think so.'

'She seemed happy enough.'

'And I'm sure, in her own way, she was.'

'So, where am I to live?'

'In a boarding house.'

'A boarding house?'

'Yes. It will of course be a respectable one. You will stay there in the week and come home to me at weekends until the time comes when you are far too busy to want to spend your weekends with me.'

'I'll never be too busy for that.'

'We'll see.'

'Maudie?'

'Yes, dear?'

'Was my mother happy? Because there were times when she seemed to drift off into a world of her own.'

'We were very different, my sister and I – she was a much nicer person than I was. We wanted different things, but we

respected each other's differences. Your mother once told me
that she didn't think she could ever love the way I did. She
didn't think that she would ever find that kind of love.'

'But what about us? Didn't she love us?'

'All I can say, dear, is that she was very fond of her family
and she was a wonderful mother.'

Isobel's eyes filled with tears. 'How terribly sad.'

'And then she met the love of her life.'

'Really?'

Maudie nodded.

'But who was it?'

'You, my darling girl. It was you.'

'Me?'

'Yes, you. Now, off you go and get dolled up – I'm in the
mood for a bit of shopping.'

As Isobel was about to leave the room, she turned around:
'Maudie?'

'Yes, dear?'

'My father wasn't tall.'

Maudie smiled at her: 'Actually, he was, dear, but that's
another story for another day.'

Isobel's life with Maudie had been nothing like the life she had
lived at home. Maudie had booked her on a six-week course on
deportment, run by a once-famous old lady called Mrs De
Bouche, who lived in a basement flat in a dodgy part of Dublin.
The walls were covered in colourful scarves and she was
covered in very heavy jewellery. Every finger had a clunky ring
on it, which must have weighed a ton.

'Call me Blanche,' she'd said, holding out a blue-veined
hand that put Isobel in mind of the cheese that Maudie was
partial to. Maudie ate a lot of cheese and very little else. Isobel

got a book from the library and learned to cook, otherwise she might well have starved to death.

Maudie was throwing so much information at her that Isobel feared she would never take it all in. She gave her books to read, starting with *Brave New World* by Aldous Huxley.

Try as she might, Isobel could make no sense of it at all.

'Haven't you finished that book yet, Isobel?' said Maudie. 'I gave it to you weeks ago.'

'It's awfully long, Maudie.'

'For heaven's sake, girl, you don't have to read the entire book! I've never read a whole book in my life.'

'Haven't you?'

'No, dear, life's too short. All you need is a smattering of the classics so that if you find yourself in a group of literary sorts, you can at least contribute to the conversation.'

'But don't you want to know how the story ends?'

'No, dear – I still don't know what became of poor little Jane Eyre.'

'She married Mr Rochester,' said Isobel.

'Silly girl,' said Maudie. 'I shall stop worrying about her then.'

Isobel laughed. 'You don't care what happened to her, do you?'

'No, dear. I found the child rather feeble.'

They spent a week in London, staying in a guest house in Park Lane, whose glory days were long gone.

'It's the address that counts, Isobel,' said Maudie. 'Better to stay in a hovel in Park Lane than a palace in Islington.'

They travelled by taxi to Oxford and sat under shady trees in front of the university, eating sandwiches supplied by the guest house.

'Back in the day, a group of poets, philosophers and writers studied here,' said Maudie. 'They were known as the Bloomsbury Group and generally thought of as a bunch of self-congrat-ulatory snobs. Boring as hell, I should think.'

'Why didn't I learn all this, Maudie?'

'Your mother did her best, dear, but you were denied any culture. In fact, living with your sisters, it's a wonder you learned to tie your own shoelaces.'

Isobel nodded.

'Our very own Oscar Wilde also graced these hallowed halls,' said Maudie.

'What did he write?'

'Quite wonderful plays but the poor man ended up in prison.'

'Why?'

'That, Isobel, is another story for another day.'

They saw plays and musicals and concerts and ballets. Isobel liked the musicals best. *The King and I, Kiss Me, Kate*, and her favourite – *Carousel* – but it was a performance of *The Sleeping Beauty* that would stay with her forever. As the orchestra swelled and echoed around the beautiful space, it touched something inside of her that she had never felt before. It didn't make her feel happy, it made her feel sad and angry and gave her a kind of yearning for something she had never known. All her life, her sisters had made her feel as if she was nothing and that is what she came to be believe. They would pass her on the stairs and not acknowledge her; there were times when she thought she was disappearing and there were times when she wished she would.

The music broke her heart and she didn't understand why. She had cried in Maudie's arms as they travelled across London and back to the guest house. She was still crying as Maudie tucked her into bed and sat beside her.

'Why did my sisters dislike me so much?' she asked.

Maudie held her hand. 'I thought you would ask me that one day, my darling.'

'I was never unkind to them – I wanted to be their friend, but they just ignored me as if I wasn't even there. I was so lonely in that house, Maudie.'

'I know you were, my dear. The truth is, Isobel, that it wasn't really all their fault.'

'Was it mine?'

Maudie shook her head. 'No, my darling girl, it wasn't your fault, it was never your fault.'

'Whose then?'

'I'm afraid it was your mother's.'

'But she loved me, she was the one who loved me.'

'She was obsessed with you, Isobel, and that is not a very healthy kind of love.'

'I don't understand.'

'Since the moment you were born, your mother loved you to the exclusion of everything and everyone else. She had no time for your sisters – they were three young girls who were deprived of a mother's love. They were fed and they were clothed but their mother was so full of love for you that there was none left for her other children. The three of them clung together because they only had each other and the sad thing was that they blamed you.'

'Oh, Maudie,' said Isobel, 'I never knew. If I'd known, things might have been different. They might have liked me.'

'Jealousy is such a negative thing, my dear, and so sometimes it's the wrong sort of love.'

'I want to go home, Maudie.'

'Then we shall, my dear. Now go to sleep, tomorrow is another day.'

CHAPTER 46

Isobel

'Today, Isobel,' said Maudie, 'we are going to meet a very good friend of mine. His name is Mr Kieron Walsh and he is the manager of Clerys.'

'Why are we going to meet him?'

'To have a little chat, dear.'

'Does it concern me, Maudie?'

'Oh yes. I have already spoken to him and he is expecting us. He is looking forward to meeting you.'

Isobel frowned. 'I don't understand.'

'Of course you don't, dear, but you will,' said Maudie. 'The taxi's due any minute so run along and change into something understated but classy. And when we step into Clerys, I want you to walk tall. No shuffling or bowing your head. Own your height, Isobel, because if I'm right, and I usually am, your height is going to be your fortune.'

'Good heavens,' said Isobel.

As they walked into Clerys department store, Maudie turned to Isobel: 'Now don't forget, dear, head up.'

They were greeted with a smile from the young girl behind the reception desk: 'Mr Walsh is expecting you, Mrs Sullivan. I'll take you upstairs.'

'I know the way, dear,' said Maudie. 'Save your feet.'

The young girl smiled at her. 'Thanks,' she said, picking up the phone. 'I'll let him know you're here.'

Isobel followed Maudie up the beautiful staircase. A man was standing at the top, smiling down at them. 'Lovely to see you, Maudie, and this must be your niece,' he said, shaking Isobel's hand.

'It is, Kieron.'

'It's a pleasure to meet you, Isobel. Maudie has spoken about you in such glowing terms and if I may say so, she hasn't been wrong. Now, before we have a chat, I've arranged a bit of a treat for you both, come along with me.'

The room they walked into was beautiful. The curtains and carpet were of the palest blue and a crystal chandelier hung from the ceiling, sparkling in the morning sunshine that shone through the long windows. It had a narrow strip down the centre, surrounded by rows of chairs, most of which were occupied. Soft music was playing in the background amid muted conversation from the spectators. Mr Walsh escorted them to the front row, where they sat down. They didn't have long to wait before a woman walked onto the runway.

'Welcome to Clerys,' she said, smiling. 'My name is Anna and if you have any questions, please see me afterwards when I will be very happy to discuss them with you. So, sit back, ladies, relax and enjoy today's showing of our beautiful spring collection. All our clothes come in different sizes and are made to order here in the store. Our lovely models today are Catherine and Emer. Thank you.

Isobel was mesmerised as one after the other, the girls seemed to glide down the catwalk in the centre of the room. They looked so elegant and confident and Isobel knew this was why Maudie had brought her here, but Maudie had been wrong this time because she could never look like them. She had been a clumsy child who'd turned into a clumsy young woman. She would trip over and end up on someone's lap, she just knew she would. It would take some persuading to change Maudie's mind, but she couldn't do this, she just couldn't. She wasn't statuesque, she was a plain, awkward beanpole, just like her sisters said she was.

After the show was over, Mr Walsh escorted them to Clerys café and over tea and scones, they talked.

'Now,' said Mr Walsh, smiling, 'your aunt Maudie mentioned that a modelling career might suit you very well and I have to say that I agree with her. You have the perfect attributes for modelling.'

'I couldn't do it,' Isobel blurted out. 'Even if you think I can, I just couldn't.'

'Couldn't do what?' said Mr Walsh.

'I couldn't parade up and down like that with people watching me – I'm not like those girls.'

'Of course you're not,' said Mr Walsh, smiling. 'You are your own special, unique self, as are we all. You don't have to look like someone else to be acceptable in this life – that would be a very unfortunate way to live, don't you think?'

Isobel nodded. 'I suppose so.'

'There is no suppose about it, Isobel. It would be a very dull life indeed if we all looked the same.'

'I'm sorry, Mr Walsh.'

'I'll tell you what,' he said, 'before you rule it out altogether, why not meet some of our models? You could come here, say, a couple of days a week and they could show you the ropes. There would be no audiences, you might even find you enjoy it.'

'No one would be watching me?'

'No one.'

'Then yes,' said Isobel, smiling, 'I'll give it a go.'

'I'm very pleased to hear it and if you still find that it's not for you – well, nothing has been lost, has it?'

'No,' said Isobel.

Mr Walsh smiled at her. 'Why not have a chat with the girls now? Would you like that?'

'Alright,' said Isobel, not looking very sure at all.

'Well, you stay here and I'll send them up.'

'And I'll see you later,' said Maudie. 'Kieron?' she added. 'Can you by any chance recommend a good boarding house for single ladies?'

'You're not thinking of moving into a boarding house surely? You have a beautiful home. Why would you want to live in a boarding house? I've known you long enough to know how much you value your own company.'

'Don't be silly, Kieron,' said Maudie, 'of course it's not for me. I'd rather be boiled in oil than live in a boarding house! No, I'm not enquiring for myself, it's Isobel I'm thinking of. You see, what I want is for her to experience some sort of independence and she won't get that living with me. It would just be weekly to start with and she would come back to me at weekends, but it must be the right one and I have no experience of these establishments.'

'Well, Maudie, this just happens to be your lucky day because I can, with no hesitation at all, recommend a fine boarding house in Merrion Square run by two lovely ladies by the names of Mary Kate Barry and Moira Kent. It is by far the best little boarding house in Dublin. The only drawback is that when people go to live there, they never seem to leave.'

'Well, I suppose that's a good sign really,' said Maudie.

Kieron smiled at her. 'I suppose it is.'

'Merrion Square, you said?'

'Number 24, it's the house with the red door. Shall I give them a ring?'

Maudie shook her head. 'I rather like the element of surprise.'

'You always have, my dear.'

'It has been lovely to see you, Kieron.'

'The pleasure has been all mine and may I say, you are looking as beautiful as ever.'

Maudie laughed. 'You don't change, do you, Kieron?'

'You bring out my romantic side, Maudie, you always have.'

'We can't turn the clock back, my dear friend.'

'Sadly no, but we certainly lived back then, didn't we?'

'We did,' said Maudie, kissing his cheek. 'We did.'

CHAPTER 47

Cathy was walking the dogs with Megan and Eliza when she suddenly stopped and clutched her tummy. They helped her to a bench and sat her down. Guinness put his paws on her lap and Charlotte jumped up beside her.

'Do you think it's a contraction?' said Megan.

'No, I've a couple of weeks to go yet. Anyway, I'm OK now,' she said, standing up.

They had only gone a few steps when she doubled over and screamed in pain.

'Do you think you can walk, Cathy?' said Megan. 'We need to get you home.'

Cathy moaned again. 'I'll try,' she said.

'Eliza,' said Megan, 'run back to the boarding house and let Mary Kate know what is happening.'

Eliza started running. She passed the row of bushes where Thomas had jumped out on them but she kept going because she had to get home. 'People don't come back from the dead,' she muttered as she ran. 'People don't come back from the dead.' She raced up the steps and into the house, yelling 'Help!' at the top of her voice.

Mary Kate and Moira ran into the hallway. Eliza was as white as a sheet and looked as if she was about to faint. Moira caught her and sat her on the stairs.

Nell came down behind her, struggling to hold onto Bull Gavin, who now weighed a ton.

'Give him to me, Nell,' said Emma. 'And fetch a glass of water for Eliza.'

'What's wrong with her?' said Nell.

'We don't know yet, love.'

'Take some deep breaths, Eliza,' said Moira.

Eliza started to cry.

'Take your time, darling,' said Mary Kate. 'Has someone hurt you, dear?'

'We can't help if we don't know what has happened,' said Moira.

Nell appeared carrying a glass of water but Eliza was shaking so hard, she couldn't hold it.

'No one hurt me,' said Eliza. 'It's Cathy.'

Moira frowned. 'Someone's hurt Cathy?'

'No, she's having her baby in the park,' she blurted out.

'Is she on her own?' said Mary Kate.

'Guinness and Charlotte are with her and Megan is helping her to walk home.'

'I'll run across and meet them,' said Emma.

'Take Rooney with you,' said Moira.

'And I'll phone for an ambulance,' said Mary Kate. 'Come with me, Eliza, and I'll get you comfy on the couch.'

At the same time as Rooney was carrying Cathy across the square, an ambulance was pulling up outside the house.

Cathy was in a lot of pain. 'I'm scared, Mary Kate,' she said. 'It hurts, it really hurts. I don't think I can do this, I don't think I can.'

Mary Kate held her hand. 'It will soon be over, my love, and you will have your baby in your arms. I promise I won't leave you, you won't be on your own.'

'Moira, ring the bookshop and get Mrs Lamb home.'

'Of course,' said Moira. 'I'll take her place in the café and get her a taxi.'

'Good girl.'

Cathy was lifted into the ambulance and Mary Kate climbed in after her. 'I'll ring as soon as I have news,' she said as the doors closed behind them.

The others stood on the steps and watched until they were out of sight, then went back into the house. Eliza was lying on the couch: 'Will Cathy be alright now?' she said.

'She'll be grand,' said Moira. 'She's in good hands and she has Mary Kate with her. You have nothing to worry about.'

Eliza sat up. 'I was scared,' she said.

Moira sat down beside her. 'What scared you?'

'The trees – I thought the bad man was there.'

Moira felt awful. It hadn't occurred to her that Eliza had run back through the park on her own in the very place where Abby had been snatched away.

'Well, I think it was a very brave thing you did, Eliza.'

'I don't think I'll be scared again.'

Moira smiled. 'Don't you?'

Eliza shook her head. 'Did you know that people don't come back from the dead?'

'I had heard that,' said Moira.

'Good job, isn't it?'

'A very good job.'

Moira heard a car pulling up and walked across to the window: 'Your mammy's here, Eliza.'

Mrs Lamb hurried up the steps and into the house. Moira met her in the hallway.

'Emma told me what has happened. Is Eliza alright?'

'She's much better, she was very shaken by what happened. I have just learned that it wasn't Cathy being in pain that scared her, it was running through the park alone to get help. It brought it all back and yet she kept running – you have a very special girl there, Mrs Lamb.'

'And I've always known it.'

Moira gave her a hug. 'She's resting on the couch and the colour is back in her cheeks.'

'Thank you for taking care of her, dear.'

Mrs Lamb went into the room and sat beside her daughter. 'Now what's all this?' she said gently.

'Cathy is having a baby, Mammy. She went off in an ambulance. Mary Kate is going to let us know when it comes out. We don't know if it's going to be a boy or a girl because you can't choose. You just get what you're given, but I don't mind what it is.'

'And I'm sure that Cathy doesn't either.'

Eliza nodded. 'I don't think she'll mind as long as she gets one.'

'Were you just a little bit frightened, Eliza?'

'I was a bit, Mammy, but I'm alright now – you see people don't come back from the dead.'

'That's right, my love. They don't. If they did, the world would be a terrible crowded place.'

'Please can I have some pancakes, Mammy?'

'You can, of course. Why don't we make them together? No one can stir batter like you, Eliza.'

'I wouldn't say no to one,' said Moira, smiling.

'There you go then. Let's make a pile of them.'

Cathy's little girl was born as the clock struck twelve. Mary Kate cut the cord and was so overwhelmed that she started sobbing: 'She's beautiful, Cathy.'

Bull Gavin had been a big strong baby but she was tiny, an amazing little person in miniature, from her perfectly round head to her button nose. Her fists were scrunched up by her cheeks and now and again her pink tongue tapped against her lips. Mary Kate gently traced the outline of her face with her finger and smiled at the tiny toes peeking out from below the blanket. She was fascinated by this beautiful little girl: 'This child is going to be ruined when we get her home.'

Cathy smiled. 'Well, I hope Bull Gavin won't be jealous.'

'Have you thought about what you are going to call her?' said Mary Kate.

'I'm going to call her Nancy,' said Cathy, looking down at her baby.

'I've always loved that name,' said Mary Kate. 'Have you named her after someone?'

'My best friend Nan,' said Cathy. 'We grew up together in the orphanage. I wish she could see her.'

'Is she still in the orphanage?'

'She might be, but I don't know. She couldn't get fostered because of her gammy leg and I couldn't get fostered because I was a baggage of a child.'

'Oh, Cathy,' said Mary Kate, smiling. 'I'm sure you weren't.'

'Oh, I was. A few families took me in but they all sent me back.'

'How sad,' said Mary Kate.

Cathy grinned. 'I didn't mind. They were a load of eejits who thought they were doing me a favour. You have to be grateful and humble if you want to get fostered, but I wasn't, so I didn't. I preferred the orphanage where I could be with Nan and Sister Breda. It was Sister Breda who taught me to cook.'

'So, you were happy there?'

'It was all I knew; it was home and I had Nan, who was like a sister. Yes, I was happy there.'

'Would you like to see your friend again, Cathy?'

'I'd love to see her again.'

Mary Kate leaned down and kissed the baby's soft little cheek. Cathy needed her help, just as Colleen had. She smiled. 'I've just had a thought,' she said.

CHAPTER 48

Isobel

Isobel had been terrified at the thought of living in a boarding house but Maudie insisted that it was high time she learned to be independent.

'But I won't know anyone,' she'd said.

'Don't whine, Isobel. Of course you won't know anyone – none of us know anyone until we meet them, do we? And you're not going to meet them living here with me.'

'They might not like me, Maudie.'

'And you might not like *them* dear, it's called life. But until you dip your toe in the water, you'll never know, will you?'

Her aunt had of course been right and Isobel had been living happily in the boarding house for over a month and loving it. She wondered what on earth she had been so worried about because everyone was friendly, she felt as if she had known them all her life. Mrs Lamb gave her cookery lessons down in the kitchen, which Maudie paid for. She fell in love with Bull Gavin and Guinness. Sometimes she went to the cinema with Cathy, who she had got very close to. In fact, there were times when she was just too busy to go back to Maudie's at the weekend and she knew that was exactly what Maudie had hoped for.

With help from Catherine and Emer, she watched and she learned and today was her first day as a Clerys model.

Isobel gave a last twirl and disappeared back behind the curtain.

Catherine and Emer were waiting for her with huge smiles on their faces.

'You did it, darling ,and you were wonderful,' said Emer, giving her a huge hug.

Catherine grinned. 'And you did it in front of real live people, with eyes and ears and arms and legs and...'

'Stop,' said Isobel, laughing. 'You're teasing me.'

'I'm sorry, darling, but you have to admit that you are very easy to wind up.'

Isobel had grown very fond of them both. It was the first time in her life that she had friends of her own age. She realised that she had a lot of growing up to do but she was learning and loving it.

'Seriously though,' said Emer, 'you're a natural model, Isobel. It took me ages to walk in a straight line without wobbling, but you can just do it.'

'Well, I did have a few lessons.'

'Who with?'

'A French lady called Mrs De Bouche. '

Catherine started laughing. 'She's no more French than my cat! Don't tell me that old crone is still touting herself around.'

'She was a bit odd,' said Isobel, grinning. 'But she did teach me to walk, at least I think she did.'

'She must be ninety if she's a day, poor old thing,' said Emer.

'I'm sorry I teased you,' said Catherine. 'Sometimes I forget what a sensitive little soul you are.'

'My sisters used to tease me a lot, I think that's why I don't have much confidence.'

'I hate them,' said Emer.

'So do I,' said Catherine. 'And I promise never to tease you again, ever.'

'Oh, I don't mind it coming from you, because I know you don't mean to hurt me. The thing is, my sisters did hurt me. When our mother died, they wanted to put me into an asylum.'

'Why?'

Isobel shrugged her shoulders. 'I suppose it was because I wasn't like them.'

'Good job too, I should think,' said Emer. 'They sound perfectly awful.'

Catherine screwed up her face. 'Please don't tell me you live with them?'

'Gosh, no,' said Isobel. 'They didn't want me living with them. I live with my Aunt Maudie at weekends and I stay in a boarding house during the week.'

'Didn't she want you either?'

Isobel laughed. 'Maudie is very fond of me, but she decided that it was time I had some independence. She says it's an essential part of my education.'

'But a boarding house?' said Catherine. 'How dreadful!'

'It's not dreadful at all,' said Isobel. 'It's really rather lovely. It's full of babies and dogs and the sweetest people. I help Rooney in the garden and Mrs Lamb in the kitchen and sometimes I take Bull Gavin out in his pram.'

'Who on earth is Bull Gavin?' said Emer.

'Nell's baby boy.'

'She called her baby Bull?'

Isobel nodded. 'Isn't it lovely?'

'It's unusual alright, sort of alternative. On reflection, there's nothing wrong with alternative.'

'It suits him,' said Isobel. 'I couldn't imagine him being

called anything else. Do you two live at home with your parents?'

'Good Lord, no,' said Catherine. 'We share a flat the size of a postage stamp in the dodgy part of Dublin.'

'At least we do for now,' said Emer. 'We're getting chucked out next week. We've been looking for somewhere else to lay our weary heads.'

'But the places we've seen aren't fit for human habitation,' said Catherine, 'let alone two beautiful young girls like us so maybe we *will* have to move back home – we might not have a choice.'

'I'd rather be eaten by ravenous dogs than move back there,' said Emer. 'My twin brothers are barely one step up from Neanderthals.'

'I have a house,' said Isobel.

'Your aunts?'

'No, I own a house.'

'In Dublin?' said Catherine.

Isobel nodded. 'Fitzwilliam Drive. It was left to me by my mother.'

The girls stared at her. 'You actually own a whole house in Fitzwilliam Drive?'

Isobel laughed. 'Yes, I actually do.'

'What, swanky Fitzwilliam Drive?'

'I suppose it is,' said Isobel. 'I've never really thought about it.'

'So why in heaven's name don't you live there?' said Catherine.

'You're going to think me very childish but well, I didn't want to live there on my own.'

'We don't think you're childish, do we, Emer?'

'Not at all,' said Emer, grinning. 'But isn't it a shame you couldn't find someone to share it with you? I'm sure there are lots of poor homeless girls who would be delighted to live in a whole house in Fitz-bloody-William Drive.'

'You mean you two?' said Isobel, laughing. 'You'd really share the house with me?'

'Well,' said Emer. 'I mean, if it would help you out, I suppose we could.' Then she threw her arms around Isobel. 'Of course, we'd love to live with you, you daft girl.'

'Unless of course something better comes up,' said Catherine, grinning.

It was Saturday, so Maudie had sent a taxi to collect Isobel for the weekend. She couldn't wait to tell her the news.

'Well, you look pleased with yourself, Isobel,' said Maudie as she walked into the house. 'I'm guessing that the show went well?'

'It did, Maudie, and I'm sorry you weren't there, but I couldn't have coped if you'd witnessed me making a complete idiot of myself.'

'But you didn't?'

'No, I didn't, and I have news.'

'You're going to be whisked off to Milan?'

'Better than that.'

'I'm intrigued, dear,' said Maudie, going over to the drinks cabinet. 'But first, let's have some wine. I find that whether the news is good or bad, it is significantly easier to swallow with a glass of something sparkling in your hand. The floor is yours.'

'I'm going to move back into my house.'

'Now that *is* good news and I couldn't be more pleased. So, you feel ready to live on your own now?'

'That's the best bit. I won't be on my own, Catherine and Emer are going to share with me.'

'This is what I have always wanted for you, Isobel, and I can't tell you how proud I am of all you've achieved.'

'I couldn't have done it without you, Maudie.'

'I have a feeling that you could – it might just have taken a bit longer. Now, when are you thinking of moving in?'

'The girls have to get out of their flat in a week's time.'

'So, we have a lot to do. Your sisters took very little from the house, just your mother's jewellery and some paintings. The house will need cleaning and a good airing, I'll get someone in to do all that. I shall also order new bedding from Clerys.'

'Thank you so much, Maudie, for everything.'

'Tish tosh,' said Maudie. 'I enjoyed the ride.'

'So did I, but I'd like to make things up with my sisters.'

'Really?' said Maudie, making a face.

'Well, I don't really like them very much but they *are* my sisters and I still love them.'

'If you must. So, why don't we have a big moving-in party and invite them?'

'But wouldn't that be rubbing their noses in it? I mean, they did grow up there.'

'You are a much better person that I ever was. I might have taught you a few things, Isobel, but you have taught me a whole lot more.'

Isobel smiled. 'In your own words, all I have to say about that is tish tosh.'

'Touché!' said Maudie, grinning. 'Now, the first thing we must do is let Mrs Barry know that you will be moving out of the boarding house.'

'I shall miss it and I didn't think that I would say that. But they have all been so lovely to me and I've grown very fond of them all.'

'You can always visit, my darling. I'm sure they will welcome you back with open arms.'

'I can't quite believe how wonderful my life has become.'

'Of course you can't, my pet, and I have a feeling this is just the beginning.'

'Maudie?'

'Yes, Isobel.'

'About my father?'

'Let's not spoil things, dear,' said Maudie. 'We need more than a glass of wine for that conversation.'

CHAPTER 49

Cathy

'Hurry up, Cathy,' shouted Mary Kate, 'or we'll miss the train.'

'Coming,' said Cathy, running down the stairs. 'Aren't you going to tell me where we're going?'

'It's a surprise.'

'But I can't leave Nancy for long.'

'We won't be long and Emma will take good care of her.'

'I wish you'd tell me what the surprise is,' said Cathy. 'I'm not that fond of surprises.'

Mary Kate smiled. 'I think you're going to like this one. Now we have to go, our taxi is outside.'

They arrived at the station just as the train was coming in. Mary Kate sat down on a bench.

'Aren't we getting on it?' said Cathy.

'Not today.'

'Then why are we here?'

'You'll see.'

Just then, a young girl stepped off the train and onto the platform. 'Nan,' screamed Cathy, running towards her.

Nan dropped her case and fell into Cathy's arms. They were both laughing and crying.

'Is it really you, Nan?'

'I do hope so,' said Nan. 'Oh, Cathy, you look wonderful.'

'So do you – oh, Nan, I've missed you.'

'I thought you'd forgotten me.'

'I never forgot you, Nan, but life sort of got in the way – I'm sorry.'

'It doesn't matter now because I'm here.'

'How long can you stay?'

Mary Kate walked up to them, smiling: 'As long as she wants,' she said.

Cathy frowned. 'I don't understand.'

'Let's go and have a cup of tea and we can chat about it.'

Cathy picked up Nan's suitcase. 'Dear God, Nan, it weighs a ton.'

Nan laughed. 'Sister Breda sent a load of food. Oh, and a bag of new knickers and vests.'

'She didn't,' said Cathy.

'No, she didn't,' said Nan, laughing.

As they walked over to the café, Mary Kate noticed that Nan was limping and then she remembered Cathy telling her about her about the young girl's leg. Cathy and Nan sat down, while Mary Kate ordered tea and cakes for them all.

Cathy grinned. 'I'd forgotten all about the knickers and vests. Oh, I'm so glad you're here, Nan. You're the only one in the world who really knows who I am. I'm so sorry I haven't contacted you all this time. I'm guessing that Mary Kate wrote to you.'

Nan nodded. 'She asked if I would like to come here for a visit and I said that I would like nothing more.'

'What did she tell you about me?'

'Only that you lived in her boarding house.'

'Nothing else?' said Cathy.

'What else is there to know?'

'I have a baby, Nan. A little girl.'

Nan's eyes filled with tears. 'You have a baby? You're a mother?'

Cathy nodded. 'I'm a mother.'

'Why didn't you let me know? I would have been there for you. Sister Breda would have been there for you. Oh, Cathy, why didn't you come to us?'

'I went to England, Nan, and I had every intention of coming back after I'd sorted things out.'

'But you didn't?'

She shook her head. 'I couldn't.'

Nan reached across the table and held her hand. 'Then you are a brave girl, Cathy Doyle, and me and your baby are very glad that you couldn't do it.'

Mary Kate came back and sat down. 'So, have you enjoyed catching up?'

'It's been wonderful,' said Nan. 'Cathy told me about the baby. I wish I had known, I would have helped.'

'Well, you're here now and that's exactly what I wanted to speak to you both about. How would you feel about staying here, Nan?'

'In your boarding house?'

'Not exactly, dear.'

'Are you talking about the café, Mary Kate?' said Cathy.

'I am. What do you think?'

'Nan, would you like to share a flat with me and Nancy?'

'Let me explain,' said Mary Kate. 'Jessie and Aishling are very special friends of mine, Nan. They run a lovely little book-shop in Dublin. They have recently extended into the café next door and they need help. It has a flat over the top. What do you think?'

Tears started to roll down Nan's cheeks.

'What's wrong, Nan?' said Cathy gently.

'I've been desperate to leave the orphanage, Cathy, but I had nowhere to go. I'm the oldest one there now and I've no life.'

'Then please say yes, Nan. Oh, please say yes,' said Cathy.

'Yes, Mrs Barry,' said Nan. 'Yes, please.'

'That's what I was hoping you'd say,' said Mary Kate, smiling. 'Now let's tuck into these buns.'

'Cathy?' said Nan. 'Who's Nancy?'

'My little girl.'

'You named your baby after me?'

'Now, who else would I be naming her after?' said Cathy.

CHAPTER 50

Mary Kate

The doorbell rang and Mary Kate answered it. There was a young man standing outside.

'I don't think we've met,' he said, holding out his hand. 'My name is Liam Flynn, I'm Norah's husband.'

'Of course,' said Mary Kate, smiling at him. 'Do come in.'

They went into the lounge. 'Please sit down, now how can I help you?'

'You know that Norah was badly hurt in the fall?'

'I do,' said Mary Kate.

'She has been in the hospital and was beginning to get better. The doctors were quietly optimistic that in time she would fully recover and be able to come home.' Liam's eyes filled with tears and Mary Kate waited until he was able to carry on. 'They were wrong, she will never be coming home. Norah is dying, Mrs Barry.'

'Oh, Liam, I'm so terribly sorry,' said Mary Kate.

'It's very sad,' said Liam. 'I don't think that I've fully taken it in – I'm going to be lost without her.'

'Your wife is a good person and a very brave one too – we will never forget what she did for Abby that night.'

'She's a strong woman alright,' said Liam sadly. 'I hadn't realised just how strong, until now.'

'Is there anything at all that I can do?'

'There's nothing anybody can do. She knows she's dying and is at peace with it.'

'But she wants to see Abby?'

'She hasn't asked, she doesn't think she has any right to, but I know that it would mean so much if she could see the little girl one last time. I will of course understand if you are against it, but I thought that I would try.'

'I'm not against it,' said Mary Kate. 'But the decision lies with Moira and not with me. Would you mind waiting while I get her?'

'Of course.'

Mary Kate called Moira's name but there was no answer, then she heard laughter coming from the kitchen and ran down the stairs.

Moira smiled at her. 'You must have a slice of this cake, Mary Kate. The girls made it and it's delicious.'

'It looks lovely,' said Mary Kate. 'Can I have a word, Moira?'

She nodded and they went upstairs: 'What's wrong?'

'Norah's husband Liam is in the front room,' said Mary Kate quietly.

'What does he want?' said Moira.

'Norah is dying and Liam is asking if she could see Abby. He says he understands if you're against it.'

'She's dying?'

Mary Kate nodded.

Moira didn't know how to feel. She had been scared of Abby's first mother, jealous even. She wanted to be the only mother that Abby had ever had. Now she was dying and what she felt was shame.

'What do you think, Mary Kate?'

'It doesn't matter what either of us thinks, Moira. The important thing is what Abby wants and I feel she would like to see her – in fact, I think she needs to see her. We have never lied to her, have we? And if she finds out later that Norah has died and we've kept it from her, she might feel that we've let her down. You're her mother, Moira, and the decision is yours but I think you should leave it up to Abby to decide.'

'You're right, Mary Kate. Of course you're right.'

Moira took Abby into the garden and they sat together on the bench.

'You look sad, Mammy. Why are you sad?'

'I'm afraid that we've had some bad news, Abby.'

'What news?'

'It's about your first mammy.'

Abby frowned. 'Did she die?'

'No, but she's very poorly.'

'Is she still in the hospital?'

'Yes.'

'Can I go and see her?'

'Is that what you want?'

'Yes, I think she likes me.'

'She definitely likes you, Abby.'

Abby stared down at the grass and didn't speak.

'Is there something you want to say?' said Moira.

Abby sighed and looked up: 'It's my fault that she's poorly, isn't it?'

'Oh, my darling child, is that what you think?'

Abby started to cry and Moira held her. 'What happened was not your fault, Abby – it was never your fault, my love.'

'But if I'd never been born, she wouldn't be sick, would she? So, it *is* my fault.'

Moira didn't know what to say, she felt so terribly sad. Abby was only a child, too young to be carrying all that guilt around inside her: 'Oh, Abby, what can I do?'

Abby shrugged her shoulders.

'Do you think it would help if you shared those thoughts with her?'

'I don't know. Maybe I could, maybe I could say that I was sorry.'

'Is that what you want to do?'

'Yes.'

'Shall we go and see her then?'

Abby nodded. 'But what can I bring?'

'What do you mean, darling?'

'Eliza said that when you visit someone in the hospital, you have to bring a present. She says it's the law – I brought two biscuits last time.'

Moira couldn't help but smile. 'Let's go and see what Mrs Lamb can rustle up for you.'

They were silent as Liam drove towards the hospital. Abby cuddled into Moira and Moira stroked her hair: 'You'll be alright, my love,' she said.

They walked down the corridor towards Norah's room. Moira sat down on a chair while Liam and Abby went inside.

'I've brought a little visitor to see you, Norah,' said Liam.

Norah opened her eyes. 'You've brought Alice?'

'She's right here, my darling.'

'Please help me to sit up.'

Norah put her arms around Liam's neck as he gently moved her further up the bed. Then he plumped up the pillows and she lay back against them. 'That's better,' she said, smiling.

'I'll leave you ladies to chat,' said Liam. 'Will you be alright?'

'Oh yes, my love, and Liam?'

'Yes.'

'Thank you.'

After Liam had left the room, Abby and Norah stared at each other. 'I'm so glad you came,' said Norah.

'I've brought sausage rolls,' said Abby, handing Norah a paper bag. 'Mrs Lamb made them this morning. I hope you like sausage rolls – Mrs Lamb says most people like them.'

'They're my favourite, thank you.'

'Are you feeling a bit better?'

'I am now you're here, Alice – do you mind me calling you Alice?'

'No,' said Abby. I think it's a nice name. Like *Alice in Wonderland* – I've read that book.'

'So have I,' said Norah. 'Do you like reading?'

'I love reading.'

'And I do.'

'Is that why you named me Alice? After the book?'

Norah smiled at her. 'I named you after my mother. Your grandmother, Alice.'

'I have a grandmother?'

'Not now, darling, she died when she was very old, but I think you would have liked her. I know she would have liked you. You have her eyes.'

'Do I?'

Norah nodded. 'My eyes are grey but hers were blue, just like yours.'

'Did I have a grandaddy too?'

Norah made a face. 'Miserable old sod, he was.'

Abby started giggling. 'I shall tell Eliza you said that – Eliza likes bad words, she gets them from her mammy. It will make her laugh.'

'Her mammy sounds like fun.'

Abby grinned. 'She is.'

'There's a bag on the floor,' said Norah. 'Can you pick it up for me?'

Abby nodded and handed it to her.

'It's yours,' said Norah.

'Mine?'

'Yes, I've been looking after it for a very long time – I always hoped that I could give it to you one day.'

Abby looked inside the bag and took out a doll. 'Did you buy this for me?'

'No, darling. A very lovely lady called Bertha gave it to you.'

Abby frowned. 'Bertha?'

'Do you remember that name?' said Norah.

Abby didn't answer but stared down at the doll.

'She took care of you, Alice. She took care of you when I couldn't.'

'She was kind?' said Abby.

Norah smiled. 'Very kind and she loved you.'

'Did I love her?'

'I think that maybe you did.'

'Where is she now?'

'It was a long time ago and she was very old.'

'Is she dead?'

'I think she might be.'

'I shall call my doll Bertha.'

'I think that would make her very happy.'

Norah leaned over and held Abby's hand. 'We won't see each other again, darling. You do know that, don't you?'

Abby nodded. 'Yes, and it makes me sad.'

'It makes me sad too, but let's not be sad today because today, we're together. There'll be time for sadness, but not today.'

'OK,' said Abby.

'Is there anything you want to say to me, Alice?'

'I'm not sure.'

'You can say anything, you know.'

'There is something,' said Abby quietly, 'but it's too hard to say.'

'Sometimes it helps to talk about it.'

Abby took a deep breath: 'I wanted to say that I'm sorry.'

'What for?'

'For making you poorly, I'm sorry for making you poorly.'

Norah shook her head. 'It's not your fault that I'm poorly, Alice. How could it be your fault?'

'If you hadn't had me, you wouldn't be sick.'

Norah's eyes filled with tears. 'The day you were born was the happiest day of my life. You were the best thing that ever happened to me. I loved you so much, Alice, but I couldn't be a proper mammy to you. A mammy's job is to protect her child, to keep her baby safe and warm, and I did none of those things. There is only one person in this room who needs to say sorry and it's not you, Alice, it was never you.'

Abby climbed onto the bed and into Norah's arms. They didn't speak, there was nothing else to say. The time for talking and regrets was gone and they were both at peace.

EPILOGUE

WINTER, 1965

Mary Kate was sitting in the lounge, writing in her diary. It was cold and rainy outside but warm and cosy in the house. When her beloved grandfather was dying, he had made her promise that at the beginning of every year, she would buy a diary. 'Why would I have the need of a diary, Grandad?' she'd asked, because she knew that she would never have anything worth writing down in a book.

'To keep account of your life, Mary Kate, to mark your red-letter days, to gain wisdom from your failures and take pride in your successes. Never throw them away but read them now and again for they will remind you of how far you have come.'

And so she had kept her promise and for fifteen years, she had bought a diary and for fifteen years, they sat unopened on a filthy floor in whatever filthy boarding house she was living in.

Her grandfather had been wise beyond his years; he had come from poverty and had never learned to read. But he hadn't needed to open a book or to write anything down for it was all there, stored inside him. Mary Kate became the keeper of all his wisdom and all the memories she had learned from being a child at his knee. Both her grandmother and grandfather encouraged her to learn all she could and in the dark evenings, by the light of a candle, they would listen to her reading from the penny books she brought home from school.

When her life began to change, she started to fill the pages with every wonderful thing that had come her way. She wrote everything down, from her first meeting with James, who had become her dearest friend, to Jenny, who had taken her to Clerys and helped her to choose beautiful outfits and who gave her the handkerchief with the letter J embroidered in the corner.

She now had everything she could ever have wanted but she remained the same; she couldn't change who she was and wouldn't have wanted to. She knew where she came from and that remained the core of her.

Every soul who had made their way through the red door also made their way into the pages of her books. Strangers who had become her dearest friends, each with their own stories to tell. They were all there, every single one of them. She put down her pen and rubbed her eyes – perhaps it was time to purchase a pair of glasses. She tired easily these days and only left the house when she absolutely had to.

She stood at the window and watched Moira walking Biscuit around the square.

Losing Guinness had been like losing another piece of Sean, for that beautiful dog had been there at the beginning and she still missed him every day. She had never known his age, so she never knew how long she would have him, but she was grateful for the years they had spent together and for the love he had brought into the house. This loyal, gentle dog had been loved by everyone who had known him and the house was never quite the same again.

James's wife Erin had drawn a picture of him. It stood in a silver frame in the fireplace, which had been his favourite spot.

Biscuit lay there now but there were still times when it was only Guinness that she saw.

The house that had once been filled with noise and laughter was now silent.

Darling Abby was studying English Literature at Cambridge University and loving it.

Emma and Rooney were married and living in the cottage in Glendalough. Emma had kept her promise and taken Nell back to her beloved hillside. They had stood on the top and shown Bull Gavin the River Blackwater. Emma had worried that Nell would want to stay but it had all been too much for her. They had visited their daddy's grave and said goodbye to their old life. Nell and Bull Gavin were now living with Emma and Rooney, beneath the beautiful Wicklow Hills, and she had found another hillside.

Cathy, Nan and little Nancy were living their best lives in the little flat over the café, which had turned out to be a huge success, just as James had predicted. And Megan and Charlotte had moved next door to Mrs Finn in Tanners Row. James had travelled to the Rhondda Valley to sort out the sale of her house – Megan would never need to work again.

The dodgy solicitor had tracked down the Schwartzes. They were cross that Megan had stolen their dog, but realised that no one was going to love Charlotte the way the little Welsh woman had. Megan was relieved to hear that she was no longer a wanted person and that Charlotte was officially hers. They returned in their droves and then the house became alive again. Those were her red-letter days. So many lives, so many memories and so much love – how blessed she had been.

Moira opened the door and Biscuit headed for the fire, where she flopped down: 'You look tired, Mary Kate.'

'I can hardly keep my eyes open.'

'Why don't you have an early night? You can have breakfast in bed for a treat, I'll bring it up.'

Mary Kate smiled. 'You're spoiling me, Moira.'

'Well, if anyone deserves spoiling, you do, Mrs Barry.'

'I think I *will* go up. Right now, I could sleep on a clothes line.'

'I'll see you in the morning,' said Moira. 'We can have breakfast together.'

'That will be lovely.'

Mary Kate lay down, pulled the covers around her shoulders and sank into the soft pillows.

It was still dark when she opened her eyes. She tried to focus, but it was hard to see anything at all. She wasn't worried, in fact she had never been more at peace. Her body felt heavy, as if something was weighing it down but she welcomed the heaviness for she was warm and cosy and safe. Her heart was filled with such complete joy and happiness, as if all her red-letter days had come at once.

It was Christmas morning and she was sitting in church beside her grandparents. Her grandaddy gave her a penny to light a candle, the glow from the yellow flame flickered around the bedroom and shone through the darkness. And then they came, they all came; they filled the room, every face that she had ever loved. Her grandparents stood together, holding hands and smiling down at her. She closed her eyes and when she opened them, they had all gone. Only one face remained and it was the face she had waited for.

Sean opened his arms and she walked towards him.

The next morning, Moira came into the room, carrying the breakfast. She was surprised to see Eliza sitting beside the bed: 'Is Mary Kate still asleep?' she said, placing the tray on the dressing table.

'I don't think so,' said Eliza.

'What do you mean?'

'I don't think she's asleep.'

Moira went across to the bed. 'Well of course she...' then stopped. She put her arms around Mary Kate and sobbed. 'My darling friend, what will I do without you? What will any of us do without you?'

She looked over at Eliza. 'She's dead, Eliza, Mary Kate is dead, do you understand?'

Eliza nodded.

'And she died alone, no one should die alone.'

'I don't think she did,' said Eliza.

'What do you mean?'

'I mean, I don't think she was on her own.'

'Did she have visitors this morning?'

'I don't know exactly when they came, but I think there were people here – I think there were lots of people here. I get these feelings, you see.'

Moira looked down at her beloved friend, the best friend she had ever had, and her heart was breaking. She touched her cheek that was still warm. She looked so peaceful, there was almost the hint of a smile on her lips. She looked across at Eliza: 'I think you're right, my love. I don't think she was alone at all.'

A LETTER FROM SANDY

Dear reader,

Thank you so much for choosing to read *Return to the Irish Boarding House*. I do hope that you enjoyed Mary Kate's story. I really enjoyed writing it. If you did enjoy it, and want to keep up to date with all my latest releases, just sign up at the following link. Your email address will never be shared and you can unsubscribe at any time.

www.bookouture.com/sandy-taylor

I would be very grateful if you could write a review. I'd love to hear what you think and it makes such a difference helping new readers to discover one of my books for the first time.

I love hearing from my readers – you can get in touch with me on social media.

Thank you again,

Sandy x

facebook.com/SandyTaylorAuthor

x.com/SandyTaylorAuth

ACKNOWLEDGEMENTS

I am so lucky to have such a precious family and wonderful friends. You have celebrated my successes and urged me on through the difficult times. Kate, Iain, Millie, Archie, Emma, Peppa and Beau, you are my world and I love you to the moon and back.

Thank you to the wonderful team that is Bookouture for your encouragement, understanding and kindness. I feel blessed to have found you. A huge thank you to my beautiful editor, Natasha Harding, who has been so supportive, always there for me and always so kind and patient. It has been a pleasure to have you beside me, you are lovely.

Thank you to my beautiful family: Marge and John, Mag and Pad, my nieces and nephews and my family in Ireland. You are all so very special to me.

To darling Clive, one in a million and my dearest friend.

Thank you to my fabulous friends: Louie and Steve, Wenny and Andy. Izzy, Lis, Becky and Phil (you can start screaming now, Becky), Angela, Lynda and Lesley, Julie B, Martyn and Juliette. And Nikki Baber. With love.

To my cabana girlies, Jan, Julie, Irene, Jane, Sue B and Sue Chenie – what fun we have had together and what fun there is still to come. Thank you for all the good times.

I would like to thank all my readers, bloggers and reviewers, including Linda Fetzer Boyer, Lola Ostrofsky, Jenny Nelson and Patti, to name but a few. Thank you all for your continued loyalty, it means so much. I love hearing from you and I will always respond to your lovely messages. You really are the best and I appreciate you all.

My agent and friend, the fabulous Kate Hordern. What can I say? Except thank you for everything you have done for me. What an adventure we have been on, Kate, and how wonderful it has been.

To my darling son, Bo, who I love and miss every day. And to Linda. Life has been a little less exciting without you, my friend.

PUBLISHING TEAM

Turning a manuscript into a book requires the efforts of many people. The publishing team at Bookouture would like to acknowledge everyone who contributed to this publication.

Contracts
Peta Nightingale

Commercial
Lauren Morrissette
Hannah Richmond
Imogen Allport

Cover design
Eileen Carey

Data and analysis
Mark Alder
Mohamed Bussuri

Editorial
Natasha Harding
Lizzie Brien

Copyeditor
Laura Gerrard

Printed in Great Britain
by Amazon

42820010R00179